Game On

A Hometown Players Novel

Victoria Denault

New York   Boston

Copyright © 2017 by Victoria Denault
Excerpt from *Slammed* Copyright © 2017 by Victoria Denault
Cover design by Elizabeth Turner
Cover photography by Claudio Marinesco
Cover copyright © 2017 by Hachette Book Group, Inc.

Forever Yours
Hachette Book Group
1290 Avenue of the Americas, New York, NY 10104
forever-romance.com
twitter.com/foreverromance

First published as an ebook and as a print on demand: October 2017

Forever Yours is an imprint of Grand Central Publishing. The Forever Yours name and logo are trademarks of Hachette Book Group, Inc.

The publisher is not responsible for websites (or their content) that are not owned by the publisher.

The Hachette Speakers Bureau provides a wide range of authors for speaking events. To find out more, go to www.hachettespeakersbureau.com or call (866) 376-6591.

ISBNs: 978-1-5387-2701-0 (print on demand edition), 978-1-5387-2700-3 (ebook)

For my dad, who is always there to talk hockey with me.

Acknowledgments

Hometown Players started as a trilogy. Three books about three loving, sometimes wild sisters and their hockey hunks that I wrote "for fun." My husband was working overnights and I was bored and trying to save money so I jumped back into my childhood hobby (writing) to avoid boredom and going out and spending money. And here we are, two and a half years and six Hometown books later, and I'm stunned, thrilled and so damn grateful.

Absolutely none of this would have happened without my agent Kimberly Brower. Thank you for taking a chance on me, for all your amazing hard work and for talking me off all the ledges.

Thank you Leah Hultenschmidt for being a fantastic, enthusiastic and supportive editor. The schedule has been crazy at times throughout this series but your positivity and willingness to talk through anything and everything has made the craziness manageable. Thank you to the rest of the fabulous team at Forever Yours who touched this book and this series in some way. From the cover art to the promotion you guys have been nothing short of amazing.

To my husband, Jack, thank you for being my personal cheerleader. I couldn't do this without your positivity and support. To my family and friends who have been so supportive, I don't know what I did to deserve you all but I am forever grateful.

To the authors who have created such a strong, supportive community and welcomed me into it, thank you. To the bloggers and readers who not only gave this series a chance but embraced it and loved it—I owe you everything. Thank you.

Game On

Chapter 1

Alex

As I stand on the busy Brooklyn sidewalk waiting for the light to change, I notice a boy, about eight, looking at me. His mom is saying something about their plans after school but he's not listening. He keeps glancing over his shoulder at me, sneaking quick glimpses and then looking away. When we make eye contact, I smile.

"Are you Alex Larue?" he asks and I can tell it's a courageous act for him. He turns instantly red. His mother stops talking and looks back at me, confused.

"I am," I reply and his whole face lights up brighter than a Christmas tree. "What's your name?"

"I'm Dylan," he announces. "And I'm super excited you're playing for my team now."

"I'm super excited to be playing here too," I tell him and his mom looks more confused so I introduce myself to her. "Alex Larue. I play for the Brooklyn Barons hockey team."

"Oh! Yeah he loves them," she says as she smiles. "His dad takes him to a few games a year."

"I didn't like you when you played for San Diego because you always made our players mad and they end up punching you and getting penalties," Dylan explains and I can't help but chuckle. His mom looks worried about his candor. "But then my dad said that now that you play for us you'll make other teams mad instead so I decided to like you."

"Thanks, Dylan. I'll try my best," I vow and smile. "Hey, do you want your mom to take a picture of us?"

"That would be awesome!" he says as his eyes light up in excitement. After his mother takes a picture and I say goodbye, I make my way toward the Starbucks where I said I would meet one of my new teammates.

It's great that Dylan is happy to have me in Brooklyn. I'm a little shocked to be here. The season started three weeks ago and I assumed San Diego was going to keep me since they'd made a bunch of trades in the summer and I wasn't one of them. But here we are—middle of October, only one week into the season—and I'm suddenly a Baron.

Luc Richard is waiting just inside. He smiles at me. "*Bonjour!*" He gives me a quick man hug. "How was your flight?"

"Good. Came in a little late so I didn't get to the hotel until three in the morning," I explain. "You want anything to drink?"

He wrinkles his nose and shakes his head. "I don't do caffeine during the season. And I never do Starbucks. Overpriced toilet water."

"Tell me how you really feel." I laugh. "I actually like their coffee."

Starbucks is comforting to me. I've lived in a bunch of different cities and one thing is a constant—there's always a Starbucks. I don't tell him this because it makes me look like a pussy. Luc and I are acquaintances and I like him because all the people I trust in this world like him a lot, but I don't really know him. That means I go into my usual happy-go-lucky, jokester mode. Honestly, even the few people I trust haven't seen much else.

"To each his own." Luc shrugs as I walk over to stand in line.

"So did management pick you to be my buddy because we're both French?"

"Nah, it's because no one else wanted to do it," Luc says with a grin so I know he's kidding. The team management always assigns a new player a veteran to help them assimilate to the team and the city. "It might be the French thing but I don't think they put that much thought into it. We have so many new rookies or trades that anyone who has been on the team more than a year has a buddy this season."

I nod. "Yeah they really cleaned house in the off-season. You and Devin must be psyched you get to play with Jordan."

Luc's face lights up. Luc grew up with Jordan and Devin Garrison playing hockey in Maine. Devin is the captain of the Barons and Luc was traded here a couple years ago. This summer so was Jordan, who incidentally I used to play with in Seattle. "Yeah. It's pretty stellar. I didn't expect that would happen during our careers. But I think the girls are more excited than we are."

Right. Devin and Jordan married sisters, Callie and Jessie Caplan, and Luc is engaged to their younger sister, Rose. Luc smiles again as he runs a hand through his long shaggy hair. "How about your family? Are they excited about your trade or do they wish you'd stayed in San Diego?"

I shift from one foot to the other and pretend to examine the menu board. "I get traded every couple of years, so this is no big deal."

He nods, thankfully accepting my nonanswer. "So I was wondering if you wanted the name of the real estate broker Rose and I used when I was traded here. She's fantastic."

"Yeah! Definitely," I reply as the line inches forward. "The sooner I can get out of the hotel the better."

"Yeah, we spend enough time in them on the road," Luc agrees.

I glance down the line to see how much longer it'll be and that's when I see her. She's right there in front of us and honestly, I'm ashamed of myself for not noticing her the second we entered. I must be slipping. Long, shapely legs in a charcoal pencil skirt. She's wearing dark stockings with the line in the back, which is seriously hot, and a pair of red leather heels. I can't see her face but between that body and the long, thick, rich brown hair, hell, I'm getting hard.

"Elle est jolie." I nod toward her. A bonus of having a fellow Frenchman on the team is that we can have candid conversations and no one here will understand us. She'll never know I was calling her pretty.

Luc looks up and his eyes do a swift up and down but he seems unimpressed. *"Oui."*

He's head over heels in love with his fiancée Rose so I don't take it as a reflection of my taste. It could be a supermodel in front of us and he'd react the same. Still, I push it further like I'm known to do. I'm nothing if not consistent.

"Regardez ce cul." My eyes linger on the perfect curve of her ass under that tight skirt. *"C'est manifique."*

She's got her head tipped down and her phone up. Clearly she's absorbed in something on the screen. We could probably talk English and she wouldn't even notice. But I don't. I miss talking in French. I don't do it nearly enough.

"Jordan est correct," Luc tells me and chuckles. *"Tu n'as pas un filtre."*

I grin and shrug at his comment that Jordan is right about me not having a filter. The line shuffles forward and I check out her ass again, only to realize she's spun around. I immediately, and probably way too abruptly not to be noticed, snap my head up. She's just as pretty from the front as the back. The chestnut color of her hair is mimicked by her big doe eyes. Her skin is flawless and her lips are full and pouty and glossed with the perfect cherry color.

"You're French?" she asks, her eyes darting from me to Luc.

I glance at Luc and he looks like he's shitting his pants. I give her a relaxed smile because I'm confident that just because she recognized the language doesn't mean she understood the words. "Yes."

"We're both from Quebec, originally," Luc explains. "We play—"

"Hockey?" she finishes for him and we both nod. "Yeah, I thought so. I mean with the arena just down the block. I figure there's a lot of French Canadian hockey players around here."

"Are you a fan of the Barons?" I ask. She doesn't look like a typical hockey fan and she definitely doesn't come across as a puck bunny, but you never know. And there's something about her that feels like déjà vu, which is odd because even if she was a Barons' superfan, I've only been a Baron for forty-eight hours. That said I've slept with a lot of women on previous road trips to New York. But I would remember if I saw her naked.

"I'm Alex Larue," I extend my hand. She places hers in mine, but it's reluctant. Her hand is warm and delicate but her handshake is firm. I cock my head to the side. "This is my teammate Luc Richard."

Luc extends his hand and I realize she's far less hesitant giving her hand to him. "I'm Brie."

The line shuffles forward again and it's her turn to order. She asks for a grande sugarfree vanilla iced latte with an extra shot, soy milk and extra ice. Most high-maintenance drink I've ever heard and it might be a red flag to a guy looking to date her, but that's never been what I've looked for. Besides, the high-maintenance ones are usually fantastic in bed. She starts to pull out her wallet to pay but I step forward and gently place a hand on her back.

It's meant as a friendly gesture but she swiftly steps away from it. I ignore that and address the cashier. "I'll pay for her drink. And an Americano for me, please."

The cashier nods. Brie looks at me, a frown fighting for

control of her face. "You don't have to do that."

"I know. But I'd like to, Brie." I give her my best, most dazzling smile. "And if you're interested in a hockey game I'd love to give you some tickets. I would just need your phone number."

She smiles. It's pretty but it's also guarded. Very. "That's not necessary, but thank you for the offer."

I think I know what the problem is—she must have a boyfriend so I say, "You and your boyfriend could make it a date night."

Her smile softens. She looks amused. "This isn't about whether I have a boyfriend. I'm just not interested...in hockey tickets."

She's shooting me down. I glance at Luc who looks like he thinks it's hysterical. The barista calls out my Americano but her drink, being the Mensa project that it is, is still being made so instead of going to grab some cream at the condiment stand, I use the extra time to hit on her again. Since I've already been shot down, might as well add flames to the wreckage.

"Have you lived in New York long?" I ask her.

"Since I was eight years old," she replies.

I smile again. "You must know the city well."

"Like the back of my hand," she replies absently as her big brown eyes look over my shoulder at the barista.

"I'm just got here last night. I would love someone to show me around," I tell her and that finally brings her eyes back to me. "I'm betting you'd be a perfect fit."

I say that line casually but then realize the innuendo in it. I have a bad habit of saying stuff that can be taken the wrong way. I think it's because English is my second language and I learned it on the street, not in a classroom. I usually don't mind it 'cause most people just think I'm that kind of guy, which makes it easier for me to be looked at as the jokester, but at the same time, I don't want to offend people. In this case though, I let the inadvertent innuendo stand. I can tell by the way her eyes widen that she catches it. She's as smart as she looks.

The barista calls out her drink. We both reach for it at the same time; our fingers touch. Neither one of us pulls away. She looks me straight in the eye, shoulders back. She's not tense, she's just confident and it lights a fire in me in places she's made clear she's not interested in.

"You have your teammates like Luc here to show you around," she reminds me coolly but then she takes a step closer and the fire inside me gets hotter. She's a few inches away and she's even more stunning this close. Flawless skin and thick lashes and a scent like warm vanilla. "Thank you, again, for the drink."

She steps back, gently tugging the drink and her hand away from me and she takes a few steps toward the entrance to the Starbucks. My mind is racing as I stare at that perfect ass and try to figure out one last way to get her number. I hate losing. Luc is snickering beside me because apparently me getting shutdown is entertaining.

She stops with her hand on the glass door and turns her head back toward me so quickly that long, luxurious mane of hair flies about her head. "When is your next game?"

She's reconsidering?

"We play tomorrow night at seven," I tell her.

"*Marquer un but pour ma manifique cul demain soir, Alex,*" she replies in perfect French with a perfectly smug smile on her lips.

My mouth falls open. She just told me to score a goal for her perfect ass. Luc bursts out laughing. Brie disappears out the door and into Brooklyn's morning foot traffic. She understood everything I said about her. Every. Single. Word.

Luc is still laughing—loudly. I want to punch him. "I thought for a second there all those rumors about your mad skills with the ladies was exaggerated," he says, "but apparently it just sucks with ones who can understand you."

"Yeah, yeah." I shrug like it's no big deal but I'm actually feeling a little embarrassed, which hasn't happened in decades. "I was just being honest. Seriously, she was gorgeous."

"She's pretty and pretty smart if she's staying clear of you." Luc grins and I give his shoulder a shove.

"Let's go. I don't want to be late to my first practice." I start toward the door and he follows. Outside we head east toward the arena, which is just a few blocks down. I can't help but scan the faces of people passing by, hoping I'll see her again but of course I don't.

When we get to the arena we head straight to the locker room. Most of the team is already there and as soon as I walk in the guys start to holler and clap and I get that warm rush inside me that I only ever get from being on a team. Devin Garrison stands up and walks over. "Glad to have ya, Rue."

He gives me a quick hug. Jordan stands up and walks over, grinning. "Brother! We're reunited at last!" He hugs me, hard and long and the warm rush inside me gets warmer.

"No one I'd rather play with again," I tell him and I mean it.

As Jordan walks back to his locker I walk over to mine. My name is written in Sharpie and stuck to my locker with hockey tape like it always is when a player is new. I should be getting a nameplate soon. If it doesn't show up by the end of the week I'll make one myself. I hate the tape thing.

Temporary, half-ass stuff like that reminds me of my childhood. In the foster system most of the time you only get a garbage bag to schlep your belongings to a new home because suitcases aren't in the budget. It's disheartening and degrading and for some reason the tape reminds me of that.

As we change Luc decides to regale everyone with our Starbucks encounter. Jordan looks up at me and grins his goofy lopsided smile when Luc finishes the story. "These New York girls will eat you alive, Rue. You should have settled down before they traded you."

"I'll never settle down." I remind him what I've told him since I met him his first year in the league. "Besides, you and your brothers stole all the good women."

Devin smirks at that from where he's lacing up his skates. "Yeah we did."

"So you're just going to spend your life breaking hearts?" Jordan questions. This from the guy who went through women faster than underwear before he got back together with Jessie.

"I don't break hearts. I break headboards," I reply and wink. He groans and thankfully Devin changes the subject.

I love Jordan. He and a few other guys I've played with throughout my career, like Avery Westwood and Sebastian Deveau, are the closest thing to family I have, and I'm happy they've all found someone they can see themselves spending their life with. I love their girlfriends and wives but when I see them together, it's kind of like watching an out-of-focus foreign movie without subtitles. It's vaguely fascinating but completely incomprehensible.

Practice goes well. I feel comfortable right away, maybe because of how many players I already know or because I'm getting used to playing on a new team every couple of years. But Coach doesn't seem impressed with me. I keep telling myself he's just sussing out a new player, but then he pops his head into the locker room when I get out of the shower. "Larue, swing by my office on your way out."

I nod. "Yes, sir."

I look at Devin because he's the Barons' captain and probably knows the coach better than anyone else on the team. He gives me a reassuring smile. "Coach is a good guy. Nothing to worry about."

I change quickly and as I grab my jacket and shove my feet into my shoes, Luc calls out. "I'll text you the Realtor's info."

"Thanks, buddy." I head out the door and down the long hall to the coach's office. He's sitting behind his desk and motions me in.

As I step into the office he says, "Close the door."

I feel like a kid in the principal's office. I sit down and he sighs, which feels like another bad sign. "So, you were management's pick. I wanted to keep Allen. He was having trouble scoring, but he liked to keep a low profile on the ice. You like to push buttons and cause opponents to take penalties. That *might* give us a chance to score, but it's drama. I don't like drama."

Fuck.

"But management thinks you're some kind of team unifier." He gives me a shrug. "I think our team morale is fine, but they think you can make it better than fine. I don't think we need a locker room hero. I was outvoted, so prove me wrong."

"I will." I've won over coaches before, and he's not going to be any different. He sighs again, clearly unconvinced, so I add, "I wasn't drafted, so I had to bust my ass to earn a walk-on chance with the Royales. If it's grit and determination you're worried about, I promise I have that. I will give you all I've got."

He stares at me for a long moment and then gives me a terse nod. It's not a sigh, so I take it as a win. If you're not a superstar, being bounced from team to team every few years is the norm. I'm a good player but not a great one, so I knew this would be my fate when I joined the league, but I've never had to deal with a coach who actively didn't want me before. He grabs a piece of paper off his desk. "In the meantime, the management was asked to have a player featured on the sports show *Off the Ice.*"

He hands me a piece of paper. "They do day-in-the-life kind of profiles, right?"

"Yep." He rolls his eyes and the crease between them deepens. "It's another distraction no one needs but the fans like it and they buy the tickets, so once again I got outvoted.

So the team wants the profile to be on you. Our tickets sales were down last year and didn't pick up the first month of this season, and they think your profile will put more butts in seats. Like I said, you weren't hired for your on-ice abilities."

Ouch. And fuck. I nod even though the last thing I want in this world is to have a television crew follow me anywhere. When I played in Seattle they profiled one of the guys and it looked like a nightmare. They followed him everywhere except the shitter and I'm sure they tried. But I just nod again because I'll take it up with PR, not Coach. He's pissed off enough as it is, the last thing I should be doing is complaining to him. He leans back in his chair. "So contact Liz in PR. She'll set things up for you. Her number is on the sheet. I'll see you on the plane tomorrow. Be early. Not on time, not late. Early."

I stand up and give him an easy confident smile. "Yes, sir."

He turns to his computer screen so I head out the door. Well, that kind of sucks donkey's balls, I think. There is no way in hell I am doing a TV show that's going to expose my personal life to the masses. It's Jordan or Luc or Devin or hell even that quirky young kid Tommy with the wild slap shot they should be profiling, not me.

I frown as I step out into the chilly fall air and walk across the arena parking lot toward the subway. My phone buzzes with a text from Luc with the name, email and number of his real estate broker. I contemplate calling her now, but decide I'll email her later since I have somewhere to be. I usually find a group home or charity to volunteer at after I get settled in a new city and while I was unable to sleep last night, I looked up some places online. Normally I would give myself a couple weeks to settle in, but this place I've decided to volunteer at only does orientations and applications for new volunteers once every few months, so I either go today or I wait months. That'd be way too long. Too much free time without focus. When my teammates are with their families I volunteer. It's the only thing that I feel connected to outside of hockey.

As I approach the subway entrance I see a young, too skinny guy sitting on a dirty duffel bag holding a shitty piece of cardboard that says "Any help is appreciated" but he's spelled "appreciated" wrong. He's probably in his early twenties and looks like life has kicked him in the teeth for at least half that time. He briefly makes eye contact as I approach.

"You hungry?"

He looks up and blinks and for a second I think he doesn't realize I'm talking to him. "Always," he says quietly.

I glance past the subway entrance and see a little deli on the corner. "Wait here, I'll grab you a sandwich. Any preference?"

He hesitates before answering. "Honestly, anything would be great."

I head to the deli. It's tiny and packed. I glance at the time on my phone screen. I'm not sure how long it takes to get from one place to another in this city but I think I'm flirting with being late for the volunteer thing. I hope I'm wrong. Ten minutes later I hand the guy a paper bag with a ham and cheese sandwich, a pastrami on rye, two apples, and a bottle of water. Then I hand him forty bucks and a hot coffee.

"Thanks, man, you're the best."

"Hope things get better for you, man." I nod and walk to the corner, pulling up Lyft on my phone. When the car shows up I ask the driver how long it'll take to get there and he winces. "Hope you're not in a hurry, dude. That's on the other side of town and traffic is a disaster."

"It is what it is," I reply and try not to groan in his face. I'm going to be late. Of course. Because the only kind of karma I have is bad. Ugh. This whole first day in the Big Apple can bite me.

Chapter 2

Brie

I hate today," I declare dramatically and Len laughs in my face.

"Thanks, pal," she replies tartly. "Since you spent the last three hours in here with me, I appreciate that."

I smile sheepishly at my best friend, who also happens to be my accountant. "You know I love you. It's just I hate math. I hate paperwork. I hate numbers."

"Yeah, yeah." Len nods, her eyes back on the laptop screen in front of her. One hand zips around the track pad and the other twirls one of her dark curls around her finger. "I swear we're only friends because together we are a whole, fully functional person. Separately we're disasters."

I nod. We've been saying that since we met at age twelve in school. I'm intuitive and street smart, she's analytical and book smart. She tutored me in high school when I was struggling with calculus and I, more than once, have saved her from sketchy potential suitors and internet scams.

"We're almost done here and then you can get back to your precious children," Len says and smiles to offset her judgy tone. She loves these kids as much as I do, she's just too scared to admit it. If she didn't she wouldn't volunteer here at Daphne's House, which is the charity for homeless teens that I founded. She offered to teach a budgeting class as soon as the doors opened; I didn't even have to ask or beg and I would have done both.

"Yeah but before I leave here you're going to give me that horrible number and it will put me in a bad mood," I sigh, dramatically again. The number I'm referring to is the amount of donations we need for the last quarter of the year.

We're doing a fund-raiser in a few weeks and if the number we have to hit is astronomical I'm going to get depressed. I would dip into my own savings again, but at this point if I do, I won't be able to pay my own bills. This year we just haven't gotten the media exposure we have in the past and if people don't know about us, they can't donate. I've tapped out all my personal contacts. My parents have been more than generous with donations and would help me out if I ask, but my dad just retired and I am not eating away at his hard-earned savings. He and Mom have made plans for that money and they deserve to keep them.

"I wouldn't worry about it," Len says and gives me a comforting smile. "Just have Vic invite all his snooty friends to the fund-raiser. They love to throw money at things they think makes them look like a good person. It's easier than actually being one."

I let that go like I always do because Len has every right to be bitchy and I am still feeling guilty for setting her up with

Robert, one of Victor's close friends, who dated her for almost two months and then completely ghosted her. Instead I correct her on the one thing I can without feeling bad. "Victor. You know he hates being called Vic."

Her wide, perfectly glossed mouth takes a downward turn. "See? Snooty."

I can't help but laugh. I've known since almost day one that Len didn't like Victor. But she tolerates him and respects my decision to date him. Still, I get the distinct impression she didn't think it would last six days let alone six months.

I glance at the clock. "How much longer, tax master? I have a new volunteers coming in here and need to prep the classroom for the GED lesson."

"Fifty grand...give or take ten grand," Len says firmly. Her blue eyes finally look up and meet mine and when she sees my pale face she adds. "Not too bad. I think you'll be able to make that at the Hamptons thing."

"So sixty thousand dollars?" I croak, feeling sick.

"Fifty...give or take ten grand," she repeats, pauses, and relents. "Yeah. Sixty. It just feels less painful the other way."

"Fuck. Fuck. Fuckity, fuck, fuck."

"Brie, seriously, we can do this." Len covers my hand with hers on the desk. "I'm bringing everyone I know. And I will make sure they donate. We can do this."

"I hope so," I say and force myself not to dwell on it. I'll panic after the fund-raiser, if I have to, not now. I can't even think about losing this place. I won't. I stand up. "Time to tackle the classroom. The art teacher who came in last night to teach sketching didn't clean up afterward."

Len looks up. "How's Hesperia? Have you heard from her?"

I smile. She loves to pretend she's an ice queen but Eleanor Levitt is a big old ball of mush. Hesperia is one of our recent success stories. She came to Daphne's House two years ago when she was sixteen after she'd run away from her fifteenth foster home. She was easily angered and had major trust issues, but we convinced the judge to let her into our unsupervised housing facility and skills program and he did. Hesperia stuck with the program here, taking all our life skill classes and seminars and even earned her GED. She never once broke the rules. She left seven months ago after snagging a job and finding a room to rent in the Bronx. "Yes. She's passed her probation period at work and got a bit of a pay bump. She's loving the job and her roommates. She said she's even started a little savings account and is thinking of taking college courses online."

"Yes!" Len raises her hand for a high five and I give her one.

"I invited her to the fund-raiser so you can get her to praise your amazing accounting courses when you see her there," I say with a chuckle.

Len feigns offense. "I don't do it for the praise. That's just something I have to endure, because I am an inspiring and incredible human. Not my fault."

"Eleanor Levitt, don't ever change," I giggle.

"You either, Gabrielle Bennett." She winks at me. "I'm going to stick around and get some other work done. Can I squat here?"

"Of course," I say, heading for the door. "Feel free to come help me clean if you're bored."

"I'll never be that bored, sweetheart."

I'm smiling as I close the door and head down the hall to the classroom. I feel pride as I walk down the long, narrow first-floor hallway. Daphne's House has been my dream since I was little. It's a last chance for kids who haven't had any luck. It's not a shelter or a group home. It's a semi-independent living facility, set up like a boardinghouse. The teens have their own bedrooms with locking doors, but they share bathrooms, a kitchen and living space. Everyone lives rent-free but must go to school or be working on their GEDs and take at least three of our offered life skill classes—be it cooking, fitness and nutrition or the budgeting and accounting classes. We also offer GED classes and art therapy, as well as yoga and meditation. We give them a safe place to start living on their own and the skills to do it successfully.

I turn into the large classroom and get started cleaning up. As I start putting away easels, I hear Selena, one of our full-time employees, talking in the hall. She's doing the orientation for the prospective volunteers. I was hoping to do it with her but I'm more behind than I realized.

"And what's the age range for the kids?" a female voice asks Selena.

"All of the kids are between the ages of sixteen and seventeen and they've all been approved by the courts for this type of living. They move out when they turn eighteen. Of course we help find them living situations afterward and have even cosigned leases for them."

"That's amazing," I hear someone else say. I turn off the water I'm currently washing some brushes in and gently place them in the sink. "I'm impressed."

"I was impressed too when I researched this place. I'm even more impressed now that I work here," Selena tells him as I turn from the sink to look at the entryway. I can't see them. I want to go out there, but I don't want to interrupt either. Selena is doing a great job on her own. "They do really great work. The owner is incredibly dedicated to the cause."

"So is there an age restriction?" another voice asks.

"We've never had someone come here under sixteen," Selena tells him. "It's much harder to get the courts to allow someone much younger to live in such an unrestricted environment. For some reason they still think that sticking them in a foster home with an adult that they don't know or trust is better than no adult at all."

Selena goes back into explaining what we do here. As I'm about to step in the hall to greet everyone, I hear the front door buzz behind me. I glance over my shoulder as a person seems to explode into the room. He's a blur of broad shoulders and dark fabric and towers over me more than any kid here. He must have been expecting to run or something after he entered because his forward motion is so aggressive that he bumps into me before he can stop himself. I stumble about as gracefully as a drunk chicken. I grab the wall to stop myself from slamming into it. I turn to fully take in whoever the hell just did that.

Our eyes lock and it's like we're colliding again.

"*Colisse!*" He exhales the French swear word under his breath.

"What are you doing here?" I demand. Did this jackass hockey player follow me? Oh my God that would be insane. Is he insane?

"I'm here for the volunteer info session," he replies.

"You're Alex?" Selena interrupts looking at the clipboard in her hand. "I thought you weren't going to make it."

"I'm sorry I'm late. I'm new to the city and I under-estimated my commute," he explains to her and then he somehow manages to give her a fairly dazzling smile, which she returns with her typical friendly one. "Well if you want to join the rest of the tour, I can explain what you missed af-terward."

"I'll explain it to him afterward," I tell Selena and then glance at the rest of the group. "My name is Brie Bennett and I'm the director of Daphne's House."

I smile brightly at all of them and make sure to let it dim a little as my eyes connect with Alex Larue again. But he smiles back, bright but lopsided. "Of course you are," he mumbles and his dark blue eyes lift to the ceiling. I know he's cursing God or the universe, or both. I'd do the same if I didn't think it was unprofessional.

Instead I turn back to the group. "Come this way into our classroom and Selena will explain more about the classes we offer the kids, all of which are taught by professionals who are donating their time and sometimes supplies, like charcoals and paper for our art class."

The group filters by me into the large room. Selena smiles at me as she passes and makes her way to the front as she con-tinues talking. Alex hangs back, closer to me than I would like. I get a whiff of his cologne, which is dark and warm and earthy. Not unpleasant even though it kind of makes me think of a lumberjack.

Those dark blue eyes keep stealing furtive glances in my

direction, which makes all the glaring I'm doing worth it. It would be wasted energy if he didn't see it. I can't help but really take in his face, since I'm trying to melt it with my angry gaze. He's got really dark, really thick five-o'clock shadow but it's nicked in places by white scars like the two on his chin. There's also one by his eye and through his eyebrow. He's like an alley cat, all marked up and probably proud of it. Surprisingly for a hockey player, his nose is straight and smooth. His mouth is wide and his lips not overly full or thin but perfectly symmetrical. He'd be attractive if he wasn't a sleazeball.

I glance over at Selena as she starts to lead the volunteers out into the hall again. "Selena will finish up the tour by taking you up to the common areas the kids share on the second and third floors." I pause and make sure I'm looking only at the Don Juan of hockey. "We want to work with people who are willing and able, but we understand if it's not the right fit for you. So take your time, look around, ask any and all questions you have. We want it to be an exceptional experience for both you and the kids. And feel free to ask me anything as well. I'll be here in the classroom."

I give the other three potential volunteers another warm smile as everyone, including Alex, follows Selena upstairs. I go back to cleaning up, but my brain is stuck on Alex. How in the hell is he here? What kind of absurd coincidence is this? I realize now, from the look on his face and the fact that I never gave him my last name when we met, that it has to be a coincidence. He certainly didn't follow me here from Starbucks and without my last name he couldn't have Googled me and figured out where I worked. But I have a hard time believing a guy like him would take it upon himself to volunteer here—or anywhere other than maybe a strip club on amateur lap dance night.

I have to admit I loved the look on his face when I spoke to him in French in Starbucks and I was tempted to stick around and really enjoy the blush on his cheeks but I didn't want to risk being late for a meeting with a perspective donor my mom had set up for me. Still, the encounter wasn't easy to forget and as I headed back here a couple hours later I found myself reliving it and then punching his name into Google on my phone. BIG mistake.

Judging by the stories, he's a world-class flirt. Tons of women—sometimes in nothing more than skimpy bikinis or cocktail dresses—have posted photos with him on social media, and almost always with his lips on their cheek or ear or neck and vice versa. His own social media is filled with half-naked selfies. The guy appears to be about as deep as a puddle.

There's a knock and I put down the easel I'm carrying and turn around. *"Parler du diable."*

He grins at my "speak of the devil" comment. I have to admit it's a good grin. *"J'ai été appelé pire."*

"Yeah, I'm not surprised you've been called worse," I say, frowning. "Why are you here?"

He steps into the room, the grin falling off his face, and shoves his hands in the pockets of his jeans. "Orientation is over and I wanted to apologize for being late and let you know I really do want to volunteer."

I pick up an easel and carry it into the corner where the others are stacked. "Is this a court-ordered thing or something?"

"Excuse me?" he asks, completely baffled. I turn back to him and he's moved to the last easel, picking it up much more easily than I do, and carrying it over to the stack where I'm standing.

"Were you ordered by the courts to do some kind of community service?" I repeat. I'm honestly not trying to offend him I just can't for the life of me picture him willingly giving up time to be with kids when he could be hitting on women or taking half-naked selfies for his one million Instagram followers.

"Are you serious?" He sighs. "No. I like helping kids. Is that so hard to believe?"

I shrug. "You don't come across as someone who cares about much more than hockey and hitting on women."

"You have spent five minutes with me." He looks at me with an annoyed expression.

"It could have been seven minutes if you had showed up on time for the volunteer program you say you are so interested in," I snap back.

He rolls his eyes and crosses his arms over his ample chest. "Well here's a little bit more about me. I prefer sunrises to sunsets. I like cats more than dogs. I will always offer a homeless person food, which is what made me late today, and I also like to donate to fund-raisers that help kids so I was going to offer hockey tickets as one of the prizes for yours."

I absorb every word he says with a weird inner satisfaction, like I was hungry for the information and I didn't know it. While the superficial information is interesting it's the last two statements that shock me. He was late because he was buying food for a homeless person, which makes me an ass for thinking he was just being inconsiderate of our schedule, and he wants to donate to the fund-raiser. *My* fund-raiser? "Who told you about the fund-raiser?"

"Selena. She mentioned it to everyone at the end of the tour."

"Why would she do that?" I question, annoyed.

"Why wouldn't she? Is it a secret?" That big, bold obnoxious grin takes over his smug face again. "Just a little advice. Secret fund-raisers don't raise as much money as the ones you tell people about."

"You're hilarious," I remark dryly and uncross my arms because they're starting to ache I've had them crossed so tightly for so long. He must take that as a sign of concession, like I've waved a white flag.

"I told Selena I would come by for my first volunteer shift on Friday. Meet all the kids and figure out what their fitness goals are," he tells me and then he hesitates before he asks, "Okay?"

I've asked professional athletes to come and just give a talk but no one has taken me up on it. Now this guy is here offering to help and even give me tickets, which would be a big draw for the fund-raiser. I may not trust him as far as I can throw him—and trust me with all that towering height and sculpted muscle I can't throw him—but I can't say no. "Okay but, again, I need my volunteers to take this seriously."

"I do and I will." He gives me one more of those confident grins. "You'll see."

Len pops into view behind him. "Sorry to interrupt. I'm going for an afternoon coffee run. Can I get you—"

Alex has turned around and that has made Len stop talking for some reason. Her big blue eyes bug out of her head. "You're Alex Larue."

"The one and only." He smirks as he extends his hand. "And what is your name, beautiful?"

Len's eyes fly to my face as she extends her hand. "Did you know this is Alex Larue?"

"Yes."

"I'm Len Levitt. I volunteer here teaching kids budget and money basics," she explains. "Are you volunteering here?"

"Yes," he answers and I can't see his expression but Len's cheeks actually start to pink. "Although I had a hard time selling Ms. Bennett here on the idea."

Len's eyes shift to me again. "She doesn't watch sports. She has no idea you're a fan favorite for every team you've ever played for. The kids will be so psyched to meet you. Oh my God! You should come to her fund-raiser! Brie, invite him to the fund-raiser!"

She's fangirling. Full-on. Alex glances over at me and winks. "Are you going to invite me to the fund-raiser?"

I sigh loudly. "Anyone who donates a prize gets an automatic invite. So yes, you're invited. But it's in the Hamptons and you're probably busy."

"As long as I'm not on a road trip I'll be there," he promises. "With bells on."

"It's formal, so you should probably wear more than bells," I snark but it just deepens that grin on his face. "You might even have to buy a suit."

"I'm a hockey player," he reminds me. "We wear suits to every game. You know, I can get you some tickets if you ever want to check out a game yourself."

"Like Len said, I don't watch sports."

Len shoots me a weird look and then steps closer to Alex. "It's nothing personal. She barely watches anything. I'm surprised she even owns a TV. Or a house for that matter since she practically lives here. This place is her baby," she rambles on. "In fact it's more her baby than an actual baby would be. If she had kids they'd have to get a room here to see her, she's here that much. Not that she would be a bad parent. She's great. She'd be a great parent if she had a kid but she doesn't have any and doesn't want any—ever—so you know . . . anyway she's got these kids and that's why this place is her baby."

"You should grab that coffee now, Len," I blurt out before she can dig a deeper hole. Dear God, is this how most woman act around him? "And you should make it a decaf."

"Right. Okay. Yes. Nice meeting you, Alex Larue."

He chuckles. "You can just call me Alex. And why don't I walk you out since I'm leaving anyway?"

"Actually, Len, I need you for a moment so stick around," I interrupt because the absolute last thing I want in the universe right now is for Len and Alex to spend more time together while she's become this unhinged crazy lady.

Len nods. "See you Friday. And good luck on your road trip tomorrow."

"Thank you." He glances back at me and nods, with the slightest trace of a smile dusting his lips. It's a smile that says *See, this is how a proper woman reacts to me.* I return it with an eye roll.

I wait until I hear the front door close and see the top of his head pass by the window and then I unleash on Len. "Are you insane? Why are you insane? Why did you just verbally upchuck all over him? About me!"

Len shrugs sheepishly. "I don't know you were just being so cold to him. And he's a freaking celebrity, Brie. He's the type of person you've been trying to get to volunteer here! He's a guy who can bring us more attention and you were acting like he smelled like dog poop!"

She probably has a point but I'm still a little mortified. "'The place is her baby. She would be a good mom but she doesn't want babies—ever.' What the hell was that?"

Len turns bright red and laughs nervously. "I'm sorry. I guess that was TMI, but he's just...Did you look at him? He's stunning. All rugged edges and rock-hard body. I mean come on..."

I can't help but smile at her despite her insanity. "Is he good-looking? I can't see his features. His ego is blocking my view."

"Oh come on, he's a millionaire athlete who has won a damn Stanley Cup. Your ego would be massive too. It's part of his charm and that French accent is..." She fans herself. Actually fans herself.

"I don't need him for a French accent," I say in my heaviest French Canadian speak dropping Hs and rolling Rs. Len laughs. Then I tell her about the encounter with him and his teammate earlier at Starbucks. "Isn't the way he seems to think he's hot shit and that he can say whatever he wants annoying?"

"Nope. Not a bit. Because clearly he's a good guy if he's here, right?" Len replies. "You should ask him if we can use his name and his prize in the advertising. So many more people will buy tickets if we can say he'll be there."

"You think?" I sound as skeptical as I feel.

She nods so emphatically that her ringlets are flying every which way. "Ask Vic, he'll tell you. Every hockey fan with money will be there. Alex is a darling of the league. He's a media favorite even though he's not a grade-A player. They love his witty banter in interviews and apparently he's a locker room leader."

"What the hell is that and how do you know any of this?" I ask and stare at her like she's not my best friend. Because my best friend has never brought up hockey before in any conversation we've ever had.

Len is looking back at me like I'm the insane one. "You're the only child, not me. My brothers have both been hockey fanatics since they were kids. My grandpa got them into it. And remember my college obsession?"

"Stuart?" I question. Len fell instantly and madly in love with a guy named Stuart who she went on and on about for all four years but never actually dated him or even said more than two words to him that I know of. "He was a massive hockey fan. Huge. Loved it. I started following it a little bit in school so I could have something to talk to him about. Not that I ever did, but it was there in my back pocket if I needed it."

"You are a strange bird." I shake my head.

She grins. "Yep. And you're an even stranger bird for not thinking that boy is hot."

I picture Alex Larue in my head. I have to admit when I first turned around to look at him in that coffee line, I was surprised. Tall, broad, sculpted, with that unkempt brown hair and those nicks and scars on his face. He looked like a model who decided to become a MMA fighter—and lost a few rounds. If he hadn't been vulgarly giving a review of my ass, I might have found all those features attractive. But thanks to the demeaning way he was talking about me, I didn't have that reaction. What I did react to, because I couldn't control it, were those stormy blue eyes. When I looked into them, I had trouble looking away. Something about him commands my attention, even if I don't think much of him, I'm oddly transfixed by him.

"Brie? Hello!"

"What? Sorry. What?"

"Where did you go?" Len questions. "I asked if you wanted coffee. I'm still going."

"Umm...yeah. Thanks. Today let's go for a half pump hazelnut iced latte with coconut milk."

"Got it." Len leaves and I walk out of the art room and head to my office.

Isaac, one of the sixteen-year-olds who has been living at Daphne's House for almost year, walks in the back door. I smile at him. "Welcome home. Have a good day at school?"

"It was school," he says with a shrug but gives me a small smile. "I'm going to try and get my homework done before the budget class so I can play video games tonight."

I laugh. "Okay you do that."

He heads straight for the stairs up to the living area. I pause and turn back to him. "Isaac! Have you ever heard of Alex Larue?"

He stops walking and scrunches up his nose as he thinks about it. "The hockey player?"

I nod. He smiles. "Yeah. That guy is cool. I saw an interview he did online with ESPN and he was funny. Why?"

"He's going to be volunteering here starting Friday," I explain.

Isaac's smile gets bigger. "Sweet!"

He heads up the stairs, taking them two at a time. Okay . . . so I'm the only one who doesn't like this guy.

Chapter 3

Alex

The first few road trips of the season are always a bitch for most of the players. They're used to staying in one time zone all summer long. Since I don't have a hometown with family to go back to when the season is over, I usually spend the summer jumping around the globe visiting teammates and friends everywhere from Canada to Sweden and all over America so travel is not exhausting to me. When you never stop traveling, you don't get jet lag.

Because of that, I'm annoying the fuck out of Devin by being in his room right now when I know he'd rather be napping. But I hate sitting around my hotel room by myself and Jordan didn't answer his cell when I called to see if he wanted to do something so I decided to latch on to Devin when I saw him in the hall. Being the great guy that he is, he isn't kicking me out. Probably because I'm new to the team and as captain he feels like he needs to get to know me better and help me settle in.

"Find a place yet?" he asks me, his voice heavy as he lies on his bed with an arm over his face as if to block out the sun coming in through the open curtains.

"Yeah, actually," I say and think back to that loft in Tribeca that the broker showed me. "Snagged a place in Tribeca."

"You sure you don't want Park Slope?" Devin questions.

"Nah, man. I need the city," I reply and add cheekily, "I'm not an old married dad like you."

Devin has a son from his first marriage, which sadly blew up a few years ago and he and his wife divorced. Callie happened to move to New York for work at the exact same time Devin's life imploded and she helped him get through everything and, from what Jordan says, accidentally fell madly in love with him. Luckily he'd already fallen in love with her.

Devin chuckles at my insult. "I'm barely older than you, Rue, you shit. And if a girl like Callie ever gave you the time of day you'd be off the market in a hot second."

I just shrug as he peeks at me from under the crook of his elbow. "Speaking of the missus, how's she doing?"

"Conner brought home the flu a while ago and it's been clinging to Callie. But I think she's on the mend, finally. Oh, which reminds me, she wanted me to invite you over for dinner. Friday night?" Devin says. "She's an incredible cook and she loves welcoming new teammates. She's says it's her duty as the captain's wife, but honestly she just likes hosting dinner parties. You won't regret giving up a Friday night of debauchery with the guys to eat her food. I promise. Even if it does mean you have to do it sitting next to my kid."

I laugh. "I don't mind kids at all. In fact we usually get along great. And as for the night of debauchery, all you doofuses are married and lame now and I've got no interest in running around bars with the rookies like their chaperone."

Devin moves his arm and looks over at me. "So you'll come to dinner?"

"Yep." I pause as I remember my volunteer shift at Daphne's House. "But I have a thing Friday. Any chance we can do the following Friday instead?"

"Yeah that should work." He yawns—loudly.

I pull my ass out of the chair I've been parked in for the better part of two hours to let him grab the nap he desperately wants. I played in Seattle for almost four years and I have a lot of friends in town I could go see. "I'm going to head out."

"Like out? Out of the hotel?"

"Yeah. Seattle has got way better food than the buffet the hotel will be serving us later," I explain and walk toward the door. There's always a dedicated room for meals, supplied by the hotel, during road trips but there's no rule that says we can't go out.

Devin sits up and looks at me with concerned eyes. "Listen . . . I know you're still friends with a lot of guys on the Winterhawks, but Coach hates when his guys are out with other players. He used to even give me grief about hanging out with Jordan and Luc after games when they were on other teams."

"Oh," I reply flatly and try not to frown. "That seems excessive."

Devin looks apologetic. "I know. But it is what it is. I'm not saying you can't hang out with Deveau or whoever, but

I'd wait until the next trip. I wouldn't purposely rock the boat right now, you know?"

I lean my back against the closed door and fold my arms across my chest and decide to deal with the elephant in the room directly. "My existence rocks his boat enough, eh?"

Devin's remorseful expression magnifies. "He's butt hurt. It'll pass. Besides I don't know one player who isn't happy to have you with us, dude."

I try not to frown as I inhale deeply and let it out long and slow. I fucking hate feeling like I have something to prove. I've earned my way into this league and I did it the hard way.

"You're a great addition to the team, Rue, no matter how you got here," Devin reminds me like the good captain he is. I can imagine what it was like for Jordan growing up with Devin in his corner. Sure, they love to press each other's buttons but the fact is, they are each other's biggest fans. I fought my way through hockey—and life—as a kid with no one having my back. It sucked.

"Thanks, man." I nod. "Tell Callie I'm in for dinner. And to make a lot of food because I eat like ten men."

He chuckles. "Yeah, she's used to that."

The door to his hotel room swishes closed behind me and I make my way back to my room. My cell rings from the pocket of my sweats. I pull it out but hesitate on answering because I don't recognize the number.

I decide to do it anyway, in case it's Kristi about the loft apartment I want so badly.

"Alex?"

"Yes?" I don't recognize the voice.

"This is Brie Bennett from Daphne's House. Do you have a moment?"

"Yes," I reply and instantly worry she's calling because she's changed her mind about letting me volunteer.

"I just wanted to confirm that you'll be coming in on Friday?" She sounds different. Unsure. She's been nothing but a ball of condescending confidence since I met her so this is odd.

"Yep. Do you make personal confirmation calls to all your volunteers before every shift?" I ask, knowing I'm being a little bit snarky. But the way she thought that the only reason I would volunteer was if it'd been court ordered has been really eating at me.

"No. Just you...because I also wanted to ask you if you were serious about donating some Barons tickets for our fundraiser that's a week from Saturday," she says, her voice still abnormally timid.

This is a woman not used to asking for things. I have that figured out now after a little Googling. So you bet your ass I'm going to make her beg for it. Sure I didn't make the best first impression but the level of shade she threw at me the first two times we met seemed excessive. And now that I've done a little research on Brie Bennett I'd bet my paycheck she'd have been less of an ice queen if I were a billionaire or a prince, since she's hung out with both, according to Page Six.

"I mean...maybe." I can hear her sharp intake of breath at my nonanswer, and it makes me smile as I pull my key card out and slip it into my door. "Do you want the tickets? It's just hockey."

"Yes. I absolutely do," she says swiftly. "I personally don't know much about hockey but I've been told by more than a few people it would be a great addition to our prizes."

"Oh well okay I guess," I say and bite my bottom lip to keep a snicker from escaping. My hotel room door swishes closed behind me. "Maybe I can get a couple for you."

"I'm not trying to pressure you but if that maybe can be a hard yes then I can add it to our online advertising and we can hopefully get some more tickets sold," she explains and seriously, the need in her voice is adorable.

"You need a *hard* yes from me?" Oh yeah, I am totally moving this into innuendo territory.

"Ah...yes?" Now the awkward discomfort in her voice is being quelled by the indignation she's trying, and failing, at taming.

"I'm good at hard," I explain to her. "So I'll give you a hard yes."

"Thank you." Her tone is clipped now and it's really hard not to chuckle. She takes an audible breath. "So because you're donating a prize you'll be given a complimentary ticket to the event. Will you be joining us?"

"In the Hamptons? Why the hell not," I fall onto my bed.

"Great! So I assume it's okay to add your name to the information then..."

"What? Put my name where?"

"On the advertising," she explains like it's no big deal at all. "We often mention specific prizes as well as famous attendees. I hear you'd be a pretty big draw and since you're so behind the cause I thought—"

"You thought wrong," I interrupt sharply and then pause to rein in the harshness in my tone. "I don't want to advertise my involvement. Mention the tickets as a prize, fine, but I don't want to be promoted. Not me personally."

"But I just assumed...I mean you're a media personality so..." She seems perplexed and that adds to my annoyance.

"I'm not a media personality. I'm an athlete," I correct her.

"Yes but you're always giving interviews and stuff," she argues. "You've done ads for Gatorade and Nike and even a car dealership in San Diego."

"Those were endorsement deals or one-offs for corporate sponsors for the team I work for," I explain tersely and I can feel the muscles in my shoulders and neck start to knot with tension. "I don't make my charity work media fodder."

"Oh, so you'll put your name on something only if someone pays you to do it?' she challenges and I automatically want to groan. Of course, she'd take it that way. She has a shitty opinion of me and wants to stick to it.

"I keep my personal life personal," I say and I know it's a vague answer but I don't want to get into it too deeply with her. If I start publicizing my involvement with charities, everyone is going to want to know why. Everyone loves a personal sob story to get behind a cause and I am not giving mine. Not now, not ever.

"You did a five-minute YouTube interview with some internet sports reporter about the pros and cons of boxers and briefs," she says. "That doesn't make it seem like privacy is your issue."

"Look, I know you're not used to being told no, but the answer is no," I reply. There is an intended sharpness to my tone.

"What is that supposed to mean?" she demands. I could tell I've hit a hot button with her.

"You're not the only one who can do an internet search," I bark. "I picked Daphne's House because I have a soft spot for kids beat up by the system, but I didn't research it too much until after I met you. I know it's run by a company your parents own."

There's a long, hard pause. When she speaks, her tone is dripping in ice. "So?"

"So you assume I will be anyone's media whore and I assume a girl whose parents gave her a business to run straight out of college isn't used to hearing no," I tell her and I swear I can feel her anger boiling up through the phone. I'm actually surprised it doesn't get hot in my hand like a curling iron. "But you're hearing it now. I want to volunteer and I will donate game tickets. Hell, I will donate an entire row of tickets but I'm not going to pimp myself out. Sorry."

I wait for her response. I even hold the phone half an inch off my ear so if she yells she doesn't make me deaf. But instead of her voice I get nothing more than a dull beeping sound. I glance at the screen and see the end button flash once before the screen goes dark. She hung up.

"*Merde.*" I swear and drop the phone onto the bed as I stand up, too agitated now to lie down anymore. I know I just made this volunteering gig a hundred times harder but I don't care. When I started Googling Brie Bennett the other night it was because I needed a distraction more than actual curiosity. I had woken up from yet another nightmare and was looking for a simple distraction to get my head out of the darkness that always lingers after a bad dream so I could hopefully fall back asleep.

I didn't find out who owned Daphne's House until after finding out a lot of other information—from social media sites and New York–based blogs—which made me realize if you looked up "silver spoon" in the dictionary you'd find this woman's picture. Her father was CEO of a Fortune 500 company. Her mom is a socialite who helped organize just about every ball or charity event in Manhattan. Brie's an only child. She also has an open Instagram account that she hasn't posted on since two years ago, but it shows pictures of her skiing in Aspen, beaching in the Bahamas and boating on Lake Como. Not to mention all the food pictures of meals from Michelin Star restaurants and the pictures of her partying in designer dresses in VIP sections of clubs.

I didn't actually resent her for it, because it's not her fault she's privileged, but she and I are from two separate worlds. It's funny because both times I met her, I kind of had this weird feeling of potential with her—like despite the attitude she was throwing at me, which should have come with a windchill warning, I might actually connect with her. Like maybe she was just challenging me to work harder to impress her. I thought it seemed like a worthy challenge, but now I realize it's not. Sure, it seemed noble at first that she would want to run a place like Daphne's House when she could clearly just jet around the world and be nothing more than a social media selfie queen, but it's easy to care when Daddy buys you a place to do it.

Frustrated, I grab my jacket and my wallet. Fuck the coach, I'm going to hang out with my friends. People who get me.

An hour later I'm sitting at the juice bar at Elevate Fitness staring across a thick green smoothie at Shayne Beckford. Shayne started dating my friend and former teammate Sebastian Deveau shortly after I was traded from the Winterhawks. I got to know her pretty well over the summer when I came here to Seattle to visit him. She's gutsy and bold and a total sweetheart, which is exactly what Seb needs. "This is not what I expected when I decided to come here to see you."

"Then you don't know me at all," she quips with a snarky smile.

Sebastian had a late-afternoon practice and a team meeting so he told me to swing by here and hang with Shayne until he was done. She somehow roped me into spending the time taking her yoga class and now she's making me drink this kale goop . She takes the dirty blender and starts to rinse it under the faucet in the sink. "You need some good food in you. When was the last time you had something green?"

"I prefer having things that are blond, brunette and redheaded," I joke and she laughs. But then she frowns and reaches across the bar and presses down on both my shoulders with the palms of her hands. I feel them drop a couple inches. "There. Much better. You shouldn't look so tense after a yoga class, buddy."

"Sorry. It's not you or the class. I'm just still annoyed by this woman," I mutter and sip my smoothie. I hate to say it, but it's actually not bad. It's got a limey pineapple taste despite all the green leaves she threw in the blender. When I look up from my cup she's staring at me in amusement with one eyebrow cocked.

"A woman has gotten under your skin?"

"She gets under my skin like it's her job." I frown and sip more of the oddly tasty drink.

She leans her elbows on the counter between us and says in a rapt whisper. "Tell me more."

"It's not like that," I warn her because she's looking at me like this is some missed love connection and it's not. "I mean she's hot and everything, but we couldn't be more different. We honestly have nothing in common, which is normally not a deal breaker, but she's an exception."

Shayne lets out a huff and I give her a sheepish smile. "What? You know me, I don't have to like someone for my dick to want to be inside them. But trust me, even he is annoyed by this woman."

I point down at my pants.

Shayne's eyes follow my pointed finger and then snap up. "Men are ridiculous. Anyway who is this woman?"

"Just some woman I keep running into," I reply vaguely.

Shayne, luckily, doesn't push for more information. "Why doesn't she like you? You're adorable and charming."

"And don't forget the captivating French accent, *ma belle*," I add.

She laughs. "Oh I can't forget that. I fell victim to that sucker myself."

"Sebastian learned everything he knows from me," I tell her.

"And remember, I hated him too in the beginning," Shayne replies. "Well, at least I wanted to. Desperately. And look at us now."

She waves her left hand at me. Her big diamond ring glints in the glow of the lights above us. I almost choke on the green stuff in my mouth. "Shay, kiddo. Trust me. That's not the ending here. Not with her or anyone. Not for me."

Shayne looks honestly devastated for a second and then it turns to disbelief. "Come on, Alex, it's just me and you. I saw how happy you were for Seb and I when we got engaged. And how happy you were for Jordan and Jessie at their wedding. I won't tell your hockey buddies but admit it. You love love."

"I do love love," I say and dare to take another quick sip of my drink. "It makes my friends happy. I want you all to be happy, even if that means you take away my wingmen one by one."

"Ha. Ha," she says, rolling her eyes. "So why not get your own piece of happiness?"

"My happiness isn't a picket fence, two-point-five kids and a hybrid," I explain flatly. "I'm not wired that way."

"Are your parents still married?"

I get that wave of darkness that envelops me when someone brings up my family . . . it's like being in the ocean in the pitch black of night and being hit with this cold, dark wave out of nowhere. I hate it. It's so empty and all consuming. My shoulders must have risen again because she reaches over and presses them down gently with her palms again. She thinks she knows why and gives me a soft smile. "It's okay. I get it. My parents were not exactly the shining example of how to have a happy, well-adjusted relationship." She pats my hand. Shayne's dad is an ex-NHL player who cheated on her mom throughout his career. "But if I can get over all my relationship issues and be madly, completely, head over heels in love with a hockey player, you can eventually settle down too. I promise. In fact, I would bet money on it."

"You would lose." I give her a wink to soften the firmness of my words. I wish I had her faith. I wish the darkness that swirled inside me could be lightened.

"Did your parents ever come to Seattle when you played here?" She starts to wipe down the bar top with a damp cloth.

"I'm not in contact with my family." I offer a half-truth

Her eyes soften again. "I've been there too. Still am there I guess since I haven't talked to my dad in months. I haven't even told him I'm engaged. I assume my mother has."

She takes a deep breath and releases it heavy and slow. "Family doesn't have to be blood." I say what I've told myself for decades because she looks like she needs to hear it too.

She smiles. "Truth."

Her eyes move up to the clock on the wall and she drops the rag in the sink and starts to untie her apron. "Shift is over. Let's go meet Seb for dinner. He should be done with his team meeting by now."

"Cool." I pause to inhale the last of the smoothie and she laughs as she comes around the bar to stand next to me. I give her a grin. "You're right. It didn't taste like wet grass after all."

She gives me a side hug as we walk to the changing rooms. "I'm always right. You'll be saying that again in a few years when you're all in love and settled down."

"Ha!" I give her a shove and head into the men's locker room to change.

The next morning I wake up feeling grounded and content...for about three minutes until my phone starts ringing. I grope for it on the nightstand knocking my bottle of water and the change I pulled from my pocket last night to the floor. I curse and rub the sleep from my eyes so I can read the name on the screen.

"Hey, Avery. What's up?" Avery Westwood, former captain of the Winterhawks and current captain of the team I was just traded from, the San Diego Saints, is probably the person I'd consider my best friend.

"You're banging Shay."

"What the fuck are you talking about?" I'm wide awake now. I sit up so quickly I get light-headed.

"Someone took your photo with her. At the gym. You two look cozy," he explains. "They posted it on Instagram and of course now everything thinks you're sleeping with Seb's girl. The puck bunny brigade are posting it everywhere else calling her a whore and you a dirt bag."

"I am not—"

"I know. We all know," Avery cuts me off with his reassuring words. "Stephanie called Sebastian as soon as she saw it and he knows it's not true. But I would call him anyway, before the game."

"I will. I fucking hate social media."

"We all do, buddy," Avery says with a sigh. "Hang in there and have a great game tonight. Just watch Seb's left hook. It's killer."

Avery hangs up with a chuckle. Ugh. I never thought hanging out with Shayne would result in this.

I throw off the covers and grab a pair of sweats out of my suitcase and pull them on with one hand while I dial Seb's number with the other. He answers on the second ring.

"I am going to rip your head off and shove it down your

throat you son of a bitch," he hisses. My chest constricts as my heart falls to the floor. But before I can make words come out of my mouth, he starts laughing maniacally. "I'm kidding, Rue!"

"*Mon Dieu, tabernac,*" I swear in French. "Not funny, dude. Not fucking funny!"

"Really? Because I can't stop laughing," he responds.

"I would never, ever touch Shayne. Not like that. I need you to know that," I reply, dead serious even though he's still laughing.

"Of course I know that. You don't need to worry," Sebastian replies as he finally stops laughing. "The girl who first posted has been stalking Shay's classes for weeks asking about me and other hockey players. She's a wannabe bunny and Shay's finally got a reason to ban her from the gym. I gotta go. We have a morning skate. And then I want to hit the gym and practice some boxing so I can knock you out like I did Westwood."

"Still not funny!" I bark but he's laughing anyway.

I say good-bye, hang up and throw on a hoodie to head to the breakfast room. I Google my name and Shayne's and the picture pops up from several different sources, including the infamous puck bunny site called the Warren. I click on it and my anger grows. It was taken as we walked to the changing rooms and she gave me that side hug. I'm looking down at her and she's got her head kind of turned and it looks like we're about to kiss. It was a millisecond in time that is totally misleading. Fuck.

As soon as I walk into our meal room, the snickering starts. I glance around. "It's all bullshit."

"What else are you going to say?" a rookie asks and I flip

him the bird as he shovels oatmeal into his mouth.

Jordan, Luc and Devin are all sitting at a table near the buffet and I grab some oatmeal and berries and a blueberry muffin before joining them. "It didn't fucking happen."

"We know," Jordan says and Luc and Devin both nod.

"But there would be no picture to explain if you'd just stayed in like I suggested," Devin mutters.

"You're right. I fucked up." I scoop some oatmeal into my mouth and then almost choke as Coach walks in.

"Morning, boys," he says in his usual gruff tone. His eyes scan the room and make contact with my own but he keeps moving toward the buffet, grabbing a coffee and taking his time as he pours cream and stirs it. I force myself to look innocent and shovel another spoonful of oatmeal into my mouth. I try not to look at him as he leaves the buffet but I have no choice when he stops beside our table.

"Everyone get a good night's sleep last night?" he questions and Jordan and Luc nod while Devin gives him a verbal "'yes." He turns his eyes on me.

"Slept great. Ready to go." I try to smile but I'm certain it looks far from natural.

"Oh it doesn't matter," he says calmly. "You're a healthy scratch tonight."

He turns and exits the room, leaving me stunned. "Healthy scratch" means the coach is choosing not to play me even though I'm not injured. I open my mouth but stop myself from speaking because I can't challenge him—it would make things worse—and he's gone anyway. I look around the table and am met with looks of sympathy. Devin says, "I'll talk to him."

"Don't. You're right. I did this. You said he'd be pissed and he is." I push aside my half-eaten oatmeal and stand up, grabbing the muffin. "I won't give him a reason to punish me again."

As I make my way to my room, I can't help but blame Brie for this a little bit. She got me angry and caused me to not want to be alone. This woman isn't good for me. I contemplate finding a new charity to volunteer at, but decide I'm going to stay at this one and just try my best to annoy the crap out of her the way she annoys me. As infantile as it may be, that'll bring me some satisfaction.

Chapter 4

Brie

Well the kids love him, I tell myself as I watch Alex take questions after his talk on his health and fitness routine. It was actually a fantastic workshop. I've had a lot of experts come in and give presentations on stuff like this before. And they were good but most forget that these kids are on their own and the money they have to spend on anything isn't a lot. Alex realizes that and he's made a point of referencing cost-efficient ways to eat healthy when he talks about food and all the exercise stuff he references doesn't need a fancy gym membership. He's also, I hate to admit, really funny, adding just the right amount of jokes and silly references to keep it interesting.

The talk wraps up and the kids leave, every single one of them stopping to thank him personally. He also brought them all Barons hats that he had the entire team sign. "If you're not a fan, sell them on eBay. I won't be offended."

I laugh at that and his eyes find mine. I cover my mouth

and force myself to stop. After the last kid leaves, he walks over to me. "You liked my talk."

"I like that they liked your talk," I reply and give him a small, polite smile. "And it's very sweet of you to give out the hats."

"I was going to ask if I could start a running club for the kids," he says and rakes a hand through his thick brown hair, sending it every which way, yet somehow it still looks perfect.

"Sure. But that would be a really big commitment." I am a little stunned he would volunteer that. We've had one athlete volunteer here since we opened—a baseball player. He came twice, promised a whole bunch of things, got the kids excited and then never came back. I should have known his motives were self-promotion and not helping the kids when he showed up with a photographer. I don't want to be that naïve again. Although I have to admit Alex seems a lot more dedicated about this than the baseball player did. And since he flat out, and rather hostilely, refused to let me mention his name for the fund-raiser, he's clearly not here for the publicity.

He shrugs his broad, strong shoulders. "We'd meet once a week. And I'd have to probably change the day around every now and then because of road trips, but if that's okay I'd love to do it."

"That would be fantastic."

"Great. Oh and one of the girls...Mary Hope." He says her name without the H like most French Canadians, so it comes out "Ope" and it makes me smile. I don't remember much about my years living in Quebec but somehow that accent feels like home and soothes me. "She said you used to have yoga classes but the instructor quit."

I nod. "Yeah, she moved upstate to start her own studio. I'm going to try and find a new one this week but it's not easy finding people that will work for free."

"I have a friend in Seattle who teaches yoga. She goes to national conferences all the time and she might know someone local willing to help," he tells me and I can't help but think of the stuff I saw online about him in Seattle at a gym getting cozy with a fitness instructor that dates another hockey player. "Would you like me to call Shay and ask?"

"You were just in Seattle weren't you?" I ask casually.

He smiles that damn cocky, lopsided grin again. I wonder why the right side of his face doesn't lift up like his left. A puck to the face maybe or a stick? "You've been following my schedule? I thought you didn't watch hockey."

"I don't," I counter. "But you made the paper for stuff other than hockey on that trip."

His smile fades and his shoulders seem to tense. He swallows and I watch his Adam's apple bob under what has to be two-day-old growth at least. He's almost sporting a beard . . . I've never kissed a man with a beard. Not that I want to kiss him. It's just an observation. He clears his throat and my eyes pop back up to his face. "I should have known you followed gossip sites."

I'm about to argue that I don't, but Len sent it to me when she found the article because she does, in fact, follow gossip sites. But before I can open my mouth Selena pops in, her arms loaded with boxes. Alex immediately darts to her to take them from her. "We got that donation of art supplies from the place in Queens."

"Fantastic!" I nod. "Thanks, Selena. I'll put them away."

"Need help?" She smiles at Alex.

"I can help," Alex volunteers immediately so Selena simply nods and disappears.

Our eyes meet and he still looks a little pissed about our earlier conversation. "Follow me." I march over to the walk-in closet in the corner. "I don't read gossip sites but I happened to see the picture."

"Shayne is my friend's fiancée. It wasn't what it looked like," he replies tersely. "Not that I expect you to believe that."

"It doesn't matter what I think," I reply. "What you do with your personal life isn't my business as long as you act professional here."

"So do you want me to help find a new yoga instructor?"

"Yes, please. I'll take all the help I can get," I admit as I open the closet door and step in, reaching up for the string attached to the light bulb. "I just have to find some space for the box."

I glance back at him. Alex has his head dipped, his eyes roaming over the contents of the box, which is probably paints, brushes and charcoal pencils. He walks up casually, but as soon as he sees me in the closet he stops, bends down and puts the box on the ground and turns to leave.

"I thought you were going to help," I tell him. "I could use those muscles of yours to move around some of these boxes to make room for the new one."

"Sorry. Can't," he says gruffly. "Maybe Len or Selena can help you."

I'm more than a little pissed off. "Len's not here today and Selena just left because you said you would help."

"I have to get going. I have a team thing," he says and it's clear he's shitty at lying.

I frown and put my hands on my hips. "When you came in today you said it was a rest day. I know what 'rest day' means. It means no game. No practice."

Everything about him shifts. He starts to look annoyed—really annoyed, like borderline angry. "Look, I came to give the talk not be a maintenance guy. I'm sorry I have somewhere to be."

"Oh. Okay. I get it." Clearly he's a lot more like the baseball guy than I thought. He's only interested in helping with things like talking to the kids who fawn all over him. Or being the hero finding me a yoga instructor. God forbid the guy built like a Greek god actually do five seconds of physical labor. I turn to the shelves piled with boxes and I pick up one. I assume he's going to leave but when I glance back he's standing there, just on the other side of the door.

"You get what?"

I readjust the box in my arms and fix him with a cold stare. "That you'll volunteer as long as it means having the kids adore you but you don't want to do anything that doesn't involve instant gratification. It's fine. Now I know and it's not even shocking to be honest. I've had volunteers like you before and I've managed."

I find an empty spot on the shelves that line the left side of the closet and slide the box onto it. I hear him whisper a French obscenity under his breath, but I ignore him and reach for one of the other boxes on the floor. Why won't he just go?

I pick it up. The cardboard is old and it's heavy. I think it's some of the summer patio stuff I had Selena box up last week. I scan the shelves again, fully aware that he's still standing there, staring at me.

"I thought you had somewhere to be," I remind him tersely as I spot a place on the top shelf that looks big enough for the box.

"I'm not the jerk you think I am." He says it low, and soft, and I can't help but turn my head to look at him. He looks kind of wounded. And for a brief, intense moment his stormy blue eyes drop and his jaw softens in defeat and I have this wave of déjà vu. But it carries an ominous feeling with it and I suddenly feel as jumpy as he looked earlier.

"I'm not the spoiled rich kid you clearly think I am either," I snap back but my words are wobbly, not firm. I turn away from his and start to lift the box, but the top shelf is high and the box is heavy and the higher I lift the more off balance I feel. I push myself up on my tiptoes and the corner of the box hits the edge of the shelf instead of sliding onto it and I realize in a panic-filled second that I'm going to drop it.

I let out a squeak and then suddenly there's another set of arms in my face and the box is ripped from me. Everything happens so fast it's a blur. He steps into the closet, saves the box from landing on my head and then the floor, and shoves it onto a shelf and then disappears—all in the time it took me to blink and steady myself.

I leave the closet and catch a blur of him as he storms out of the room. What the fuck is his issue? I follow him but he's out the front door before I even get to the hallway. I reach out and catch the door seconds before it closes and call his name but he's already halfway down the street.

"What the f—" I catch myself before the rest of that word

comes out of my mouth because I will not swear at work in case a kid hears me. We're always on them to clean up their language. Sighing, I let the door close and turn and head back into the closet.

Seriously, I do not get that guy.

An hour later, I'm explaining the whole thing to Victor as we share a cab to my place. Normally I take the subway home but when he meets me after work he never wants to take the subway. In the whole time we've been dating, we've never taken the subway. I sometimes wonder if he's ever been on it. As a native New Yorker, I would guess yes but with Victor it's highly possible he hasn't.

"I told you before, he sounds like a self-absorbed athlete," Victor surmises when I'm done explaining the closet incident. He already knows about the phone argument and the way he showed up late for the orientation. I haven't, and I won't, tell him about how he hit on me in Starbucks. "I don't know why you let it get to you. These men are as superficial as they come. They get fawned all over for skating a straight line. He's not volunteering to do good, he's volunteering to look good."

He shifts his dark brown eyes down to his phone in his hand and a wisp of his perfectly styled dark hair falls forward. He brushes it off his forehead, annoyed, which is too bad because he looks better when he's mussed up.

"But then why won't he let me use his name on the posters?" I question because I think Victor is probably right, but that one fact goes against our theory.

Victor pats my knee and I try not to bristle. He does that a lot. It feels condescending, like he's placating me. I told him that once and he got completely offended and explained it's a gesture of love and support so now I grin and bear it. "Brie, baby, he's an adult playing a game for a living. He's a man-child. Don't take it personally. And besides you don't need his name to sell tickets. Half my office is coming and your dad will corral all his rich friends. It'll be fine."

I sigh. "I need the interest in this place to grow. I don't want it to always be your colleagues, my dad's friends and my trust fund supporting this place. His name would bring in a different group of potential donors."

His hand has left my knee and is now wrapped around his phone as he reads his emails. He's not paying attention at all. I don't even need the lackluster "uh-huh" he gives me as a sign.

I reach up and softly graze my fingers through the back of his hair. "You tuned me out again."

He blinks his dark eyes and lifts them from his phone screen. "I'm sorry. It's work."

"It's always work," I whisper.

"So I should stop paying attention to my work so I can listen to you complain about yours?" he questions and his words are a little clipped but he smiles at me like he's half kidding. I realize his point, even if I don't agree with it. I don't say a word when he refocuses on his phone screen. I turn and look out the window instead. The Upper East Side flies by through the rain splattered window.

"You can always go into private practice, use that psychology degree you spent all that time, money and effort on," he says signifying he's done with his emails and that he was paying more attention than I gave him credit for a minute ago. I turn to look at him. His face holds a tentative expression and his words are gentle. "If this charity project doesn't work out long-term, I mean. You'll still be doing a good thing. And you can set your own hours and I can see you more. We can finally talk about the future because we'll have time to plan it."

I can't believe he's saying this. Just the thought of closing Daphne's House makes me sick to my stomach. Literally. I can feel it churning. I put a hand on my belly and take a deep breath. "The House can't and won't fail. And your job is a big part of why we're not spending as much time together too."

"Okay relax, I'm not trying to play the blame game here." He frowns, his wide mouth turning down, and loosens his tie a little. "I'm just saying... right now you help, about what? Twelve kids a year? If you had your own private psychology practice you'd be helping that many a day and making money at it."

"But I want to help the ones who can't afford to pay," I reply, my voice hard. Victor was so supportive and interested when I told him about what I did for a living when we first met. And he knows about my past, and why this is so important to me.

He calmly pats my knee again. "You could do free work with these kids—at shelters. You don't have to take it all on yourself. The charity is wonderful, don't get me wrong, But I honestly don't know how you're going to keep it going and move forward with your own life. It's too all consuming."

I clench my jaw to keep from saying something about that last comment. Victor wants to get married. He's been dropping that hint for about a month as subtly as you'd drop a boulder on a pinkie toe. But he hasn't come out and asked me, officially, because he thinks I'm not ready. He's right. I'm not. If this was two months ago, I would have probably said yes but the last few weeks Victor has made it clear that he either isn't listening to the things I tell him about who I am and what I want or else he doesn't believe I'm serious.

"Victor, your work is all consuming too," I argue back in a resolute tone and shift so his hand falls onto the seat between us. "Remember, I could have easily turned into one of those kids. If my parents hadn't seen my story on the news, I would have spent my life in foster care."

"You said yourself you don't remember much about foster care. You were four," he says as the cab slows to a stop in the gridlock just a block from my house. If it hadn't started raining I would've gotten out and walked the rest of the way but I don't have an umbrella.

"I remember crying. A lot. And I remember being scared and I remember the paramedics and police when they came to take us away from that horrible house." I remind him of everything I've shared with him already. "I'm never going to stop fighting for kids so they don't end up in places like that."

He moves his hand to pat my knee but I cover it with my own to prevent him from doing that again. He takes my hand in his and lifts it to his mouth, kissing the back of my knuckles. "We don't have to talk about this. The charity is your job right now. And if nothing else it shows what a wonderful, protective heart you have for kids, which means you'll be a great mom one day."

The cab finally turns onto my street and stops outside

my door. As Victor pays the cabbie, I jump out and run up my front stairs . By the time I get the door open he's right behind me and we scurry into the front hall. I love my townhouse. It's huge in New York terms—two stories with two bedrooms, two bathrooms and archways, crown moldings, and big lead glass windows. I adore it. Both the townhouse and the building where Daphne's House is located were willed to me by my grandmother when she passed away. I don't need a place this big to live, but I'm clinging to it because it reminds me of my grandmother. Eventually, if I have to, I'll sell it, get something smaller and put the profit toward Daphne's House.

Victor closes the door behind us and helps me out of my coat.

"What do you want for dinner?" I ask.

"You," Victor says and kisses my shoulder.

I smile and turn in his arms to face him, but I pull back when he tries to kiss me. "I'm not on the menu tonight, honey."

He looks confused for a minute and then he groans. "We haven't had time alone in weeks and now you're on your period?!"

"It's not like I planned it," I remind him because it somehow feels like he's accusing me.

"But you could have told me," he replies, clearly annoyed. "There's a mixer for my alma mater tonight I am skipping for this."

"Not to spend time with me, just to have sex with me?"

His mouth opens, but closes without a debate. He sighs. "Why are you constantly trying to twists my words lately?"

"I'm not. You're being an ass," I tell him bluntly.

He takes several deep breaths and steps back, his long, lean frame blocking the small light I leave on that sits on the hall table. The narrow hall gets as dark as my mood. "I don't want to fight with you."

I don't want to fight with him either, but it's all we've been doing for a couple of weeks now. I've been ignoring it and trying to tell myself it's not big deal, because I don't want confront him, or honestly even myself, with what might be the cold hard truth—this isn't working out. "I'm not going to be a mother one day." It's a whisper but it's stern and resolute. "I've told you that. I am not risking passing on my bum genes to someone else."

"Sweetheart, you also told me you don't know if you carry the same gene your birth mother did," Victor replies calmly and then he steps closer and pulls me to his chest. He has always known the right time to hug me. I have to give him that. "And even if you do carry it, it doesn't mean you'll pass it on."

"But I could," I reply. "And if I have it I could die of ovarian cancer as young as my mom did and leave my kids motherless."

"Or you could not have it, or have it and not get cancer and not pass it on," Victor replies and runs a hand over the back of my hair. "You know what my endgame is, Brie, honey. Marriage and a family. If you're going to let this gene dictate what you do with your life, then you need to get tested and find out if you have it so I know what I'm dealing with."

"What *you're* dealing with?" I repeat. And this is exactly why I never told him I got the test done last year but never picked up the results. Because he would pester me relentlessly to find out and I'm not ready to face the news.

"I want a family, Brie. That does not make me a monster."

I stare into his hazel eyes. "There are other ways to have a family. I'm living proof of that. I'm not against adoption or fostering, you know that. In fact I feel very strongly that I want to do that one day."

He lets go of me.

"I know." He averts his gaze, heaves a deep breath and loosens his tie a little. "Jesus, how did this conversation get so heavy. Can we change the subject?"

"Go to your mixer." I give him a peck on the cheek and hang my coat on the antique coatrack before I head through the living room into the kitchen. I open the cupboards and examine the contents waiting for the sound of the front door opening and closing. It doesn't come. And a second later I hear the oak floorboards creak and his hands are on my hips as he gazes into the cupboard from over my shoulder.

"We could order sushi," he suggests.

I shrug. "Honestly, Victor, if you want to go to the mixer, go. It's fine. I swear. I've had a long day and I'll probably just make mac and cheese and go to bed."

"But you love those spicy shrimp rolls at the place on the corner," he reminds me and I glance over my shoulder at him. He gives me his best dashing smile and squeezes my hips. "Screw the mixer."

I feel lighter. Like maybe things are turning around. God I hope so. I don't deal well with giant upheaval or changes. It comes from all the upheaval and changes I faced when I was little. I've been to psychologists my whole life, my parents were very proactive knowing my past. I knew even before I became a professional myself that I tend to hang on to things—people—longer than I should because my childhood traumas made me feel like jumping out of the frying pan always meant you landed in the fryer. Of course knowing my issues and actually facing them are two different things. So I smile back at Victor and hunt around in my junk drawer for the menu from the sushi place.

Chapter 5

Alex

I wake up screaming. I don't know how long I've been screaming, but my throat is raw so I'm guessing it was a while. The sheets are damp with sweat and twisted around my legs. I know without even looking that I've dug my fingernails into my palms again and they're bleeding. I can feel the sting and sticky dampness of the blood. I struggle to get air into my lungs and reach for the bedside lamp. I squint against the light and stare at my palms. There are little half-moon fingernail imprints across them both. Only a couple on each palm broke the skin though and they're not too deep, but there is blood and it's on the hotel sheets too.

Fuck. I am so sick of this.

The nightmare is the same as it's been since I was eight. I'm trapped in that damn concrete room—the "time-out room" as the foster monsters used to call it—and it's cold and for some reason it shrinks. And shrinks. And it makes me call out for help because I'm panicked and it won't stop shrinking.

And I'm crying and I'm terrified and then all the concrete—all the walls and the ceiling are pressing into every part of me, cold and hard, and I scream.

The thing that always makes me angry after the dreams is that I'm calling for help. I learned in the first couple of weeks of being at that foster home that there was no help. I always sat silently for the hours, sometimes all day, that I was in there. I didn't cry and I didn't call for help. But in my dream I do, and I even sometimes know I shouldn't. But I can't stop.

I sit up, untangle myself from the sheets and head to the bathroom. I leave the light off, but it's not completely dark because the bedside light is filtering in through the open door. As I'm running my hands through the water to clean the small wounds, there's a firm knock on my door. I yank off a bunch of toilet paper and press it into my left palm because it's got the most cuts and then grab a towel and wipe my right hand on it. There's another firm knock. I'm only wearing my underwear so I grab the complimentary bathrobe off the back of the door and throw it on.

I'm just about to open the door when it starts to open for me and one of the hotel's security guards is standing there. He looks startled to see me. I'm annoyed to see him. "I'm sorry, Mr. Larue. We normally would never enter your room without permission. However, we called and you didn't answer."

"I was sleeping," I reply tersely and shove the bloody toilet paper in the pocket of the robe before crossing my arms. "I sleep deeply."

"Oh. Again, apologies, it's just that we had a noise complaint," he explains and starts to look a little uncomfortable and I know exactly why he's here. Someone heard me screaming.

"The screaming?" I question and he nods. "Yeah, I fell asleep with the television on and I guess there was some cheesy horror movie on. It woke me up too."

"Oh. Okay." He glances toward the television, which is clearly off, but as far as he's concerned it's because I shut it off. "Again we're sorry to bother you but when you didn't answer the phone and someone reports screaming we have to—"

"Yeah. Sure. No problem," I cut him off. "I'd like to go back to bed now."

"Yes, sir. Have a good rest of your night." He leaves, closing the door behind him. I throw the latch on the door so he can't just walk in again if I fall back asleep and start screaming again. It's doubtful that'll happen anyway. I glance at the clock. It's four in the morning. I got four hours sleep. Oh well. Better than nothing. I'm meeting Kristi for the keys to my new apartment at ten.

I shrug out of the robe, leaving it on the floor and throw on some sweats, a hoodie and my sneakers. Might as well go for a run. Staying in this tiny room isn't going to stop the nightmares from coming again if I go back to sleep. I hadn't had one in almost two weeks, but I know that incident in the closet with Brie triggered it. I really wasn't trying to be an asshole about not helping her. I just can't do confined spaces. That closet didn't have concrete walls and wasn't in a dank root cellar, but it was the same long, narrow shape and...I just couldn't. I should have told her I was claustrophobic, but that woman is so damn judgmental.

I grab my iPod and headphones and leave the hotel. It's

colder than I anticipated. Locals probably wouldn't find it cold at all, but I still have California blood from living in San Diego. I suck it up and start to jog. I head straight for the bridge so I can run to Manhattan. I can't wait to live there. As much as I love my teammates—and I honestly do—I don't think living near them is the best thing. Being a third wheel is fine in small doses, but now there's no Jordan without Jessie, Devin without Callie, Luc without Rose. The girls are all fantastic, truly, but they don't want me around all the time and I don't want to be around all the time.

It's not that it's hard seeing them all in love and everything. It isn't. I don't miss what I've never had. But it's a distinct reminder that my life—these friends I've considered family—are getting their own families and I'm not. I'm happy for them. I'm just not particularly looking forward to the next phase of my life.

I'm fucking thirty. And I'm feeling thirty. Late nights before a practice or a game affect me now. I'm sluggish and achy and foggy mentally. Also, I'm kind of over the puck bunny thing. I'd never admit that to the guys, because I have a reputation to uphold but yeah . . . not feeling it anymore.

I jog across the bridge and then slow to a walk. I don't want to overexert myself because I have practice this afternoon. I'm run-walking for about an hour and stumble across a Dunkin' Donuts. I head inside and order a coffee and a Boston Kreme donut. I sit at the small counter against the window and scarf down the donut, then order one more and take it with me, gulping down the last of my coffee and tossing it in the trash can as I exit.

The city is getting busier. Of course it wasn't exactly

empty when I started this run, even at four in the morning. With any luck, the city is lively enough to meet some new single friends. Maybe. Hopefully.

I decide I'm going to grab the subway home so I wander down the block in the general direction I think it might be. The music in my ears suddenly disappears. I pull my iPod from my pocket and see the battery is dead. Damn it. Well at least it didn't crap out on my run. As I start to pull my earbuds out I hear a female voice—loud and firm. "Don't!"

I stop and look around. There's a woman walking about ten feet ahead of me, but she's by herself. Across the street there's a guy in a business suit and another one a few feet back in jeans. No other women though.

"Stop!"

Same voice, only this time it's louder and filled with fear. And I can tell it's coming from behind me. I start walking backward. One step. Two steps. On the third step I'm parallel with an alley. Halfway down it I see this big, hulking dude leaning over a very skinny, scraggly-haired woman. She's pressed against the side of the building and he's grabbed her by the arm of her ripped puffy coat. He's speaking, but his voice is low and I can't make out the words, only a rumbling sound.

I start to walk toward them. They don't notice and when I'm about ten feet away I stand straight, pull my shoulders back and in my deepest voice I say, "Hey! You all right, lady?"

Her head snaps over and I realize she's not a lady. She's a kid with dirt-stained, coffee-colored skin and matted curly hair and light eyes. Is she even a teenager? I take a few steps closer and try to look calm and not shocked. The guy glares at me. He's meaty but not muscled, which bodes well for me if I have to get physical. And he's dirty, stains on his jacket and tears in his jeans; not the fashionable kind.

"She's my kid. Mind your business," he warns and yanks her away from the wall and turns her and himself away from me. He starts to drag-walk her down the alley. She looks back at me, eyes wide and filled with fear.

"Hey!" I take more steps toward them. "Kid! Is he your dad?"

"No!"

"Fucking bitch!" he barks, but doesn't let her go and starts drag-walking her faster.

I pick up my pace too and clamp a hand on his shoulder. He spins to face me quickly, arms up. He doesn't swing, he doesn't seem to be holding a knife or a gun and more importantly, he lets her go.

I reach out and motion for her to get behind me. She does with quick, quiet steps. He turns his glare to her. "You fucking owe me, Mac!"

"I owe you nothing!" she yells back.

He bares his teeth, what's left of them, and swears again taking a step toward us so I step toward him. "Fuck you..." he hisses at me. "I'm going to fucking find you and I'm going to make you pay."

"What does she owe you?" I ask. But I'm really not sure I want the answer. She's a street kid, clearly, so the answer could be anything from money to clothes to sexual acts. Oh please let it not be sexual acts.

"Not your fucking business."

"I looted his Dumpster," she blurts out.

Ah. Turf war. Okay. I sigh in relief because I can fix this. I reach into the pocket of my hoodie and pinch some, but not all of the bills I have in between my fingers and pull them out. A twenty and a five. "Twenty-five bucks to forget about whatever she took from your Dumpster."

He rips the money out of my extended hand. "Tell her not to do it again."

"She won't. Right, Mac?" I glance over my shoulder. She's not there. The entire alley behind me is empty. "What the fuck?"

I start to jog. When I get to the sidewalk I look right and then left. She's across the street, half a block up. I sprint and catch up to her in no time. I even manage not to be hit by any cars when I jaywalk to get to her faster. "Mac!"

She doesn't turn. Instead she starts walking faster and then she breaks into a run. I speed up. She's fast, but she's not a professional athlete with over a decade of endurance training. I reach her before she even gets half a block. She turns on me when I grab her arm and she's ferocious, like a wild animal in a trap. It's meant to be intimidating and to scare me and I'm thinking it works on a lot of people, but not me. I've been her. I know the tricks.

"I'll scream. I'll tell them you touched me," she threatens.

"But then you won't get the sixty bucks I want to give you," I explain calmly, quietly, as I reach into the kangaroo pocket of my hoodie with the other hand and pull out the bag with the now mostly crushed donut. "And this."

Her eyes, which are a light green color, dart down to bag and then back to my face, harder than ever. "It's probably laced with roofies."

I laugh. This girl is tough. "They wouldn't dissolve like they do in drinks. You'd see them. And I swear on my life I just bought it a second before I ran into you. It's my favorite donut in the world and I'm giving it to you, so take it before I change my mind."

She wrenches her arm free and for a split second I think she might bolt again, but instead she snatches the donut bag out of my hand. She pulls it out. Most of the chocolate frosting is gone, it must be stuck to the inside of the bag. I figure she'll take a bite but she just holds it, still a skeptic. "You don't look like a guy who eats donuts."

I laugh. "I'm not supposed to. You're saving me from myself."

She still looks skeptical but she takes a giant bite anyway. "Thanks," she manages through chewing. "It tastes much better than the stale ones they dump out back after close."

Oh God, this kid is killing me. "How long have you been on the street?"

"Who said I was?" she challenges.

"Everything about you says you are," I reply bluntly. "I know because I've been there."

"Ha!" she blurts out without a drop of humor. "Bullshit."

"Swear to God," I promise and something in that hard as nails face softens. I decide to push a little more. "How old are you?"

"Eighteen."

She's maybe five foot one or two. She's got the frame of a twelve-year-old but that can happen even to an adult when you're malnourished. However, her still chubby youthful cheeks tell me this isn't just malnourishment. She's a baby.

"I'm guessing twelve?"

"Fuck you! I'm sixteen."

"No you're not," I counter. "You're young enough that your potty mouth is extra offensive."

She stops chewing at that. Frowns and swallows what's in her mouth. "You're not my boss."

"Nope. Just stating facts."

"Sorry."

Okay. She's not lost yet. My heart feels less heavy. I pull out the remaining cash in my hoodie pocket. I carry cash at all times, even running at the crack of ass, for this exact reason. I hold up the three twenties. "I'll give you this no matter what, but I'd like an honest answer about your age."

"What month is it?"

"October. The twenty-first."

"I'll be fifteen next month," she admits. "But obviously I'm mature for my age. Now pay up."

"Yeah. This life will do that." I hand her the cash. She takes it quickly but with less of a swipe than the donut.

"I won't use it for gross stuff like drugs or anything," she promises.

I look around the street. "Where you living? You got a camp somewhere? With others?"

She shakes her head. "Nah. Not really. Sometimes this crazy lady Ethel lets me hang out with her under the bridge, when she's not arguing with the voices in her head. She's got a tarp and some blankets. But the cops like to raid camps and I don't wanna get nabbed. I am *not* going back to the system."

She's not good at this. She shouldn't be telling me any details. It makes me think she hasn't actually been on the street very long. I nod. I know that visceral fear and hearing it in her words floods me with unwanted memories. "I know a place. It's like a boardinghouse. Just for kids."

"Good for you."

"Mac, it's different."

"How do you know?"

"Because I researched it. I volunteer there," I explain and a guy in a business suit marches by, giving us a curious but disgusted glance. Man, I fucking hate people sometimes.

"You researched it?" Her tone is dismissive. "Yeah, lots of crap looks good on paper. The whole system is great on paper. It's a joke. I'm not going back to it."

"This is private. Not state run," I explain. "It's good."

"Have fun volunteering," she says and turns to walk away again.

I fall in step beside her. "You should check it out. It's in Brooklyn."

"Uh-huh." She is so not buying what I am selling.

"You can't keep living like you're living," I tell her and I know it's going to annoy her, to say the least.

She glares at me. "Fuck you. I can take care of myself."

"I'll get a pamphlet on the place and give it to you. So you can read about it," I offer, refusing to back down. "I'll meet you tomorrow with the info. Sound good?"

"Not interested," she replies.

"Okay, how about I make it interesting. Meet me tomorrow. Say right over there," I point to the corner across from us in front of a bakery. "At nine in the morning and I'll give you another sixty if you come and read the pamphlet."

"Are you for real?" she asks, coming to a stop.

"Real," I promise. "So? Deal?"

She nods. "But I get the cash before you start yapping."

I smile. "Okay."

She looks stunned and still a little skeptical. "I won't sleep with you like ever. No matter how much money you give me. If you try to make me I will bite your—"

"Whoa now!" I do not want to hear the end of that sentence. "I swear to God I don't want anything sexual from you. Or anything at all. I've just been in your shoes."

"I still don't believe that by the way," she replies firmly. "No one goes from this to that."

She points at me, her tiny finger sweeping up and down and then it does a flamboyant circle. I smile again. She's something else. "Do you need a place to stay tonight?"

"No," she replies. "Look I will read whatever you want for money, but I ain't your pet project. So don't go all fucking social worker on me."

"Okay. Fine. I won't." I raise my hands as if surrendering. "Tomorrow. In front of the bakery. Nine."

She nods. "Don't follow me."

I nod and watch her walk away. She keeps glancing over her shoulder until she crosses the street and disappears around a corner. I pull out my phone and take a picture of the storefront so I remember the name of it and then pull up Google maps to figure out where the fuck I am and how to get home.

I walk toward the closest subway station. She's exactly why I volunteer at charities that help kids. I don't do it for praise. I do it because if people hadn't done it for me, I wouldn't be where I am. Mac is the first street kid I've engaged this much though. I've often given them money and food or stuff like toothbrushes and clothes, but I tend to keep the interactions impersonal because I can't get attached to these kids and they can't get attached to me. At any point I could be traded. The last thing either of us needs is to be ripped away from each other.

But there was no way I was going to leave Mac there in that alley with that guy. It might be my downfall, if I get too involved and somehow let her down, but I have to try and help her.

Chapter 6

Alex

I knock on the front door of Devin and Callie's Park Slope brownstone, and Callie swings it open with a bright friendly smile. "Come in!"

"Sorry I'm early," I say. "But I brought wine."

She wipes her hands on her apron and grabs the bottle. "Thanks! Let's get this puppy open."

I follow her through the house to the kitchen at the back. She puts the bottle on the counter and opens a drawer, digging around for a corkscrew. I sit at one of the bar stools on the other side of the peninsula. "I haven't had a drink in weeks. Not since Conner brought the stomach flu home from school. He got over it in a couple days, but I struggled for weeks."

"Devin mentioned it. You're better now?" I ask as she pulls out the corkscrew and reaches for the bottle again. I inhale deeply. Something smells delicious, like tomato and cheese.

She nods, a piece of her long brown hair coming loose from the ponytail she's wearing. She tucks it behind her ear and begins to open the bottle. "Mostly."

I take another long whiff of the delicious aroma filling the kitchen. "Dinner smells amazing."

She sniffs. Pauses and sniffs again. "Really?"

I nod and her brow furrows for a second. How could she think it smells anything less than delicious? I look around the place, glancing into the dining room to the left and the archway to the family room on the right. There's a train track set up in there and a bunch of toys on the floor. "Where's Devin and the rug rat?"

"Dev is picking him up from hockey practice," Callie explains. "They'll be home soon."

"Hockey practice," I repeat and smile. "Another Garrison getting ready to make the league his bitch, huh?"

Callie laughs. "Devin sure hopes so. And Conner loves it. It's all he talks about now."

I feel a weird little sting, like a paper cut inside my chest. I am kind of jealous of what it must feel like to have a family. I haven't felt that sting since I was a teenager and couch surfing, bouncing around between the homes of other guys on my hockey team because I'd run away from my foster home. I must look like I feel because Callie's expression softens and grows curious. "You want to add another Larue to the league one day?"

I shake my head. "I don't want kids. I would have no idea how to be a good parent."

She pulls the cork out of the bottle but pauses, her brown eyes curious. "Your parents suck, huh?"

I shrug but for some reason, for the first time in a very, very long time, I don't stop there. Maybe it's because I know her childhood history is similar to mine since she and her sisters were orphaned at a young age or maybe it's because running into that Mac kid this morning has made me think about it a lot more today, but I tell Callie something I haven't told anyone since I was eighteen. "They didn't get a chance to suck. They died."

She puts the wine bottle down on the counter with a thud. Her eyes are even wider now. "Both of them?"

I nod. "Car accident."

"Holy shit. Recently?"

"Before I made the league. I don't really talk about it." The dreaded prickly feeling of humiliation starts to set in. I shift in my seat and stand up. "Wineglasses?"

She points to a cupboard next to the fridge so I walk over and open it.

"I'm going to tell you what you've heard a million times: I'm so sorry you went through that," she says and I glance at her over my shoulder. Her eyes aren't filled with sympathy but more with understanding. "My mom died before I was even a teenager and I still get condolences when people find out. I try not to bring it up because of that. It's hard."

I shake my head. "You guys avoided foster care though, right?" I take two wineglasses down, put them on the peninsula and reach for the wine.

"Thankfully," she says quietly, which is uncharacteristic for her. "Our dad's mom took us in but as soon as Jessie turned sixteen, Grandma Lily moved to Florida for nine months of the year, leaving us on our own in Maine, and we had to lie to just about everyone so they didn't put us in foster care."

"That's horrible," I tell her but still, part of me considers her lucky because she had Jessie and Rose and a house to live in, which is much more than I got once I left the foster care system. "You know things are changing now. There's a lot of private facilities for orphaned or abandoned kids. There's this one right here in Brooklyn that lets them live independently as long as they're in some kind of schooling and helps teach them life basics like budgeting and cooking and nutrition. They offer the classes to kids who don't live there too. And they have lawyers and stuff who help them for free."

She looks genuinely excited. "Oh my God, I wish there was a place like that in Silver Bay when we were growing up. I almost burned the house down like five times trying to cook that first year Grandma Lily left us."

I laugh and hand her a glass of wine, taking my own.

"You should tell Rose about this place," Callie informs me. "She's got a teaching degree and she wants to tutor kids. And of course that type of place would mean a lot to her because of our past."

I nod and make a mental note. "Cheers," I say to Callie and clink my glass against hers before taking a sip. She takes one too but instantly makes a face.

She spits the wine back into the glass. "It tastes disgusting."

I cock my head. "Really. I like it."

"How can you like it? It's like vinegar!" She sniffs her glass and I watch the color drain from her face. I'm about to ask her if she's okay but she abruptly puts the glass down on the counter and charges from the room.

Fuck! Where is Devin when you need him? This is husband territory. I set my glass down beside hers. Pause. Pick it back up and gulp down more wine. Nope. Definitely not vinegar. I put it down again and trace her steps. She went out into the main hallway and at first I'm not sure where she went from there but then I hear her groan from behind a door under the stairs. I knock on it tentatively. "Callie? Are you okay? Should I call Devin?"

I hear a toilet flush and a moment later she opens the door. She's leaning over the sink, the faucet is on and she's scooping water into her mouth with her hand and then spitting it back out. The bathroom is tiny, with no windows so I stay firmly in the hallway.

"Don't call Devin," she croaks. "He'll be home shortly anyway. I can't believe this flu is coming back. I think I really have to give in and get to the doctor."

"Callie..." I feel like I'm intruding by saying this but it seems so obvious to me. "Are you sure it's the flu?"

"You think it's something worse?" she questions, panicked. "Like salmonella? Or Ebola?"

"No." I laugh as she steps out of the bathroom closing the light and then the door. "Any chance you're pregnant?"

She freezes. "What? No. I mean. Maybe. But no. I would know. Right?"

"Umm...I think these symptoms might be your body's way of telling you," I reply and I'm more than a little stunned that she seems so confused.

"We're not trying," she confesses. "I mean...we're not

using anything but we're not trying. You know what I mean?"

"No. Honestly, I don't really have a clue." The idea of being lackadaisical about birth control is terrifying to me. "But you should probably take a test."

"I did a couple months ago when I was late, and it came out negative," she replies.

"Too much information," I blurt out and cover my ears.

"I can't be."

"You can be," I argue. There's a storm brewing in her big brown eyes as hope and fear swirl behind them.

"I have a test upstairs," she explains. "I bought a bunch."

"Okay then."

The front door opens suddenly and Devin walks in with a pint-sized version of himself. "Hey Rue," he says, sniffing deeply. "Something smells incredible."

"I..." Callie's face is still a swirl of emotions and Devin takes it in and looks instantly concerned. She tries to smile down at Conner. "Hey, Con! How was hockey?"

"It was awesome. I scored," he announces and then turns his attention to me. "Do you play?"

"Yep. With your dad. I'm Alex," I say and he extends his little hand. I want to laugh but I don't want to offend him so I extend mine and we shake.

"Nice to meet ya. I'm gonna play with my iPad now."

He marches to the back of the house and I watch him go in amusement. Devin is looking at Callie. "You okay? You don't look it."

Callie smiles. "Fine. I'm just going to run upstairs for a second. If the oven dings take out the lasagna okay?"

She charges up the stairs. I follow Devin into the kitchen again. He sees the wine and heads to the cupboard to grab another glass. "Should I be worried about her?"

"I think she's just trying to figure out if she has the flu," I explain as he pours himself a glass.

"That bug is back? Damn." He shakes his head. "I'm going to make her go to the doctor this time. She hates doctors but I'll carry her there if I have to."

"Devin," I say his name and he looks up at me. "You've been through this before. How are you not getting it?"

And then he gets it. Instantly. "No. She's . . . ?"

I shrug but nod because if I had to bet I'd bet yes. He puts his glass down on the counter again and his eyes shift toward the family room, where Conner is and back. "With Ashleigh we had to try forever. But Callie and I . . . we were just going to see what happens."

"Babies." I grin at him because he's a doofus right now. "Babies are what happens, Captain."

"I have to go check on her," he whispers, his voice excited and a giant smile spread across his face. "We were going to start trying the minute we got married but decided to wait to make sure Conner was settling into the stepmom thing and then she didn't want to be pregnant for Jessie's wedding and well, now I guess maybe she'll be pregnant for Rose's."

He moves toward the hall, but the oven beeps so first he pulls a bubbling, hot, gooey, delicious-looking lasagna out and places it on top of the stove. It smells so freaking good I already regret the next words that are about to come out of my mouth. "Is it okay if I bail on dinner?"

He's making his way toward the hallway again, to head

upstairs and check on Callie, but he stops and gives me a re-morseful smile. "You don't have to."

"Dude, this is a family moment." I tell him what I know he already knows. "It's fine. Tell Callie I'll take a rain check on that lasagna."

I walk to the family room archway, lean in and ruffle Conner's wheat-colored hair. "Nice meeting you, hockey star. See you soon."

"Bye, Alex who plays with my dad," he says, eyes never leaving the iPad in front of him. He's got some game going with loud, annoying music.

I walk to the front hall with Devin and grab my coat off the banister. Devin still looks remorseful. "Call Luc and Rosie. They're just down the street and they're always up for guests."

"Maybe."

"Devin!" Callie's voice sounds urgent as she calls his name from somewhere upstairs.

I smile as the excitement in his eyes grows. I remember Jordan telling me years ago how badly Devin wanted to be a dad. How excited he was when Conner was born. "Go. And Devin," I pause as he stops two stairs up and looks back at me. "I hope you knocked her up."

He grins. "I hope I did too."

As I make my way down the sidewalk, my stomach is rumbling in protest at leaving that lasagna behind. The weather is ominous, dark clouds hiding the sun and a blustery wind has started. I wonder where Mac is. That coat she had on seemed warm, but it was also ripped. I regret not buying her a hotel room somewhere, but I bet she'd have accused me of wanting bad things from her if I did it. Or she'd worry I was going to call the police on her. I really hope she meets me tomorrow.

I pull my phone out and text Luc like Devin suggested to see if he's free for dinner. He texts back almost right away and says he and Rose are just sitting down to order dinner at a pub a few blocks away. He tells me to come meet them and includes the address. Fifteen minutes later, half a block from the pub, the rain starts. I move faster, ducking under awnings and make it into the restaurant without getting too drenched. I spot Luc and Rose at a table near the back and wave as I make my way over.

We have two days off without games, which Luc explains Rose has packed with wedding planning. I'm almost jealous of him because at least he has something to do. Other than the fund-raiser in the Hamptons for Daphne's House tomorrow night and a practice Sunday afternoon, I've got nothing planned. I figure I'll busy myself buying new furniture for my new place, but that will probably take all of twenty minutes and a few clicks on some websites.

"I thought you were having dinner with Callie and Devin. She was making her famous lasagna," Rose says as the waiter brings our drink orders over.

I nod and then concentrate on taking the paper off my straw to buy myself some time. I don't think I can tell her Callie is in the middle of a pregnancy scare so I need the time to figure out a lie. "She thinks she still has the flu, so we postponed. I can't get sick."

"Why not? At least then the coach would have a legitimate reason to bench you," Luc quips and gives me a sympathetic smile. "He's being a dick, for the record."

"Thanks," I say, smiling.

"So since we have time off, you should have a housewarming this weekend and invite us all over," Rose announces and I almost choke on my diet Sprite. Luc shakes his head at her. She tries to look innocent. "What? He has to have a house-warming sometime. It might as well be now."

"I do?" I question and shrug. "I've never had one before."

"Well that's simply unacceptable," Rose says. "Every house needs a party to break it in, make it feel loved."

"She's a crazy person," Luc informs me with a grin that says he wouldn't have it any other way. "But if you don't plan one, she'll plan it for you."

"I'll have one, but I can't this weekend," I explain. "I'm attending a fund-raiser tomorrow and besides, I don't have any furniture other than a bed. I could still have a party with just that, but it's not a party I'd invite old married people like you to."

Luc laughs. Rose turns pink and shakes her head. "You single hockey players are the worst."

"What's your fund-raiser for?" Luc asks as the waiter comes back over with our meals. I try not to stare too longingly at the cheeseburger Rose got. I got a Greek grilled chicken wrap with a spinach salad, which are probably delicious but don't look as appealing. Luc must agree because he leans over Rose's plate and inhales deeply with his eyes closed before picking up a fork and diving into his grilled salmon.

"A thing for kids," I mutter vaguely even though Callie told me Rose would love Daphne's House. I reach into the pocket of my coat on the bench beside me and pull out the pamphlet about the place I have for Mac and slide it across the tabletop.

Rose pops a sweet potato fry into her mouth, wipes her fingers on her napkin and the takes the pamphlet. Her chewing gets slower and slower as she reads, her eyes narrowing with focus. She looks at Luc, excited. "It's like Hope House that you did a fund-raiser for back home!"

Luc, who was reading along with her nods and swallows down a hunk of salmon. "Seems similar, yeah. You were looking to volunteer at a place like that. This could be perfect."

She nods so vigorously. Luc looks over at me. "How'd you find this place?"

"I was looking for a place to volunteer." I shrug and give him a cheeky grin. "Court-ordered community service."

He laughs. Rose ignores the joke and leans forward. "Where do I get tickets to the fund-raiser? Why are you just telling us about this now?"

"It's all the way out in the Hamptons," I explain.

"Oh no. A night at the beach. How horrible," she exclaims, every word dripping with sarcasm.

I turn to Luc and smile. "I can totally tell she's related to Callie right now."

He chuffs out a laugh. "And just like Jessie when she gets set on something, there is no talking her out of it. So you should tell us where to buy tickets."

I tap the bottom of the brochure. "If there are any left, you can order them from the website. If they say sold out, text me and I'll try to pull strings. But no promises. The director kind of hates me."

"Why would he hate you?" Rose asks innocently.

I move my gaze from her to Luc. "It's a her, a woman who heard me compliment her ass in a coffee shop and got offended."

Rose looks confused, but Luc's face is awash in recognition. "Holy shit! That chick who spoke French? She's the director of this place?"

He's laughing so hard I don't think he even notices I'm frowning. Rose looks clueless. "What am I missing?"

Before I can stop him, Luc gleefully tells her about the incident at Starbucks and then Rose is laughing too. I groan and finish the last of my wrap. "Of all the women in all the youth homes . . . yeah, I have horrible luck."

"I don't know," Rose says, smiling. "Sounds like fate to me."

"Oh no . . . *Fleur*, I love you and all the romantic bones in your body, but this is not some new love story starting up," Luc tells her and leans over and kisses her cheek. "She looked at him like he was contagious."

"Thanks," I say, but I chuckle because it is true. "And she still does. You can see for yourself if you guys come to the fund-raiser."

"I'll buy tickets as soon as we get home," Rose announces happily.

"Thanks, *mon ami*," Luc gripes, but he's smiling. "I love having to wear a suit on my day off. Because wearing them to games isn't enough."

"Maybe you shouldn't take so much joy in my pain and I won't take joy in yours," I quip.

Rose rolls her eyes at us and turns to Luc. "We'll spend the night in the Hamptons. I'll find a bed-and-breakfast. I'll make it worth your while."

She has a look on her face that makes Luc's expression get darker and definitely more intimate, like he doesn't realize everyone in this place can see the lust on his face. I clear my throat to remind him I'm alive as I reach for my wallet.

"I'm going to go. My new bed was delivered this afternoon and I can't wait to give it a test drive." I drop twenty bucks on the table and lean over it, closer to Luc. "Looks like you are going to thank me for inviting you to this fund-raiser."

"I hope so," Luc replies. "I forgot how much she loves beach getaways."

Rose gets out of the booth and hugs me good-bye. "See you tomorrow night."

Chapter 7

Brie

Len smiles at me as she carries over two glasses of champagne. She hands me one and then leans in and kisses my cheek. "It's a fantastic event."

"I'm not willing to admit victory until the final numbers are in," I tell her, but I smile. We sold out of tickets and everyone is having a great time and there's been a lot of activity at the table showcasing the auction items.

"I heard two guys from your dad's office talking about outbidding each other on the deep-sea fishing trip," Len says. "And a woman was telling her friend over by the pool that she will do anything for that Barons hockey package."

I nod at that and my brain instantly goes to Alex. Len told me she saw him walk in about half an hour ago with a pretty brunette. I'd be lying if I didn't say I was looking for him. But the party is spread out all over the first floor of the house and spills out onto the sprawling backyard, since the weather is unseasonably warm for October and that pesky rain from yesterday completely disappeared. We haven't even had to turn on all the portable heaters yet and it's almost nine at night.

"Where's Vic?" Len asks as she sips champagne.

"*Victor.*" I reply pointedly, "is on the patio with his buddies from his office."

"Did he bring any cute ones this time?" Len asks. "Does he even have any cute friends?"

"Of course he has attractive friends," I reply and roll my eyes. "But I don't think any of the guys he invited tonight would be your cup of tea. Two are married, one is gay and the other is going through a rough divorce. It's all he talks about."

"Ugh," Len sighs dramatically and then perks up instantly. "Maybe you can give him therapy and make him datable again."

I laugh. "I specialize in family and child therapy, Lennie."

"Let's be honest, most men are just overgrown children, so it's not out of your wheelhouse," she says tartly and I laugh. Her blue eyes widen and she points, very obviously, at a stunning woman in a red cocktail dress. "Oh! That's the woman Alex came with. I told you she was pretty."

I take in the woman walking in from the patio. Her hair is long and silky and a rich color that may actually be more black than brown. Her skin is like flawless alabaster and the perfect amount of smoky makeup accentuates her wide dark brown eyes. The dress is flirty and cute but also clinging enough to all the right places to make sure everyone in this room knows she's got a killer figure.

"That isn't the fiancée of the Seattle teammate, is it? The one he was apparently getting jiggy with on that road trip?" Len asks in a lower whisper.

I shake my head no, because I hate to admit it but I kind of memorized that dubious photo. "That woman had longer, lighter brown hair and much lighter eyes. She seemed taller and had more of an athletic build. Not that I analyzed it or anything..."

Len barks out a "Ha!" so loud that a couple near us turns to look. I smile politely and tug her over a few feet to an area near the fireplace where no one is congregating. "Are you interested in Alex?"

"What? Oh God no!" Now it's my turn to laugh. "I have a boyfriend. And also, he's not my type."

"Let's pretend Victor doesn't exist for a second." She pauses and smiles way too happily at that idea. "You're single. You're so single you're contemplating getting a cat. Are you interested in him?"

I roll my eyes. "No. He's still not my type."

"What about him is not your type?" Len asks. "Is it the rugged, Greek god–like physique? Or is it the fact that he's got a beautiful face even with all the scars and nicks? Or wait! I know! It's the charm and sex appeal that seeps out of every pore on his body. That's not what you're looking for right? I mean what woman would want that?"

"You should give up accounting and become a comedian." I take a gulp of champagne so big the bubbles make my nose tingle. My eyes land on Alex's date again as she reaches for her own glass of champagne. "It's the fact that he reportedly messes around with women who don't belong to him."

"You don't know the details about that Seattle thing," Len reminds me.

"No, but you said he came with her and she's wearing a ring the size of a Fiat." I nod toward the mystery date again and watch as Len's eyes find what I couldn't help but notice as she reached for her champagne.

"Lordy! I bet that thing can be seen from space," Len gasps. "And here he comes!"

I turn and see Alex walking toward the girl in red. He must feel the weight of our eyes because he turns his gaze to us. Len grins and waves and I nod. He leans in to say something to the woman when he reaches her and then he's got a hand on her back, guiding her toward us.

As soon as they reach us, he opens his mouth to say something, but Len steps forward and speaks first. "Hi! I'm Len Levitt. I volunteer at Daphne's House. This is Brie Bennett, she's the director."

I extend my hand. "You must be Alex's fiancée?"

Len chokes on her champagne. Hard.

"Oh my God! Are you okay?" Red Dress asks Len, eyes filled with concern. She hands Len her cocktail napkin and gently pats her on the back. "Alex, get her some water."

"I'm fine," Len manages to spit out. "Thank you, though."

"Len and Brie, this is my friend, Rose Caplan," Alex explains, glaring at me.

"Oh. I just saw your lovely ring and I thought..." I let my sentence trail off.

"She's engaged to my teammate, Luc," Alex explains and gives me a tight smile. "She's a teacher and she's also very interested in Daphne's House."

"Nice to meet you, Rose," I say, quickly absorbing this new information. "I'd be happy to answer any of your questions about the charity, and thank you so much for attending tonight."

"If Brie doesn't have the answer I'm sure her mom and dad do," Alex says with a big, fake smile on his face. "Mommy and Daddy own the place, don't they, Brie?"

Mommy and Daddy?

I hesitate. His condescending tone makes me want to tell him the truth. I open my mouth to explain, when Luc, his friend from the Starbucks, is suddenly standing beside me. Rose's face lights up and she reaches for him. "This is my fiancé, Luc. Luc this is Brie and Len. They work with the charity."

Luc shakes both our hands. "Nice to see you again."

"You too." Len is staring at him, openmouthed, so I subtly nudge her.

"This is a great event. And a great cause. I've done a fundraiser for a similar place in Maine called Hope House. Have you heard of it?"

"Yes! I worked closely with Keith Duncan when he was starting it. He based his place on us." I'm really excited that they're genuinely interested.

"Rose has been itching to find a place like this here in New York to volunteer with," Luc says. Rose nods as he weaves their fingers together. "We both grew up without real parents so we know how necessary this type of thing is."

"Oh." I'm totally stunned by that statement. "Were you in foster care?"

Rose shakes her head and her face darkens a bit. "My

sisters and I essentially raised ourselves, and Luc was lucky enough to have family friends take him in."

I'm more than stunned; I'm blown away really. Len clearly is too. "Make sure you give us your contact info because we're always in need of volunteers."

"And our kids are always looking for tutoring help so they can improve their GPA or get help passing their GED."

"I would love to tutor them," she says.

Len pulls out her cell phone from her purse and starts to take Rose's info as I feel a warm hand on my back. I look up and see Victor. His eyes are darting from Luc to Alex. "Hey. Barons, right?"

They both nod and introduce themselves. Victor shifts his glass to his other hand and shakes with Luc and then Alex. "Larue, right? You just got traded here from San Diego? Brie mentioned you were volunteering. Taking the kids jogging something."

"Yeah. Among other things," Alex says with a nod.

"Just don't teach them how to cross-check or slew foot." Victor chuckles. "Hockey's violent, but Daphne's House isn't."

I think he thinks that's funny, but even I don't and I'm one of the only people who laughs at his jokes. Before anyone can react, or I can figure out how to subtly apologize, Victor looks at me. "They're going to start the auction, honey. The MC wanted me to get you. I guess he has some questions before he starts."

"Oh. Okay." My eyes move from Alex to Luc to Rose. "Excuse me. It was so great meeting you and I hope we can chat again before the night is over."

I take Victor's hand and tug him away with me because I don't want him to stay and keep insulting their profession. My dad is by the side of the small stage we set up under a tent on the patio. He's talking to the MC, a local radio personality he knows. His face lights up when he sees me and he pulls me into a hug. "There's my girl."

I close my eyes and absorb his hug, which I swear is a cure for everything. I instantly feel better and calmer as we break apart. He introduces me to the MC, who asks a few quick questions and then walks to the back of the stage to check on the mic.

My dad leans in and shakes Victor's hand as Victor says, "Good to see you again, sir."

My dad nods. I'm not sure he's a huge fan of Victor's, but he's never been a big fan of any of my boyfriends, so I don't let it bug me.

"The event is going well," my dad says. "Everyone is raving about the food and there's been a big buzz about the auction items."

"Good. I'm glad!" I reply. "Thanks again to you and Mom for letting me host this here. And strong-arming all your rich friends into coming."

He laughs at that, his gray eyes crinkling in the corners. "My friends didn't have to be strong armed. They know a good cause when they see it and they're more than willing to support it. Except for William. That cheap bastard had to be strong-armed. But I reminded him about all the damn stuff he made me donate to when Len, Lance and Louis were kids and involved in all those 'Save the Everything' campaigns so he owes me."

I laugh. The whole reason I know Len is because my dad and her dad have been best friends since they were children. "All those things Len supported were good causes too."

"Yeah, yeah," he says, winking at me. "Your mom is very proud too. She's around here somewhere probably pressuring people to bid on auction items."

I grin. "This is why you guys are the best parents. Because you're not above squeezing cash out of your friends to help your daughter."

He kisses the top of my head. "I'm going to go find her. Be back in a minute."

I watch Dad retreat into the crowd as my program manager Selena walks over to the stage. Victor looks confused. "She's announcing?"

"Yeah. She's so excited, she practiced her speech all week," I explain and smile at the memory.

Victor's not smiling. "But it's your show. It's your business."

"It's not a business," I argue softly. "I'm not a CEO and besides, I speak every year. I thought it might be nice for everyone to hear from someone else. Selena's been a dedicated employee since day one."

Why am I trying to justify my decision to him? Why does he care? He's still frowning. "I've just been telling everyone you're speaking. I wanted to show off my girl. It's strange to me that you wouldn't want that moment."

I just shrug. I can't trust myself not to start a fight if I respond. I'm not a prize Pomeranian to parade around on stage so people can pat Victor on the back for having such a pretty girl. What the hell is wrong with him? Luckily Selena is holding the mic and walking to the front of the stage so there's no time to argue.

She gives a great speech, talking about how many young lives she's seen changed thanks Daphne's House and how much she loves her job and then she surprises me with a part of the speech I hadn't heard her practice—she talks about me. Selena tells everyone that I'm the best boss she's ever had and that she's never met anyone with a bigger heart. I start to tear up a little.

She introduces the MC, and I hug her as he starts the auction. Everything is going for more than I expected it to, which makes me excited. We really are going to meet our goal. The last prize to be auctioned is the entire row of seats, right behind the bench, to a Barons home game. Like with every item, the bidding starts at three hundred dollars, but this item escalates even more quickly than the others. By the time it hits two thousand dollars it's basically a battle between two people—a sixty-ish man and a forty-something woman.

I notice Alex in the corner of the patio, he's holding a drink, head tilted down, surveying the bidding from under his dark lashes. I get that odd, intense wave of déjà vu for a fleeting moment. He notices me noticing him and our eyes connect, but the woman bidding says something that spins both our heads toward her.

"Five thousand dollars, if the donor will throw in dinner."

"What the fuck?" I whisper as Victor and just about everyone around me chuckles at the brazen request.

The MC looks at the card in his hand, which I know also contains the donor's name. It was also posted on the printed card everyone was given detailing the auction items so she knows exactly who she's asking to have dinner with. "Mr. Alex Larue?" he says into the mic. "Is this item sold?"

I spin around so quickly I almost lose my balance. Our eyes connect, like he was looking for me too and I slowly and clearly mouth, "You don't have to."

If he understands what I say, he doesn't make it clear. Instead he slowly looks away from me and to the MC and starts to raise his glass. "Sold!"

My jaw drops. The lady squeals at her victory and everyone claps, except me. I'm horrified. I feel like she just hired him for services, which kind of makes this event seem dirty. Ugh.

The DJ takes over and the music starts and everyone goes back to mingling, drinking and dancing.

"Sweetie, come meet my boss."

"I will in a moment, I promise," I say and reach up and kiss his cheek to lessen the blow. "I just have to speak with Alex."

"Why?"

"I don't want him to feel obligated to go on a date with that woman," I explain. "He wasn't for sale."

Victor scoffs and gives my back a condescending little rub. "Honey, it's not like he's some innocent virgin. The man is a professional athlete."

"What's that supposed to mean?"

"It means he has done worse than put out in the name of charity," Victor replies and kisses the top of my head. "I'm going to offer my boss a cigar. I've got the expensive Cuban kind he likes."

I nod but he doesn't see it. He's already walking away. I

make my way into the house because Alex is no longer standing in the corner looking broody with his scotch. I find Len
in the dining room. She grabs my arm. "That was the woman
who said she'd do anything for the Barons package, but in the
end it's Alex who will have to do anything."

She laughs. I don't. My stomach twists. "Speaking of, have
you seen him?"

She points down the long hall toward the front door. "He
went that way."

"Thanks." I turn and leave even though I know she's about
to say something else. I need to find him.

He's standing in the hall, beside the staircase, talking to
Luc. I walk over and try to give them both an easy smile, but
it must look as tight as it feels because Luc asks, "Everything
all right?"

"Yes, but do you mind if I steal Alex for a minute?"

He nods. "Sure thing. I'm going to go find Rose anyway."

Luc walks into the living room and I turn and look up at
Alex. His expression is relaxed, but I know mine isn't. "I just
wanted to let you know I don't expect you to go out with that
woman."

He looks perplexed. "But she won."

I nod and smooth my hair. "Yes, but you weren't on the
auctioning block. I'm not comfortable with this."

He laughs. It's this deep, somehow cocky sound. "Brie,
I'm a big boy. I have been used for sex more than once in my
life. I'm okay with it. In fact, I prefer it."

"Sex?" I blurt out the word way too loudly. Panicked, I
glance around. No one seems to have noticed. I lower my
voice. "No one is saying you have to have sex with her!"

His laugh gets deeper and louder. An older couple holding martinis at the end of the hall look up. So does the waiter walking by. This is so not a conversation we should continue in public. Not knowing what else to do I open the door to the powder room, grab his wrist and pull him inside. I grope for the light as soon as the door is shut and flip it on. I'm startled to find a stricken look on his rugged face. Not startled, or confused by my actions but...anguished. Like he's about to have a panic attack.

"Alex?"

"Let me out," he demands in a voice so deep and choked I don't even recognize it. I take a step back.

He turns away from me and fumbles for the door handle. I feel this overwhelming need to comfort him so I reach out and touch his shoulder. "Alex. What's wrong?"

He jerks away from my touch and flings the door open, stumbling out into the hall. Now people are really staring. He doesn't seem to notice as he storms off. I stand in the open door watching his retreating back and I realize "storm" isn't the right word. Flee. He's fleeing.

Dear God, what happened to him?

Chapter 8

Alex

I move like lightning through the house, onto the deck and then I keep going. It's an oceanfront house, thank God, because I don't even think the expansiveness of their driveway or street would be open enough to quell this hard, cold fear clogging my veins and filling my lungs. I find the stairs to the sand and run down them. My feet sink into the sand and I stumble. I close my eyes and force a deep breath into my lungs.

Chatter, laughter and music float down from the party above, adding to the chaos in my head. Everything sounds harsh and shrill and jarring. Every breath is a struggle because it feels like there's a building on my chest. Fucking hell. It hasn't been this bad since I was in my early twenties. I thought it would never be this bad again.

Fuck.

Through the screaming in my head I manage to hear her say my name. It's a cautious whisper that whips by me on the wind. I turn around and she's about two feet away, at the bottom of the stairs, barefoot in the sand, her heels dangling from her left hand. The hem of her flowy, silver-gray dress billows around her and so do wisps of her smooth dark hair that's slipped out of her low side bun. It's hard to make out her face in the pale moonlight, but that's probably a blessing. I don't want to see whatever expression she's wearing because it'll be one of the ones I fucking hate—fear, confusion, sympathy.

"I'm sorry. I'm claustrophobic," I explain tersely and move toward her. Well, not actually toward her; I'm heading for the stairs so I can finish fighting this panic attack in peace and without judgment.

I won't look at her as I pass. I keep my head down, fixated on the first step. But before I can step on it she's blocked my path, moving her body in front of me. She drops her shoes and puts a hand on each railing completely making it impossible to climb the staircase.

"Fuck," I hiss. "Why won't you just leave me alone?" I step back and run a hand through my hair and then over my face.

She steps right up to me, only a few inches away. "It's okay. Listen to the waves. Inhale and exhale in unison with them," she replies calmly. "Focus on just them. Nothing else."

If it will make her leave me alone, I'll do anything. My brain feels like a hamster on a wheel, spinning my thoughts around and around. But I force myself to listen of the rhythmic pounding of the waves. I don't know how long I'm standing there, matching my breaths to the crash of the waves, but eventually everything starts to slow. My thoughts, my heart rate, my blood in my veins, my breathing, everything begins to feel almost normal again.

I feel her hand brush mine and for some reason I can't even begin to analyze, I reach for it. It feels soft and fragile and I gently lace my fingers with hers. "You're okay."

"I'll never be okay," I confess.

"Alex." Her voice is so soft and gentle. *"Qu'est ce qui t'es arriver?"*

When she asks me what happened it's is like a lightning bolt jolting me back to the reality of who this woman is and what she thinks about me. I'm a player, a jerk and now probably insane. At least I'm sure that's what she thinks now. I'm not about to add "tortured," "pathetic," and "sad" to the list of words she associates with me. I let go of her hand and take a step back. "This was a wonderful fund-raiser. I hope it surpasses your goals. I'm going to go home now. Good night."

I leave her on the dark beach calling my name.

I wait impatiently for the valet to come back with my rental. I could have stayed in the Hamptons overnight like Rose and Luc were but I wanted to make sure I was back in the city early to look for Mac. She never showed up this morning to meet me in front of the bakery.

Brie doesn't seem to be anywhere in sight, thankfully. I turn back as another valet brings up someone else's car. A couple standing to my left gets in. My car should be next. Everyone around me is chattering away and just like before the background noise is an annoyance.

"This little hobby of hers is quite something," I hear someone say. "You must be very proud of Brie. I wish we could have been formally introduced."

Her name cuts through the rest of the voices and I focus on that one conversation with the same intensity with which I focused on the waves.

"I was hoping you could meet her too, but she's just been so busy tonight running around making sure everything is perfect. What can I say, she's a good girl with noble intentions," a second voice replies. It's familiar, so my eyes seek out the source. It's that guy, Vince or something. And he's talking about her like she's a prized show pony instead of his girlfriend.

"I'm sure she's a lovely girl, Victor," the older man commends him like he's deserving of praise for the person Brie is. "And if you keep her around I'm sure I'll get another chance to meet her."

"Oh she's not going anywhere," he replies confidently. "I'll probably pop the question later this year. I'm ready for a wife and a family. I'm just giving her a little more time to prepare the charity for someone else to take over."

I'm riveted to this conversation now, even though I know I'm eavesdropping. They're all puffing away on cigars and don't seem to even notice me. The older man exhales a plume of smoke. "Good idea. It would be hard to run something so time-consuming and be a proper wife and mother."

I almost snort at that. This guy is straight out of *Mad Men* or something. Archaic, chauvinistic douchebag. But Victor is nodding. "She's going to have to give the reins of this endeavor over to someone else one day if she wants to be Mrs. Rosenkrantz. Her friend Len will probably never marry so she could always take over."

Ouch. Jesus, what is wrong with Brie that she's with this

guy? "So does Brie want a big family?" the younger guy asks.

"Right now all she thinks about are these foster kids. She's even fantasized about possibly adopting," he says and his words are dripping with disdain that he tries to cover with a smile. To me, it looks like a sneer. "She's got such a big heart, you know, always trying to save the world."

"Very noble," the older man says but he doesn't sound impressed. "But kids are hard enough when they're your own. You don't need to take on someone else's problem."

"Brie will come to realize that eventually," Victor says dismissively. "I know once she has one of her own, she'll come to her senses."

"Sir," the valet interrupts my eavesdropping.

I look over and he's standing at the open door of my rented SUV. I hand him a tip and slip behind the wheel, pulling away before I say something inappropriate to that douchebag Brie is dating. Instead I settle for glaring at him in the rearview mirror.

Chapter 9

Brie

I reach the driveway just in time to see his body slide into the driver's seat of a black SUV. I open my mouth but stop myself from calling his name. The long circular driveway is filled with people. Not just valets and event staff, but guests. I don't want to make a scene. I start to walk quickly toward the car, intent on reaching it before he can drive away but someone calls my name. I almost ignore it but then there's a hand around my wrist and I turn and see Victor staring at me expectantly.

"Speak of the devil," he says with a big smile.

"I think you mean angel," a deeper, gruffer male voice says and I glance over Victor's shoulder to see a portly older gentleman with a cigar wedged between his plump fingers. This must be the boss Victor wanted me to meet.

"Where were you headed in such a rush, babe?" Victor asks me and I glance quickly over my shoulder in time to see Alex's SUV turn onto the road at the end of the driveway. He's gone. Damn it. I turn back to Victor. "Sorry, I was just hoping to catch Alex before he left."

Victor blinks, his face full of questions I don't want to answer, especially in front of his boss, so I turn to him and extend my hand. "Mr. Lombardi, I'm Brie Bennett. Victor speaks very highly of you; it's nice to finally meet you."

He smiles and does that thing where instead of shaking my hand he takes it in his and pats the top of it with his other hand. It's both awkward and annoying to me and as he does it a big clump of ash from his cigar plops to the pavement between us. "I'm sure he doesn't speak as highly of me as he does of you, young lady. After all I'm the one that makes him work weekends."

The men all chuckle like that was the wittiest thing anyone has ever said. Mr. Lombardi leans closer, as if about to share a secret with me and says, "This is a lovely party for a lovely cause."

"Thank you." I struggle not to choke on his foul cigar and whiskey breath.

Victor wraps an arm around my shoulder and squeezes. Mr. Lombardi shoves the cigar between his lips, reaches into his pocket and pulls out a piece of paper. "I know there are donation boxes inside but I wanted to give you this myself."

He hands me a check for twenty-five hundred dollars. "Mr. Lombardi, sir, thank you so much."

"Call me Peter, honey."

I bite my tongue to keep from responding with *Call me Brie, not "honey," honey.*

"Victor says you have a background in psychology and that you're Baxter and Helena Bennett's daughter?" he says. "I know Bax from my old position at LeBrun Industries."

I nod, not really paying attention. My mind still on Alex. I hope he's okay. I debate texting him or calling him, but I don't want to annoy him. If he wanted my help he would have asked for it, right? And since he thinks I'm some meddling, spoiled socialite, I'm the last person he'll ask for help. His expression was pure torture when I saw him on the beach, and his body was so rigid it was like marble. And when he took my hand in his, unexpectedly, it was out of need. He was freefalling and looking for an anchor. That's why I grasped it back, lacing my fingers with his and holding him in a firm and gentle grip, my thumb sliding soothingly back and forth against his wrist.

Victor says something. Peter says something else. I keep smiling. Over Peter's droopy shoulder I see Len standing on the front porch talking to the woman who bought the Barons tickets. I can't believe Alex agreed to have dinner with her. And he thinks that means he agreed to sex. Does it? Does that woman think she can buy sexual services at a freaking charity auction? And would Alex really just sleep with her like it's no big deal?

"Gabrielle!" Victor's sharp tone yanks me back to reality.

My eyes refocus and I realize by the expectant look on Peter's face that he'd asked me something. Victor's hand slips from my shoulders to my hip where he holds on firmly— much more firmly than required. "You've just always had an affinity for helping kids in need, right Brie?"

I blink. He smiles sharply at me, barely containing his annoyance. "That's why you started the charity right?"

I look back at Peter. Oh. "Well, I'm adopted and actually spent a year in foster care before I was placed with my parents.

I was very young and was blessed to be adopted out of the system and into such a loving, strong family. But I've always been aware that not all kids have been blessed like me, by no fault of their own, and so it's just always been important to me to try and help them. Change their luck, you know? And this charity is my way of doing that."

Peter looks truly moved. Dropping his cigar on the pavement and crushing it under the heel of his black dress shoe, he reaches for my hand again and gives it a squeeze. "I had no idea you'd been through that."

I smile and gently, subtly, take my hand back.

"She barely remembers it," Victor announces in a confident voice. "She's just a regular person."

What the actual fuck does that mean? I stare at him with a look I'm fairly certain could melt titanium but he's too busy staring at his boss. So I turn to Peter again too. "It was so nice meeting you and I appreciate the donation very much. If you'll excuse me for just a moment I need to discuss something with my friend Len, who is handling something for me."

"Of course, honey," Peter says with a grin. "I'm sure you have a ton of obligations. Nice meeting you."

I start to walk away, toward Len and the guest who seem to be about to wrap up their conversation, when I hear Peter ask Victor, "Is Len the one who will take over the charity after you get married?"

I freeze and turn back to them. I'm standing a little behind Peter so he doesn't know his words have caught my attention, but Victor knows because our eyes lock. I can tell by the expression on his face Bob's words are not some misunderstanding. He told Bob that I'm going to give up Daphne's House after we're married. I silently mouth three words: "What. The. Fuck?"

But I turn and walk away, continuing toward Len. I walk up beside her and she smiles and introduces me to the Barons ticket winner. I smile and extend my hand. The older lady with the way-too-low-cut dress takes it, her fingers icy. "Lizzie Cameron."

"Ms. Cameron owns Cameron Real Estate," Len explains. "She bid on the Barons tickets and got Alex to throw in dinner too."

"It's such a good cause," Lizzie says, smiling. "And if I can help you and help myself by meeting a hot athlete at the same time, I am more than willing to do it."

She laughs. I smile politely just like Len is doing. "About those Barons tickets. I think it was such a funny moment to ask for dinner but unfortunately we don't make alterations to prizes."

"Excuse me?" Lizzie looks startled.

"We don't?" Len blurts out, just as startled.

I smile calmly. "Mr. Larue was not being auctioned off."

"He volunteered to sweeten my pot," Lizzie replies icily.

"Yes, well he is a very generous, selfless man. But being the director of the charity, I wouldn't feel comfortable forcing him to go through with it," I explain, refusing to look as ruffled as I am.

"Brie, it's just dinner," Len whispers, but it's loud enough that Lizzie hears her.

"It's not," I reply to my best friend and glance over at Lizzie. "Is it?"

"It's whatever Mr. Larue and I decide it is," she replies and gives me another icy smile, her bright red lips a garish contrast to her pale skin and pale blond hair. "I can just cancel my check."

"Please do," I reply firmly and turn and walk back into the house. I make it to the kitchen before Len catches up to me.

"Holy shit. What the hell has gotten into you?" she asks a little too loudly, even though the kitchen only has some event staff cleaning up in it and the rest of the house is almost empty of guests too since the night is winding down.

"She expects more than surf and turf, Len," I explain hotly as I pace the narrow strip of marble floor between the island and the stove. "She was hoping to get laid. By Alex."

Len drops her forearms on the island and leans forward, her face filled with confusion. "So? Alex is a big boy. He can handle himself."

She might be right, but the man I saw tonight on the beach wasn't a big boy. He was a scared kid. When the dinner thing first happened, I was worried about how it looked to be auctioning off dates—and potential hookups—at an auction associated with my charity. But now I'm worried about putting him in a position that makes him feel trapped. But I can't tell Len that because I don't want to reveal what happened tonight. I know he wouldn't want me to. "Maybe I overreacted, but I'm not okay with her using this like it's a bachelor auction. It isn't."

"You needed that five grand, Brie," Len reminds me of what I already know.

I sigh and reach up and start pulling the pins out of my hair. "Not that badly."

Len looks unconvinced and shrugs. "Where is the man whose honor you're defending?"

"He left."

My mom walks into the kitchen and smiles warmly at Len before wrapping me in a hug. "I've barely had a chance to see you all night, princess."

"I know. It's been crazy."

"But good, right?" she asks, looking down at me with her kind hazel eyes. My mom is a statuesque, auburn-haired beauty who probably could have been a model. Instead she studied languages at NYU and worked as a UN translator until she met my father on the subway. They fell madly in love and when he was transferred to Quebec just four weeks later she quit her job and moved with him. She never looked back.

"I think so. Len still has to run the numbers," I reply. She hugs me again.

"I'm sure we raised enough," she declares confidently. "Now since everyone seems to be outside waiting on their vehicles, I'm going to sneak upstairs and take off these heels. I'll also make sure the bedrooms have fresh sheets. You and Len in one room. Victor in the other. I'm still old-fashioned so humor me, Brie."

She smiles and winks at me, probably figuring I'll have Len and Victor switch rooms because I've done that before.

"Don't worry about it, Mom. Victor isn't spending the night."

"Why not?"

"Because I'm about to break up with him," I reply and start to walk out of the room.

"What the fuck?" I hear Len say behind me. "Sorry, Mrs. Bennett."

"No, I think a 'What the fuck?' is appropriate, Eleanor," my mom replies to her. "Brie! What happened?"

I pause at the archway that leads to the hall. "It's a long story and I swear I will tell you both later. I just need to finish this now. And before you ask, I'm okay. It's been a long time coming and I'm ready for it."

I turn and walk toward the front door, intent on finally ending what has been dying a slow death anyway. And then, I'm going to find my phone and text Alex and make sure he's okay. Because as crazy as it makes me, I'm more concerned about him than I am about ending my relationship.

Chapter 10

Alex

I'm about to give up when I see her. I don't get my hopes up at first because I've thought I've seen her three times in the last two hours and every time it wasn't her. Luckily, I realized my mistake before I spoke to the Mac look-alikes or got too close so no one thought I was a crazy stalker or some kind of kidnapper or something. I'm right behind a girl now as she moves down the street, hood up on her puffy but tattered winter coat. I quicken my pace so I'm a little bit beside her and she glances up at me at the very same time I catch a glimpse of the tear in the arm of her coat. It's her.

"Mac!"

She looks at me, startled, then angry. "Fuck off!"

She starts to run and I run too. Today she isn't as quick as the other day. I'm able to gently grab hold of her right forearm. She yelps and tries to yank it away and yelps again. "Don't create a scene, okay? Just stop!"

She's like an animal caught it a trap, literally. She's yanking and whimpering and yelping and when she finally stills and her eyes meet mine, they're filled with tears and her expression is twisted with pain. "Please let go. I won't run, but it hurts! Let go."

I instantly drop my grip on her arm. "What's wrong?"

"Nothing. I'm fine," she barks back using the back of her left hand to wipe away her tears before they can fall. When she glances back up at me her expression is hard. "What do you want?"

"To give you this." I pull the pamphlet about Daphne's House out of my pocket. She frowns but takes it and without looking at it, shoves it in her pocket. "And also these."

I take off my expensive cashmere gloves and hand them to her but she won't take them. Her arm, the one she whimpered about, is hanging limply at her side. My heart jumps. "I'll give you a hundred bucks if you tell me what happened to your arm."

Her green eyes flare in shock and maybe a little in fear. I've never been great at giving off a harmless vibe, but I try right now. I lower my voice and try to soften the hard edges of my face. "Mac...if you're hurt I can help. No strings attached. No ulterior motives. I just want to help you."

"It's nothing. I just scratched my arm on a fence," she mutters.

"Let me see," I coax. When she doesn't move, she just stands there motionless I pull my wallet out of my back pocket and pull out all the cash I have and hold it up. She tries to swipe it with her left hand—the good one—but I hold it up over my head. She even tries to jump for it, but it's still too high. "Nice try, squirt. Show me your arm."

We stand there eyeballing each other in some sort of silent battle of wills for what feels like a full minute and then she sighs dramatically, unzips her coat and gingerly pulls her arm out. First I'm shocked she's only got a thin, dirty T-shirt on under the coat and then I'm horrified when I see her forearm. There's a deep, six-inch red jagged gash across it. It's still oozing blood and pus and the skin around it is angry looking. I reach out and touch the skin near the wound. She yanks it away, but not before I feel the heat radiating off it.

"I didn't say you could touch!" She turns and tries to leave, but I grab her shoulder.

"Sorry, but you're not going anywhere until we get that treated," I tell her and she looks furious.

"You can't tell me what the fuck to do."

"It's severely infected, and you will get very sick," I explain. "So go ahead and create a scene here and someone will call the cops and I'll tell them about your arm and they'll get you treated but also put you back in the system. Or do what I say and let me get you help and keep you out of the system."

"Hospitals ask questions," she tells me.

"Mac, I'm serious. You could die." I'm so desperate to get her the help she needs I start making promises I'm not sure I can keep. "That place in the pamphlet, I'll get them to help you. You can trust them. I swear it's good."

The fear is still all over her face like a mask, and her eyes glare at me with pure skepticism but she nods. My wave of relief is short-lived, though. I don't know where the hell to go. I glance around, like an idiot, and spot a coffee shop a few stores up. "Come with me. Let's get you something to eat first."

Inside the coffee shop I get her a juice and a bagel with extra cream cheese, as per her request, and then I sit her at a table in the corner and tell her to eat. I walk to the front of the store, keeping my eyes glued to her, and dial Daphne's House. Selena answers on the third ring.

"It's Alex," I tell her. "Is Brie there? I have a situation."

"She doesn't work weekends," Selena explains and I sigh. I have no choice but to tell her what's happening. She gives me the name of a clinic that they work with and I open my Lyft app and go to get Mac.

A little over an hour later I'm pacing outside an examination room while a doctor treats Mac. The door is open, at her request, and I keep glancing in, but all I can see is the back of the doctor's white coat. He's asked her a bunch of questions and, despite the potty mouth and attitude she gives me, she's been unexpectedly polite to him. Her answers are clipped, but she hasn't sworn once and when there's something she won't answer, like her age and her last name, she just says "I'm sorry, doctor, sir, I plead the fifth amendment." It's absurd and makes me smile. He doesn't push her.

I hear a shoe squeak on the beige linoleum and look up. Brie is walking toward me with a woman I've never seen before. She texted me late last night and again this morning, but I ignored her. I was embarrassed and didn't want to deal with it. But now, despite the way we left things, I'm relieved to see her. Her hair is in a sloppy top knot and she isn't wearing an ounce of makeup. I can't help but think she looks just as beautiful as she did all done up at the fund-raiser.

"Good, you're still here," she says, sighing in relief. Did

she really think I would just take an injured kid here and bail? "How is she?"

"I don't know. The doctor is in there with her now." I shove my hands in my pockets. I can't stop staring at her. I don't know if it's because I've never seen her so dressed down, or if it's something else. She looks so different—younger and somehow familiar.

Brie glances into the room and then reaches out and wraps her hand around my wrist. I let her pull my hand from my pocket and tug me half a foot down the hall. The other woman with her, who is in a pantsuit and trench coat, joins us. I introduce myself to her. She shakes my hand. "This is Laurie Bieksa. She's a family lawyer and does pro bono work for me."

"I told Mac no social workers. No lawyers. No police," I warn, my eyes darting back to the open door. "I promised."

"I understand that but, Alex, she's too young to stay at Daphne's House, at least not without due process," Brie explains. "We've never been awarded a kid under sixteen."

"If this ends up getting her put in foster care again, she'll hate me and I'll hate me." I feel tension ripple through every part of my body.

"I know. Selena explained the situation pretty well." Brie touches my arm again. "But she can stay with me. I'm certified to foster. Laurie will get me emergency custody. I have an extra bedroom. I don't mind taking her in while we figure something better out."

I stare at her, stunned. The tension in my body starts to evaporate, leaving a tingling feeling of shock in its wake. Is she really going to take this kid in? Into her house? "You'd do that? You haven't even met her."

"But you have and you like her enough to want to help her." Brie's big dark eyes find mine. "I trust your judgment."

I reach out and pull her into my arms. I'm so overwhelmed with relief and gratitude I can't help it. I hold on to her tightly and to my surprise she wraps me in just as tight a hug. "*Merci.*"

"I'm betting we still have a hard sell to make," Brie murmurs, her lips close to my ear. The words aren't intimate but they somehow feel like they are so I let her go and take a step back.

"Yeah, but we can convince her," I say with a smile. As usual, it's said with more confidence than I actually feel.

The doctor comes out and calls us over. "She needed a tetanus shot and she's got to have some IV antibiotics today and again tomorrow. It's the fastest way to blast her system and get that infection under control. After that she'll be on pills for another ten days and I'll want to see her at least once in that time and again to take the stitches out. She's going to have one hell of a scar. No way around that."

"Thank you, Dr. Subban. Once again, you're our hero. I can't thank you enough," Brie says, smiling. "I'll settle with you up front in a second. I just need to talk to our new friend."

The doctor nods. "She's a captive audience right now with that IV so go for it."

He walks down the hall and Brie turns and knocks on the open door. Mac looks up. Her eyes darting from Brie to me and then to Laurie. "Oh hell, no."

She starts to sit up and I dart into the room, scared she's going to rip that IV right out of her arm in order to run away.

"Wait! She's my friend. This is Brie. She runs that place I gave you the pamphlet on. Just listen to her."

Mac's eyes move across all three of us and then narrow suspiciously on Laurie, but she lies back on the treatment table again. Brie looks serene and relaxed as she walks closer to stand beside me. "Hey. Mac is it?"

"Sure."

"Is that your street name or your real name?" Brie questions calmly.

"You can read all the info I gave to the doc, so I'm sure you can figure it out," she mutters.

"Mac..." I warn softly.

She sighs. "Full name Mackenzie Brown. But I don't use a last name anymore."

"Cool." Brie reaches for the doctor's stool in the corner of the room and rolls it over so she can sit by the end of the table. "Listen, I know Alex told you about Daphne's House, but you can't stay there right away. We need special approval because you're under sixteen."

"Fine. I'll check back with you in a few weeks." Mackenzie's eyes lock with Brie's and then shift to Laurie in the corner. "You're not going to fucking let me leave."

"I'm not. I can't. The doctor can't," Brie replies bluntly. "But he can let you leave with me."

Mackenzie's face hardens into a vicious glare, like she's trying to make Brie spontaneously combust with just the power of the hate in her eyes. Brie doesn't even blink. "I'm not a foster parent. I've got the credentials, but I don't take in a bunch of kids for money and treat them like crap. I'm rich. I don't need money. I'm just helping Alex out because he's a friend and he wants you to be safe and get healthy."

Mac's death stare softens as Brie continues. "You'll have your own room. No other kids. Eat whatever you want. Watch whatever you want on TV. But no drugs, booze, sex or swearing."

"Ugh," Mackenzie groans and I know it's about the swearing. She doesn't argue, though, or lecture Brie on how she's not her parent. "For how long?"

"Until we can get the judge to approve you in our independent living facility," Brie tells her. "Could be a couple of weeks."

"Mac, this is your luck changing. I promise," I tell her.

She looks incredibly unconvinced, but she rolls her eyes and says, "Fine."

And just like that I saved this kid. Thanks to Brie.

Chapter 11

Brie

I barely slept. I kept waking up at the slightest sound and then gave up on sleep altogether and made an extra large pot of coffee and sat in the living room and waited for her to get up. When she wasn't awake by ten I panicked and peeked in on her, thinking she might not be there. Maybe she'd run away in the middle of the night. But she was in my guest room, sprawled across the bed, snoring. It hit me that she probably hadn't had a decent bed—or any bed—to sleep in lately and so she was taking advantage.

I relaxed and headed back into the living room where I laid out on the couch and turned on HGTV and fell asleep sometime during a ridiculous episode about a family of four with two huskies that want to move into a three-hundred-square-foot tiny home. I wake up to the smell of bacon and the sound of knocking on the front door. I have no idea what's happening or even where I am for a second and then reality slams me in the face. I rush to the kitchen and find

Mackenzie cooking. She looks up at me, still clad in the extra pair of pajamas I gave her last night that are swimming on her, and gives me a guarded smile. "You said I could eat anything."

"I did," I say with a nod. "Throw enough on there for me, okay?"

"Sure."

Another knock on the door. I hesitate for some reason, not wanting to leave her, but I force myself to make my way to the front door. I glance through the peephole and find Alex's rugged face staring back at me. I unlock the door and swing it open, smoothing what must be epic bed-head from my couch nap. Our eyes meet and he smiles. It's soft and even a little shy—nothing like the brash, oversexed guy I've come to know.

"Sorry to bother you at home. I know you probably didn't expect unannounced visits just because I shared an Uber with you guys last night," he starts, rubbing the back of his neck with his palm. "I have a three-day road trip and I just wanted to make sure everything is good. You know, with Mac and everything."

I nod. "It's good so far. She's cooking breakfast."

"Cool." Alex's eyes move from my face to his own feet. His shoulders are hunched and he's emoting this vibe—sadness or something else I can't define—but it makes me want to sooth him somehow. "So you're going to get her into Daphne's House?"

"That's the plan Laurie is working on," I reply. Without even thinking about it I add, "Do you have time to come in for coffee? Food?"

"What? Really?" He's as shocked I asked as I am. I nod. He hesitates. "Yeah. I've got some time."

I step out of the way so he can step into my home. As I close the door behind him I self-consciously tug at the shirt I'm wearing. I'm still in my pajamas. A faded old Tinker Bell shirt that's too small and barely hits my waist, and a pair of pajama bottoms with white and black sheep all over them. Not exactly professional, but after last night I think Alex and I are past that part of our relationship. Now I'm more than just a boss at a place he volunteers. It feels like we're kind of almost friends.

He follows me through the living room and dining room into the kitchen. "Alex stopped by to say hey."

She turns around and sees him and she smiles brighter than I've seen yet. Not actually very bright at all, but for her, it's bright. "Hey."

"Hey back. How's the arm?"

"Okay."

She reaches for the eggs in the carton on the counter as I head to the coffeepot and pour him some, handing him the mug. "Black, right?" I question and he nods, a little surprised. "I remember from Starbucks."

That shy smile comes back. "I really would prefer if you forgot that whole encounter."

I laugh. Mackenzie is watching us curiously. "Are you two a thing?"

"What?" I sound horrified. I know it and I regret it but I can't change it.

Alex's eyes dart to me and then to Mackenzie. "We don't even really know each other, Mac."

"Oh." She seems genuinely startled by that truth. She turns back to the pan, scrambling the eggs with her spatula.

"I'm going out of town for a few days and I just wanted to swing by and say good-bye," he explains.

"You're leaving?" Her normally confident voice is soft, feeble, scared.

My eyes fly to Alex's face in time to see his jaw clench at the sound of it. He clears his throat and his voice is calm. "You're in a safe place. Keep it that way, okay?"

She looks at me. She still doesn't fully trust me, clearly, but I get it and I won't push her, I'll just prove to her she can let me in. I give her a little nod, as if to back up his statement. She shrugs. "I don't make promises, but I'll probably be here when you get back."

"I guess I'll have to take that," Alex says and I motion for him to follow me back into the living room.

I sit down on one end of the couch. He stands awkwardly and looks around. I feel like he's judging me as his eyes survey the room. I start to feel defensive. He finally sits down on the edge of the chaise longue across from the couch. "Nice place."

"My grandmother left it to me," I explain. "She owned a lot of real estate, which was divided up between her grandchildren when she died. I got this place and the building where Daphne's House is located."

"Oh."

For some reason, I feel the need to impress him. Or at the very least change his opinion that I'm some spoiled rich kid who has never faced adversity. "I knew since I was young that I wanted to work with kids struggling in the foster system and give them a different choice," I explain and pause. I'm about to tell him why—the full real reason—but I chicken out. "My grandmother died when I was nineteen and the only way to start the ball rolling on Daphne's House was to have it done in my parents' name because they were the trustees on my inheritance until I turned twenty-five. The place is mine, from the idea, to the money, to the building. I just never bothered to change the paperwork once I got out of college and started running it."

Now his expression changes. Those stormy blue eyes now regard me with awe and, most importantly, respect. "Was Daphne your grandmother's name?"

"No."

"Breakfast!" Mackenzie yells.

She's carrying three plates of eggs and bacon. Alex and I stand up. I walk over to the tiny square dinner table that's set up just next to the kitchen, but Alex doesn't join.

"I already ate and I have to head to the airport," he explains and carries his half-empty coffee cup down into the kitchen. I watch him drain it and place it in the sink. Mackenzie shrugs and starts to scrape the food on his plate onto hers.

"Thanks for the coffee." He smiles at me and his eyes dart to Mackenzie, who is basically shoveling the food into her mouth at an astonishing speed. "And everything."

I get up and walk him to the door. He leaves without another word and I close the door and lock it behind him. When I sit back down at the table she's already finished half of the food on her plate.

I pick up a strip of bacon with my fingers and tear off a

piece. She's cooked it perfectly; it's crispy without being dry. Mackenzie is watching me with a hopeful look so I smile. "Delicious."

A brief but happy smile flies over her elfin features.

"How did Alex find you?"

She swallows down a mouthful of eggs. "He stopped a dude from beating me up for taking a half-eaten piece of pizza from a Dumpster."

I nod like that's no big deal, but it's gross and it breaks my heart that it was her life. I have to make sure it doesn't become her life again. She shoves and entire strip of bacon into her mouth and swallows it down after only a couple chews. I can't help but warn her. "Take your time."

She pauses and for a second I think she might be pissed off but then she admits, "I'm just used to having to rush."

I nod and for some reason I don't even want to analyze, I find myself pulling the conversation back to Alex. "So he stopped the guy from beating you up and you became buddies?"

"Not really. He bribed me with money to meet him again so he could give me info on your charity place, but I ghosted him," she tells me and pauses to eat another heaping forkful of eggs. "I didn't trust him because he fed me some crap about having been a street kid. I mean, really, street kids don't turn into him, you know?"

Wait, what? Did she just say . . .

I swallow down my own mouthful of eggs. "He said he was homeless? When? Why?"

She nods and takes in my expression. "I know, right? It's gotta be total bullshit. Anyway, I don't know if it was just dumb luck, but he found me again and made me show him my arm and well, you know the rest."

"Yeah." I chew absently on another strip of bacon, not really even tasting it.

Alex told her he was homeless? Was that just a line to get her to open up to him? He's full of lines. He is a genius at coaxing and flattering and getting what he wants. Maybe he was using those "talents" for good in this situation with her instead of evil. Because honestly, there is no way he was homeless. How does a homeless kid play hockey? And he had to have played when he was young. You don't get to the professional level without working hard as a teenager. I've got so many questions, but will he answer them if I ask?

"So what does he do for a living?" Mackenzie asks. "Is he like an actor or a model or something?"

The strangest sounding bark of a laugh escapes my mouth and she stares at me, both eyebrows raised. "Sorry. I just...No. He's not."

"He could be," Mackenzie says, shrugging. "He's handsome for an old dude in a rough action-hero kind of way, don't you think?"

I don't answer her but I answer the question internally. Yes, he is handsome, I had to admit that even when he was being a cocky player. And the man who showed up here this morning, the humble, soft-spoken, man...he was even more attractive. But I will not confess that to a child.

"He plays hockey." I answer her original question instead and stand to collect her now empty plate. "For the Brooklyn Barons."

Her green eyes nearly pop out of her head. "Wow. Plot twist. Didn't see that coming. So is he any good?"

I shrug. "I guess so. He's been playing for years for a lot of teams."

"Guess that explains all his scars."

I smile and as I carry the plates into the kitchen I realize it doesn't explain all his scars . . . and I'm suddenly more interested than ever in learning where his biggest ones came from.

Chapter 12

Alex

The three-day road trip feels like ten days. I usually love road trips. I love being around the guys twenty-four/seven. No wives, no girlfriends, just my boys and hockey. But on this trip I can't stop thinking about Mac and Brie. I've called Brie every day to check in. At first the conversations were short. I asked how it was going, she told me it was okay and we hung up. But the conversations started to get longer. After I found out how things were going with Mac we'd start talking about other things, like how our days were.

Last night we talked for almost half an hour, which stunned me when I realized it because I don't think I've ever talked to anyone on the phone for that long in my life. The conversation wasn't particularly deep. She told me about how the fund-raiser didn't make as much money as they'd hoped, but she was working on some new fund-raising ideas. Then she asked me about why a guy took a swing at me during the game, which made me smile because it meant she'd watched it.

I want to call her tonight after the game, but with the time difference it's too late. She and Mac are going to court tomorrow to see if a judge will let Mac live at Daphne's House and it's all I can think about so I decide to head down to the lobby bar for a beer. I text Jordan to see if he'll join me and he texts back that he's heading down.

I often grab a drink and unwind in the bar after a game but this trip, I haven't enjoyed it like I usually do. My brain is preoccupied worrying about Mac's case and for some reason that I can't figure out, it starts thinking of Brie when I'm getting hit on by the bunnies at the bar. Both of the previous nights I left early to call Brie.

Jordan saunters into the bar in sweatpants, a hoodie and a baseball cap. I raise an eyebrow. "You don't even try to look decent anymore."

He shrugs. "Married. I've got no one to impress here anymore."

I laugh. He sits down on the stool beside me and flags the waiter, ordering a pale ale. He yawns and turns to me. "So what have you been up to besides pissing off the coach and blowing off TV shows?"

I groan. "I didn't blow them off. I just haven't had a chance to call them yet."

Jordan gives me a look that screams *Bullshit.* He knows me too well. Thankfully the coach doesn't and when he confronted me, steam nearly pouring out his ears, for not getting in touch with the producer of *Off the Ice*, he believed that excuse. But I don't know what excuse I'll give him next because the fact is, I am not going to call them. Not ever.

"You're going to get yourself benched again, you know that right?" Jordan asks.

I lift my Guinness to my lips and shrug. "Yeah, well if it means I don't have to yack about my life in front of a TV camera, it's worth it. Now can we change the subject?"

"Okay. Tell me about this charity thing you got Rosie all pumped about," Jordan replies. "She's been bouncing off the walls about it. She says she's going to teach a GED course or something."

I'm tell him about Daphne's House and how Brie started the charity from her inheritance and how I've been volunteering there and I even mention Mac, and how I'm hoping she gets into the program.

"You know, you're not the same guy I knew in Seattle," he says, smiling. "I don't know if I should be impressed or scared. It feels like I'm witnessing some modern-day miracle or omen or something."

"Why? Because I volunteer with kids? Surprise! I did that in Seattle too," I confess and sip my beer. "I just didn't make a big deal about it."

"No, not that. I know you're a good guy and also a private guy, so I'm not surprised you do charity work and didn't tell me." His blue eyes glance around the room before landing back on me. "You're a kid in the middle of a candy shop right now and it's like you haven't even noticed."

I scan the room. Bunnies are always the most plentiful in Canadian cities so I'm not shocked that the Vancouver hotel bar is flooded with them. A very cute blonde smiles when our eyes meet. I raise my beer at her as a hello but cut off any further interaction by turning back to Jordan. "I've probably fucked half this room already," I reply since I recognize a few of the pretty faces. "I'm just taking a breather right now. I'm sure one day soon I'll feel like conquering the other half."

He chuckles and shakes his head. "And here I was thinking maybe our little Alex was growing up."

"Nah. Like I've said before, you Garrisons took all the good women."

"Despite your best efforts," Jordan adds with an evil grin. I groan. He knows I hate it when he brings up the fact that I tried to sleep with Jessie. I didn't know she was his long-lost love. "Speaking of our good women, can you keep a secret?"

"I'm a human vault," I promise him and think about the fact Devin told me at the beginning of our trip that Callie is, in fact, pregnant but the doctor suggested they wait another month before they tell anyone. He was beaming when he told me.

Jordan glances around probably to make sure none of our teammates were lingering nearby. There was a group of rookies over at a booth in the corner most with bunnies on their laps, and two other guys playing pool but no one within earshot. He gets a look really similar to his brother's earlier and he whispers, "Jessie is pregnant!"

I start to laugh, which I instantly realize is confusing by the way his eyebrows pinch and his eyes narrow. It's just the fact that I'm the only one to know that both Jessie and Callie are pregnant is hysterical. "You should be sharing this with Devin not with me."

"I can't tell Dev because he'll end up telling Callie who will tell Rose." Jordan sips his beer. "We're not supposed to tell anyone for another couple of weeks, but I'm dying here."

I reach in and hug him. "Congrats, buddy. It's going to be hysterical seeing you try to parent. You're a disaster."

"Thanks, asshole," he says, but he's smiling because he sees the humor in my expression.

"I hope it's a girl and she grows up to be hot like her mom because that'll make it even more hysterical," I add and chuckle. "You're going to have to buy a baseball bat to keep the boys away."

"Oh God, don't even joke about that," he warns. He finishes his beer and glances at the time on his phone. "I'm going to head up to my room and call Jessie."

I stand up when he does and give him another hug. "Congrats, man. Seriously."

"Please, you probably think it's a death sentence," he laughs.

"Maybe for me, but not for you," I reply honestly.

"It's terrifying," he admits quietly.

I slap his shoulder. "You've always stumbled fearlessly into any challenge. You've got this."

He grins. "Looks like someone wants to be *your* next challenge."

His eyes are looking at something over my shoulder and I turn and see the girl I raised my glass to earlier walking toward me. She's cute. Pretty, even. I'm sure she knows exactly who I am and exactly what will happen if she comes over here. But for some reason, I'm not in the mood tonight. I haven't been in the mood the entire trip. So I gulp back the rest of my beer and follow Jordan out into the lobby before she gets close enough to even say hello.

He looks at me with a confused stare. "Again? You didn't score in Toronto or Montreal either. And you always say Montreal has the best bunnies."

"I'm focusing on my game," I explain, which is true. "Coach hasn't scratched me once this trip and I intend to keep it that way."

"Yeah but we're going home in the morning," he reminds me. "And I'm sure he doesn't expect you to be a monk. None of us were ever monks."

"I'm not being a monk. I just . . . I'm not in the mood."

We step into the elevator and he looks more than confused now, he looks stupefied. "You lead the league in sleepovers. You're always in the mood."

It's a line I used to proudly boast about. Jordan might lead the league in short-handed goals, Avery in regular goals, Devin in points, Seb in penalties, Luc in hits and me in bedding women. Only this year, statistically I'd be way off. I've seen women come out of other players' rooms every road trip and I'm yet to bed a bunny. It's not a conscious decision, I just haven't wanted to. It should be as shocking to me as it is to Jordan, but I don't feel shocked. I don't feel much of anything because it doesn't feel like I'm giving up much.

"I'll make up the points in the back end of the season," I tell him jokingly. "A threesome or two after Christmas break and I'll be leading the league again."

"Yeah, there's the Alex I know and love." He laughs as the elevator opens on our floor and we say good night, since our rooms are in opposite directions. His comment leaves a cold feeling swirling in my gut and I can't figure out if it's because he's relieved he thinks I haven't changed or because, deep down, I think I have.

The next day we land around noon and, since we don't have practice or a game, I head straight to Daphne's House. Selena opens the door when I buzz and greets me with a big smile. "Hey! Are you scheduled to volunteer today?"

I shake my head. "No. But I have the tickets for the kids for the upcoming home game. And I was hoping to see Mac. Is she living here?" Selena's smile slides right off her face and my heart slides right into my boots. "She's not here?"

"Not living here, no," Selena replies and I heave out a heavy sigh. "Brie can explain. She's in her office."

I storm back there before Selena can say another word. They had an appointment with the judge first thing this morning. I was worried when Brie didn't text me, but I convinced myself it was because she knew I was flying home. And instead of texting her when I landed I decided to just come here. Now I'm worried and angry and most of all frustrated.

I shouldn't care this much. This is why I don't get involved. The door is open and I don't bother knocking. I just march right in. She's at her desk, typing away on her laptop. She looks startled when I barge in, her big brown eyes getting bigger. She stands up and she is incredible. That thought forces itself into my head even though it's completely inappropriate. She's in a formfitting skirt similar to the one she was wearing in the Starbucks the first time I saw her. It might even be the same one, I don't remember. Her sweater is also snug. I hadn't realized until right this second that her breasts were as enticing as her ass. The revelation disturbs me, and that adds to the negative feelings swirling inside me.

"You're not going to let her live here?"

The startled look on her face morphs into annoyance. "I'm good, thanks. How was your trip? Nice to see you made it home safe."

She's making me look like an ass and even though that observation would be accurate right about now, it only serves to anger me more. "Selena said Mac isn't living here. You said Laurie was petitioning the court this morning to get her placed here."

"She was and she did," Brie replies tersely. "Turns out with Mackenzie's history they aren't inclined to give her a shot at independent living right now. She skipped school a lot her last year in foster care and ran away more than once."

"So they'll just take away her chance at something that might work?" I accuse and she marches around the desk.

"Don't growl at me," she warns angrily. "I'm doing what I can."

"Yeah, everyone said that to me too," I reply before I even realize it. My eyes fly to hers. She doesn't look shocked.

"How long were you on the street as a kid?" she asks calmly, leaning her perfect butt against her desk.

"So what happened to her?" I ask trying to sound less angry because Brie has already done more than I could imagine and I need to remember that. "Is she in juvie? Did they put her in another home? Has she already run away?"

"Nice avoidance skills. I bet you're better at avoiding questions than you are at slap shots," she says tartly.

"I have a fucking great slap shot," I growl. Again. "Now can you tell me what the fuck happened to her?"

"When you answer my question," Brie replies. "How long were you homeless as a kid?"

"That's none of your business." My voice is vibrating with anger.

"Technically Mackenzie is none of your business," Brie replies, just when I think she can't be more annoying. "You're not a relative, guardian or even her foster parent."

I turn toward the door, but I don't leave. I take a breath, but it's hard, like the air is thick. "I ran away from my last foster home when I was fifteen. I slept in alleys and ate out of Dumpsters and then lucked out and went through a few years of bouncing around on couches of hockey teammates and even lived in a friend's garage for a while. Happy now?"

"Of course not," she replies in a voice barely above a whisper. I feel her hand on my shoulder. It's soft and she gives me a gentle squeeze and it's soothing and I hate it. I don't want pity, even if sometimes it feels like I need it. I spin around and face her. She's standing so close to me she has to take a step back or else our chests would bump.

"Now that you've invaded my privacy will you fucking tell me what I want to know?" I hiss.

She looks a little hurt by that, but I don't care. She forced me to share something I hate sharing. My mood is on her.

"She's at school," Brie explains and takes a step away from me, crossing her arms. "Today is her first day. The judge is allowing me to continue to foster her for now. That's a win by the way because she should be in juvie with her history. But they're overcrowded, and Laurie convinced them she'd follow the rules with me. So far she has. She's not a bad kid. A little rough—and hard—around the edges but good."

"How long are you going to keep her?" I can't imagine this is anything less than an inconvenience for Brie. She's young, rich and has a boyfriend who I know doesn't want a kid that isn't his.

She sighs. "I don't know, Alex. It'll depend on the court and on Mackenzie. But I promise you I will do whatever is best for her."

I want to argue that but I have no reason to. She's been good to this kid. I run a hand through my hair before shoving it back in the pocket of my coat. "How's your boyfriend handling all this?"

Her face changes, her lips flattening into a hard line, her eyes darting away from me to the window. "Now look who is getting personal?"

"Tit for tat," I snark.

"You know, you and I have a lot in common," she says.

I laugh out loud, which seems to offend her judging by the pissed-off look on her face.

"Why? Because you work with kids nobody wants, and I was one? Yeah, we might as well be twins."

"For someone who has seen both sides of life, you're the most presumptuous, condescending asshole I've ever met." Her stare is so fiery I bet I could toast marshmallows off it if I had any.

"Look, don't get me wrong," I say. "What you do is amazing. And I can tell you're a good person, but being around kids who have never been loved and being the kid who was never loved are two very different things." I try not to let the ache developing in my chest seep out into my voice. I do not want this woman's sympathy. I don't want anyone's and never have.

"Where did you grow up?" she asks. "Quebec?"

"Nope. I got the information I needed. I'm not telling you another thing." I turn and storm out of her office. I call over my shoulder. "Tell Mac I say hi."

I'm halfway to the front door when I remember I haven't given anyone the tickets. I promised the kids they could come see the game tomorrow night. I turn back to find Selena and give them to her. And I collide straight into Brie.

She starts to fall backward and instinctively I circle an arm around her waist. I yank her into me, her body pressing against mine and I pull her upright. It takes a second for her feet to get under her again and in that second I find myself overdosing on the feel of her warm, soft body pressed into me. Suddenly I'm well aware of how long it's been since I've been this close to a woman. It's been way too long.

She grabs my shoulders and makes this tiny little gasping sound, which I feel in my groin. Jesus, it's sexy as fuck. Our eyes lock. Her mouth is parted just enough that I can see the tip of her pink tongue. I want to know how it tastes. Because of that urge, instead of letting her go, I tighten my arm around her waist. She doesn't pull away. Her grip on my biceps gets tighter too.

When our eyes connect again, it's electric. There's a charge between us. All the animosity and anger that heated the air between us a second ago has turned into something else. Passion? Lust? Maybe both.

I dip my head, she turns hers, our lips are inches from each other. The sound of the door directly behind me buzzing because someone is coming in, feels louder than a fire alarm. It's also a wake-up call reminding me that not only do I not get along with this woman but she has a boyfriend. I pull back so quickly she stumbles again but manages to grab the staircase banister.

It's Reg coming home from his job at Dunkin' Donuts, still in his uniform. "Hey, Alex! Are we still all going to the game tomorrow?"

I pull the tickets from my pocket and hand them to him. "Yeah. Give these to Brie."

"But she's right—"

"See you tomorrow night!"

Chapter 13

Brie

"Say that again."

"No."

"Come on. Humor me," Len begs. "I have no life, romantic or otherwise, so I'm living vicariously through you right now."

I roll my eyes, but she ignores that and tugs on my arm, which she's been holding as we walk with the kids through the arena toward the gate where are seats are located. I probably shouldn't even be here. But he included a ticket for Mackenzie and she wanted to go. One of the kids didn't want to, so I offered the extra ticket to Len. And then I confessed the details about what happened yesterday in the hallway. I shouldn't talk about it. I should just ignore it and move on, act like it didn't happen, but I can't stop thinking about it. More importantly I can't stop thinking about how much I felt in those wild few seconds. Passion, lust, need, desire raged inside of me out of nowhere as soon as his arm circled my waist and he tugged me to him possessively.

"Say it!" Len urges in a harsh whisper still tugging on my arm.

I glance at the back of Mackenzie's head. She's far enough in front of me that I don't think she'll hear. So I indulge Len and I say what I said earlier that's got her so excited. "I think he was going to kiss me."

She squeals. I feel heat touch my cheeks and that now familiar shiver of desire dance down my spine like it has every time I've thought about that moment since it happened. I've never experienced anything like it. In ten seconds flat, as he grabbed me to keep me from falling, all my frustration and reservation about Alex disappeared. It was like they were never real to begin with. Like they were just a curtain veiling my attraction to him. As soon as his strong arm slipped around my waist and my body was pressed to his, the curtain fell and I was left with nothing but deep, burning desire for this man.

"It's not a big deal," I tell Len as I shush her and glance ahead to make sure the kids are still wrapped up in their own conversations. "He was just emotional and got caught up in the moment."

"I don't know, Brie," Len says softly, growing serious. "You could be this epic, like book-worthy, opposites-attract love story."

I roll my eyes again as we enter one of the entrances to the seating. The truth is we're not opposites at all, but I don't feel like I should tell Len about his childhood when he clearly didn't even want me to know. He thinks I'm some pampered princess who has lived this privileged life and I need him to know I'm not. I was just one of the lucky ones.

I don't remember much of when my luck changed, I was only four. And what I do remember are like flashes from a horror movie filled with screaming and blood and sirens, which took years of therapy to deal with, but that led my parents to me so it was lucky. It hurts my heart to think that he wasn't as fortunate when he was little.

"If you don't want to talk about Alex, talk about Victor," Len urges me, still clinging to my arm. "Since my last boyfriend just disappeared on me like I never existed, I didn't get a chance to break up with him so I want to hear all the gory details of your breakup."

I almost laugh at that. "It wasn't that gory. I mean, yeah, he was angry at first, but I also think he was a little relieved. I think he knew we wanted different things."

"And you weren't going to become the person he wanted you to be," Len adds because I'd already told her that was what I told Victor after the fund-raiser. "Because you are a perfect, smart, sassy, badass woman just as you are and if Vic doesn't like it, he can't stick it up his—"

"Whoa!" I warn, but as always the kids are chatting among themselves, oblivious to us. Still, I don't want her to finish that sentence. "Anyway, he came by to get his stuff from my place yesterday and he met Mac and that seemed to make him understand."

"Really?" Len looks shocked.

"Yeah. When he realized I was serious about fostering and he'd never turn me into his personal breeding cow, he couldn't leave fast enough."

Len's pretty face contorts with anger. "Vic is a worthless

jerk. I am beyond thrilled he is out of your life. On to bigger and better! Possibly with skates and a face like an alley cat."

"Shut up," I hiss but I'm smiling at her because her ridiculousness is kind of cute.

"Holy sh—" Mackenzie stops mid-swear and corrects herself under my glare. "Shoot! These seats are insane!"

I realize we've stopped at the first row, right behind the team bench. I glance at the number on our tickets. Yeah, this is us. Mackenzie is right, Alex outdid himself. I can tell by the looks on all the kids' faces that they've never experienced a professional sport this up close and personal. Neither have I, honestly. Victor had season tickets to the Knicks but always took one of his friends or a client.

We let the kids scoot into the row first and take the two end seats. As soon as we're seated Len leans in and whispers. "Now that Vic is out of the picture, you need to live a little! And Alex looks like a guy who knows how to make a girl feel alive."

I glance down the row to make sure the kids didn't hear. "Speaking of making women feel alive, did you tell him you canceled that woman's prize from the auction?" Len asks.

I shake my head. "I'm hoping he just forgets about it and I never have to tell him."

Len gives me a stern glare. "You'll have to tell him, and I hope he thinks you canceled because you want him all for yourself. Then maybe that almost kiss will become an actual kiss."

I glance at the kids again as I hush Len. No one is paying attention at all. Len is staring at me with a pleading look on her face like she's desperate for me to do something inappropriate with Alex. It's actually hysterical and I can't help but laugh. "You are nothing if not a hopeless romantic."

I give her a quick side hug because I adore that in her. When we first met as kids I was a little bit dark, maybe I still am. And she's always been nothing but light and sunshine and happily ever after. "He volunteers for me, so although he's not my employee, it's still not a great idea to think about dating him. Besides, he's far from the settling-down type and proud of it."

"So don't settle down," Len says with a shrug. "Keep it casual."

I take a long slow breath and even though I might regret admitting this, I tell her a truth I have barely admitted to myself. "I don't do that kind of thing. I have nothing against it I just can't. I can't turn off my feelings."

Her big blue eyes somehow get even bigger and she starts gripping my upper arm again. "Are you falling for him?"

"No. But he has this side of him I've seen a few times, like with Mac, that's way more appealing than the cocky, flirty side he shows everyone," I confess. "I think I could develop feelings for that Alex and that's not a good idea. He's...not ready for that and probably never will be and even if he was, it probably wouldn't be with me. He thinks I'm some spoiled brat."

She looks confused. "So tell him about your childhood. Pre-Bennetts."

"You know I don't really talk about that," I remind her. "It upsets my mom when I bring it up. You can literally see her heart breaking."

"So don't tell him in front of your mom," Len says with a

shrug. "Are you worried he'll be like Vic and think it makes you somehow less?"

"No. I know Alex won't react like that," I tell her. "But I don't like to bring it up with just anyone."

"Yeah, but if you've got feelings for him, he's not just anyone." Len looks excited and I know I have to squash that hope before she gets carried away.

"I said I don't have feelings for him," I remind her. "I'm trying to avoid developing them."

Len looks undeterred. "But he's kind of like a friend now, right?"

I think about all the phone conversations when he was on his trip and how they easily morphed from talking about Mac to talking about ourselves. I found myself looking forward to hearing his voice. Because of that I can't help but give Len a nod of confirmation.

"So confide in him as a friend," Len suggests. "He'll definitely stop thinking of you as a spoiled, rich princess. And it will probably bring you closer. I mean your friendship."

She uses her fingers to make air quotes when she says "friendship." Her not-so-subtle way of telling me she's still holding out for some star-crossed lovers action. I give her yet another eye roll. She has a bit of a point. Telling Alex about my own foster care experience might change the way he sees me. But then again, it might make him resent me more. I got the life he was never offered. A safe home and loving parents.

The lights dim and the crowd gets to its feet as the players funnel onto the ice, music blaring, fans cheering. I spend the entire game watching Alex. My eyes refuse to leave him whether he's on the ice or sitting on the bench waiting for his shift. He looks incredible out there. He skates so fast and hits so hard. One minute he's all aggression and the next the supportive, jubilant teammate, like when someone scores. By the time the game is over, the crush I'm not supposed to have on him is bigger. I really should not have come tonight.

As the players leave the ice, he stays at the bench and finally turns toward us and waves and smiles at the group. His eyes sweep over our row but they stop short of meeting mine. I know it's on purpose. He waves Len closer to the glass instead of me, which stings a little. Okay, a lot. She leans in and I pull out my phone and pretend I am checking texts or emails or something. Better than staring at him longingly while he ignores me.

I look back up as I see Len straighten out of my peripheral vision. Alex is heading down the tunnel and Len is grinning as she turns to the kids. "You guys want to see the locker room?"

There's a resounding yes out of every single one of them. "Alex said we can come down. Follow me."

Len starts up the stairs to the main concourse. She's so excited she's bouncing more than walking. "I wonder if any of his teammates are single?"

I laugh. "Len, this isn't your own personal Tinder."

"Why not? Romance can strike anywhere."

She's adorable in her wide-eyed optimism. I, on the other hand am feeling the burn from being ignored by Alex and am debating even going down with them to locker room. It stung enough being ignored by him with Plexiglas between us.

Everyone piles into the elevator but I don't move.

Mackenzie looks at me, her face is so excited. She looks happier than I've seen her since I met her. I know if I don't go with them it might disrupt this moment for her and I don't want to do that so I step into the elevator.

Len gives her name to the security guard standing in front of the steel door when we get off. He checks a list and then counts us and nods, opening the door. We're suddenly in a long concrete curving hall and there's another security guard smiling at us. He doesn't take us to the locker room though; he puts us in a room with leather couches, big screen TVs and a long buffet table filled with fruit, chips and candy. Of course, every single one of the kids head straight for it.

"Don't go crazy just because it's free!" Len calls out.

"Mr. Larue will be here in a minute to start your tour," the guard tells us and disappears. There's a few other people in the room. Mostly beautiful modelesque woman who must be girlfriends. Although some are wearing giant rings so I assume they're wives. A couple are chasing toddlers or holding babies. On a couch in the corner I recognize Rose from the party. She's sitting with two other women.

I walk over to say hi, hoping it'll distract me from the uneasiness in my gut about facing Alex. She looks up as I approach and her face bursts into a smile as she stands. "Brie!"

She pulls me into a hug. "Hi. Alex gave the kids at Daphne's House tickets and I tagged along."

"That's awesome." Rose turns to the women she was sitting with. "These are my sisters, Callie and Jessie. Their husbands play on the team too."

"Wow!" I can't help but blurt out. "That's got to be uncommon, you all with hockey players on the same team."

"And Jessie and I married brothers," Callie explains, adding to my shock. "So yeah, we're definitely unique."

"Remember when I told you Luc had friends to live with growing up?" Rose says quietly. "It was the Garrisons, their husbands' family, so he's basically like a brother to their husbands too."

"It makes us seem kind of inbred or something, I know," Jessie laughs.

"No. I think it's great. And sweet," I tell her.

"Rose has done nothing but talk about Daphne's House since she went to that charity event," Callie tells me. "You work there?"

"I run it," I explain and pause. "In fact, I created it."

"Well I'd love to know more about it," Callie says. "And maybe see if I could volunteer somehow like Rose is going to do."

"We can arrange that," I say and start to open my purse to pull out a business card but Rose interrupts.

"Why don't I have you over for dinner, with my sisters and Alex, and we can chat about it more?" she suggests. "We all live in Brooklyn. Callie can cook, she's incredible at it."

I hesitate. I have no problem having dinner with these women. Rose has proven herself to be warm and genuine and her sisters seem to be exactly the same, but they want Alex there too. That part makes me unsure. Things are weird between us and it would be awkward to be at dinner with him. But Rose looks so excited and hopeful and it really could do the charity a world of good if they got onboard. Even after the fund-raiser we're still short almost twenty thousand dollars of what we need to keep the place running, no thanks to me refusing to let that woman buy her date with Alex. Len and I have blitzed the local media with press releases, trying to garner some interest in getting an article or news segment on the charity but so far we haven't heard back.

"Sure," I relent.

Rose lets out a happy squeak. "Great! I'll give you the details when I stop by tomorrow for my first GED class tomorrow."

She pulls me into a bear hug just as Alex appears in the doorway over her shoulder. He's in a pair of shorts, flip-flops and a formfitting black athletic shirt. And what a form it is. The fabric embraces him like Saran Wrap. The broad expanse of his shoulders is on display along with the bulging curl of his biceps and the ripples his abs make. I didn't think bodies that perfectly ripped actually existed. I thought they were all the product of Photoshop, at least a little bit. But seriously, even the best graphic designer couldn't fake something this...gorgeous. His hair is damp with sweat and tousled. There's a glow to his skin and his eyes are brighter, lighter; like the game brought him enough joy that it lightened the stormy color in them.

This time he looks at me. It's brief but somehow still has an intensity to it that I can feel. He must feel it too because he takes a breath so sharp I can see it and then he quickly turns his head to the buffet table. "Hey! Leave some snacks for the rest of us, eh?"

I can't help but smile at his use of the little Canadian "eh" that I haven't heard in decades. The kids all turn and call out excited greetings, most walk toward him, but Mackenzie runs. For a quick second I think she might hug him, which would melt my heart, but she skitters to an abrupt halt half a foot in front of him and gives him a smile instead. "Hey, bud. Why didn't you tell me you were all famous and junk?"

Every adult in the room chuckles. Alex smiles at her and shrugs. "I'm not famous."

"Can I sell your autograph on eBay?" she questions.

"Yeah. Probably."

"Then you're famous," she concludes and pauses before adding, "Can you sign something for me?"

He reaches out and ruffles her hair. "Why don't I give you guys a VIP tour of the place before you start your eBay business, Mac."

"It was nice meeting you," I tell Jessie and Callie and give Rose another quick hug.

As I walk across the room to join the others who are filing out the door Rose calls, "I'll see you tomorrow with dinner details!"

I nod.

Alex takes us into every single room. There are medical rooms and rooms filled with fancy workout equipment and a room with a hot tub and an ice bath and a room just for massages. Finally, we end in the locker room. He introduces us to the captain, Devin Garrison, and his brother, Jordan, who I know now are married to Rose's sisters. They're rugged, good-looking men and have a real, easygoing way with the kids, showing them around the room and answering all their questions, even the weird ones, like when Reg asks if it's strange to shower together.

Alex hasn't spoken to me directly and he hasn't made eye contact again. I'm beginning to feel that sting of rejection, which makes me annoyed with him but also with myself for letting him have that effect on me. When the tour is over, and Devin has given them each their own jersey, which I'm sure costs a fortune, I thank him profusely.

"It's nothing really," he says and hands both me and Len a jersey as well.

I turn to Alex as he walks us back to the elevator, Mackenzie glued to his side. "Thank you for this. It was beyond kind."

"Yeah. It's nothing for me. Glad you enjoyed it," he says lightly and shrugs, his eyes facing forward, still refusing to look at me.

"Well, it was something big to the kids," I tell him, trying not to sound hurt or angry, but I'm both. He's the one who almost kissed me. Why is he making me feel bad about it? "Will you be by tomorrow?"

He shakes his head. "I can't tomorrow. I know I was scheduled, but something came up. I was hoping I could do the run I was planning with them on Saturday instead."

"What came up?" I can't help but ask, even though it's none of my damn business.

He doesn't like the question and his shoulders tense. "I told you when I signed up my volunteer times would have to be fluid due to my job."

"Yes. Because you have games. But you don't have a game tomorrow," I remind him but judging by the way his jaw flexes, he hasn't forgotten.

"I have a date, okay?" he barks out in a low growl of a whisper. It's like a physical punch right to my solar plexus. I feel winded and when, a second later, I take a breath it feels like I'm filling my lungs with embarrassment, not oxygen.

I glance ahead. The group is already at the elevator still talking excitedly about the night they just had. Somehow we've fallen behind. Just him and I. I'm grateful because that means no one heard our exchange.

He sighs loudly. "Selena called to ask if it was okay if you held a raffle for the tickets that weren't sold at the auction."

Shit. I told her I would handle that. She must have thought she was doing me a favor by calling him for me. He frowns down at me. "You shouldn't have refused to give the winner the prize."

"I didn't," I reply. "I simply told her you weren't part of the prize and she didn't want it without you."

"You need that five grand," he reminds me. "I had Selena give me Ms. Cameron's contact information and I am meeting her for a lunch date tomorrow. She'll also be supplying me with the check and I will be giving her the hockey tickets."

"Alex, I am not comfortable with—"

"I'm not comfortable with Daphne's House losing much needed funding because you're trying to protect my honor," he cuts me off and his voice drops into a low, penetrating whisper. "I'm not one of your kids. I don't need protecting and my honor has long since been lost so just relax. I'm doing this."

He's staring at me with this tortured look on his face, like he's pained that he had to tell me his plans and convince me to let him do it. I'd love to chalk that up to his veracious need for privacy but it's probably more about how I must be coming across like a schoolgirl with a crush. Oh my God, I'm so embarrassed.

"Saturday it is. I'll update the schedule. Good night."

"Brie. Wait!"

I don't wait. Mackenzie is looking at me quizzically as I usher her into the now open elevator with everyone else. "Wait!" she complains. "When will I see him again? Alex! When can we hang out?"

"He'll be by the Daphne's on Saturday. You can swing by and hang out. But you'll have to take his Learn to Run class," I tell her and she groans at the running part.

Alex says my name one more time just as the elevator doors close.

Two hours later, Mackenzie is in bed and I'm trying to convince myself that it's not too late to open a bottle of wine. It's almost eleven thirty and I have to be up by seven. I could have one glass, to take the edge of embarrassment off, but then I'll want two and probably three. And then I'll have trouble being a cheery foster parent in the morning. Mackenzie, I've learned since she started having to get up for school, is not a morning person—and at least one of us should be.

I'm staring longingly at my bottle of cabernet sauvignon when I hear a rapping sound. I turn from the wine rack to glance around the living room. I assume it's Mackenzie, but as soon as I step out into the hall it happens again and I realize it's coming from the front door.

I'm startled and a little fearful. No one I know would drop by this late without texting or calling me first. I force myself to inch over to the door, softly, like they might hear me, which they wouldn't…whoever they are. I stick my eye up to the peephole. It's dark and he's hunched over but

I would know that strong jaw and those eyes anywhere.

I crack open the door and our eyes connect and somehow residual embarrassment starts to flood my cheeks again. "You can see Mackenzie on Saturday. She'll go to Daphne's."

"I came to talk to you."

He reaches out and puts a hand flat against the middle of the door. He thinks I'm going to slam it in his face. I don't. In fact, I let him step over the threshold and into my front hall. "I'm sorry about tonight."

I look up at him through my lashes, with my head still tilted down, humiliation still refusing to let me have any pride in this situation. "You're allowed to switch your volunteer day, and it's not my business why. Is that why you're here? I apologize for overstepping. It won't happen again. Have a good night."

He just stands there. He doesn't move a inch, but somehow, he seems to take up more space in my narrow hall. His mood is darkening—intensifying—and that seems to be what's taking up with space. He yanks a hand out of his pocket and scrubs his face with it. He opens his mouth, running his tongue along his full bottom lip, but then he doesn't speak. Is he really going to make this even more uncomfortable for me?

"What do you want from me?" I blurt out, aggravated.

"I'm not going to sleep with that woman." I look up at him and he's staring with a look of intense discomfort on his ruggedly handsome face. He's completely out of his comfort zone, being raw and honest with someone, but he's forcing himself to do it. "Sex is just a way to have a good time. It's not emotional or deep for me and trust me, I know that's all this woman wants—a naked good time. I don't have a problem with it, but you do and that matters to me."

I don't know how to react to that confession. I'm so confused by the emotions inside me it's frustrating. I cross my arms angrily, but I also sigh in defeat. "If it's what you want to do, just do it. I don't want to stop you from being you. But I don't want you to feel like you have to fuck someone to get money for my charity."

I didn't mean to be so crass but I guess I'm just feeling as raw and emotional as he is and I'm sick of not showing it. He tilts his head slightly to the side, like he's trying to decipher something and then he says in that same low, penetrating voice he used earlier at the arena. "I don't want to fuck her. And it's because of you, but not just because I don't want to upset you. It's because I like the way you look at me lately and I like the way it feels when I look at you and when we talk and I don't want to lose that."

Those dark blue eyes that always seem to be swirling with some unexpressed emotion are as tumultuous as ever. Looking into them as he scans my face is like staring into the eye of a tornado. I don't feel unsafe, but I feel uncertain. I have no idea what's going to happen next. And of all the thoughts running through my head at lightning speed, not one of them was the idea that he would step closer, standing so close that our bodies touched. But that's what he does.

I feel dizzy and off-balance so I try to take a step back, but suddenly his arm is around my waist. His embrace is strong, urgent and heats me from the inside. The blush of humiliation on my cheeks is turning to the heat of lust. I grip his biceps just like I did yesterday, only today it's not for balance, it's because I want to make sure he doesn't pull away this time.

He dips his head and tilts it, brushing his lips against my cheek either by accident or on purpose. It causes a ripple of desire to quiver down my spine. God, I hope it was on purpose. "I want things from you I shouldn't want. You have a boyfriend."

"I don't," I reply my voice a quaking whisper. "Victor and I broke—"

I stop before the last word because his lips are brushing mine now. It's not a kiss but it's so close; it's both soothing and painful. His eyes flutter closed, his breathing gets shallow, but his grip on my waist starts to ease. I tighten my grip on his arms. And then I whisper strongly, "Do it."

His eyes open and then his lips are brushing mine again but instead of just ghosting by, they stop. I rock up onto my toes and his arm around my waist tightens, our torsos press roughly against each other and his mouth opens. The first feel of his tongue against mine makes me whimper and that seems to break him free of his hesitation. The kiss is nothing short of monumental. He's rough and wild—claiming me with abandon, his tongue searching, his lips pushing, his hand slipping to my ass as I circle his neck and tangle my fingers into his hair. But then there's a sound upstairs. A toilet flushing. And he's gone so quickly that I'm left wondering if I just had a hallucination. The door is wide open, the hallway is empty and there's nothing but cold air and a dark empty New York street. I step onto my stoop. He's already halfway down the block.

I want to chase him. I want to drag him back here and continue whatever the hell we just started. But I know he's like a wild animal and if he's chased he'll just run faster—emotionally and physically. And besides, I can't with Mackenzie in the house. I lean against the closed door and press a hand to my chest. My heart hammers against my palm. I don't know what that was, but I want it to happen again.

Chapter 14

Alex

I'm smiling as we finish the run, which actually turned into more of a walk than a run, albeit a brisk one. These kids haven't been lucky enough to be on team sports or even been in PE classes since they haven't been in school regularly, so I knew it wasn't going to be much of a run. Still, they were troopers and they all were interested in technique and tips. I had a good time and I think they did too, which makes me really happy I didn't bail like I contemplated after making out with Brie.

I feel a wave of panic just thinking about it again. *Colisse,* I swear at myself, what the hell was I thinking? I mean honestly, just last week I thought she was the most irritating person on the planet. She started to grow on me when she came to my rescue, well Mac's rescue, but then she got all nosy and pushy and I was back to being irritated. Then...I touched her. I've touched a lot of girls, with intent and without intent, and this candid moment of saving her from tripping, it was like I was hit with those defibrillator paddles at the hospital. Every single part of me, every nerve and every cell was jolted alive. With desire. I would have pulled her to the floor in her hall and done a hell of a lot more than kiss her if it wasn't for two things—the sound of that toilet flushing reminding me Mac was just feet away and the fact that this woman isn't one-night stand material, and that's all I know how to do.

Mac is staring up at me with a weird look on her face, which I've noticed even after just a week, is filling out. She looks healthier. I glance down at her. "What?"

"Were you at Brie's house after the game the other night?"

"What? Why?"

Oh shit, if Mac saw anything I will truly die.

"I thought I heard your voice."

"I . . . Umm . . . Yeah . . . I was, I guess."

Her face twists into a mix of sarcasm and judgment in a way that only a teenager can accomplish. "You guess?"

"I was. For a second."

"Why?"

We've reached Daphne's now and so I stop and say a personal good-bye to each of the kids who came on the run. They all head inside except Mac who is clearly not going to let this go. She's still looking up at me with an expectant look on her face. "I wanted to clear up something with Brie."

"At like midnight?" That look is on her face again. God, this kid is too smart for her own good.

"It wasn't midnight," I reply defensively. "And even if it was, I'm an adult. So is she, so we can have late-night conversation. It's no big deal."

She smiles. Doesn't speak, just smiles and somehow that

feels even more judgy and sarcastic than the look she was giving me before. She turns and heads into the house. "I'm going to take Len's budgeting class this afternoon."

"Cool. Have fun. Tell her hi," I say casually as she climbs the stairs to the front door.

"You can tell her yourself," I hear Len's voice behind me.

As Mac disappears inside I turn and see Len walking up the sidewalk behind me. She's smiling conspiratorially so I know she knows about the kiss before she even says a word. I must look as embarrassed as I feel because she lets out a soft, sympathetic chuckle and pats my arm as she stops in front of me. "It's okay. I'm not going to chew you out for your late-night kiss stealing."

"I didn't steal it," I mumble, my eyes firmly glued to a crack in the sidewalk between our shoes. "She gave it to me."

Len laughs again. "When you take it and run, it's stealing."

I finally pull my eyes off the pavement and look at her. "I left because I needed to stop it from going any further. Mac was there and . . ."

I can't seem to figure out how to finish that sentence so Len decides to help me. "And you didn't want her to hear you two getting it on? But also you weren't sure you should get it on right now?"

I nod but feel heat creep over my face. "Brie is great but—"

"She's fantastic," Len interrupts. "No buts about it."

I nod. "But I'm not boyfriend material and she's not the casual type."

Len rolls her eyes so hard she looks like she's having a

seizure. "Oh come on. Don't pretend that you're some stereo-typical hockey jock who wants nothing more than to get his hockey stick wet. You're not. I already know that. Those types don't volunteer with orphaned kids and they don't save girls like Mackenzie from the street."

"You're right. I'm not like that," I argue back. "But I'm not the type of guy Brie wants either."

She frowns. "Shouldn't you be talking to her about what she wants?"

"I will," I say. "I'm on my way there now."

Len looks disappointed. "Alex, I have to say if you truly feel that way then you're right. Brie has been through enough in her life. I don't want her to deal with a player. She's better than that."

I nod, not in the least offended. "She is."

"It's just, the way you are with the kids and with Macken-zie especially, makes me think you'd understand her past and you'd get Brie on levels that Victor never did," Len says qui-etly. "On levels even I don't get her on."

She adjusts the bag on her shoulder and turns and starts up the stairs. I should walk away, head over to Brie's and for-get this conversation, but I can't. I stare at her and as she digs out her key fob to open the front door I call out, "What's her past?"

"That's for her to tell you, not me," Len replies firmly and now the smile she's giving me is less friendly, less warm. "And she won't. If you won't let her in, she won't let you in."

She disappears into Daphne's House. I pull out my phone to call a Lyft to head to Brie's. What in the world could have happened in Brie's past that Len thinks only someone as broken and fucked up as me would "get" her? Then again, Len might not know my past. She probably just sees me as a rich athlete. Let's face it, most kids who play hockey grow up in comfortable families because hockey is not a cheap hobby and it costs even more if you're trying to get your kid into the NHL with off-season training sessions and what not. I doubt my history has anything in common with a girl who spent her summers in that mansion in the Hamptons.

My phone starts ringing as I wait for my ride and I see Rose's name on the call display. As soon as I answer there's a trio of voices blurting things out.

"It's Rose, Callie and Jessie! We've got you on speaker," Rose says.

"We're calling about that dinner we invited you and Brie to," Callie pipes up.

"We've decided it's going to be a small party instead," Jessie adds. "At your house."

"What?"

"Your new apartment," Callie clarifies. "A housewarming."

"Don't worry," Rose adds before I can say no. "We'll do everything from invitations to food. You just have to text me your address."

"I don't want to."

"Housewarmings are imperative or else it's not a house. It's just four walls and a roof," Callie insists. "So if you don't give us your address, I'll make Devin do it."

"It's happening Alex," Jessie assures me. "Friday after you guys come home from your game in Chicago. So try not to get punched for once. I want the steak to be for the guests, not a black eye."

"Address?" Rose demands in a happy singsong voice but it's still a demand.

I sigh as loud as I can so they know I am not pleased, even though I don't think it matters to them in the slightest. I give them my address and I can actually hear them high-fiving each other in victory. Jesus, these girls are forces of nature, like tornados or hurricanes or tsunamis.

"Thanks, Rue," Callie says happily. "You won't regret it!"

"I already do!" I reply, but they've hung up.

I sigh. What fresh hell is this?

Chapter 15

Brie

When I hear the knock on the door all the butterflies I've been trying to quell inside me take flight. I haven't seen him since that kiss. They had a game last night but he texted me before it, after his date with Lizzie, to tell me it went smoothly and asked if he could swing by today after his running clinic. Of course I said yes. I wanted to see him and figure out exactly what the hell is going on between us.

I glance at my reflection in the mirror in the hall. I spent two hours getting ready this morning. I curled my hair but then messed it up so it looked natural and applied all the natural-colored makeup I could find so I didn't look like I was actually wearing any and I even tried three lipsticks before settling on one that was only a shade darker than my natural lips. My clothing selection took almost an hour even though I ended up in just a pair of soft gray patterned leggings and an oversized, off-the-shoulder sweater. I've never tried so hard to look casual and effortless in all my life. But when I swing open the door and his eyes sweep over me and he smiles, it was worth every second.

"You're a sight for sore eyes," he says and I smile.

"Come in." I open the door wider and he steps into the hall. I motion for him to head to the living room and he does after slipping off his shoes. But he just stands in the middle of my room and stares at my furniture like he's unsure of where to sit. Although it somehow feels like a bold move, I reach out and take him by the wrist and tug him toward the long velvet couch. I drop down on one end, my back against the arm and he sits more in the middle. And then slides to the other end. Not a great start.

"Congrats on the win last night," I say to break the ice.

He smiles. "You watched?"

"Mac insisted, and I didn't mind," I confess. His eyes light up a little bit at that and he smiles. Then he reaches into his pocket and hands me a folded piece of paper.

"The check from Lizzie," he explains as I unfold it. "She got her lunch and her tickets. And absolutely nothing else, much to her dismay."

My eyes lift from the check and lock with his. He looks calm and almost amused. I'm still horrified that a woman thinks she can buy sex at a charity auction. "Was she a bitch about it?"

He nods. "Oh yeah. She told me that she was going to tell everyone the rumors weren't true and that I couldn't possibly be great in bed and I was probably impotent or something."

I am one hundred percent horrified and I'm clearly not

hiding it because he starts to chuckle. "I can't even... I mean who does that?"

"Lots of women come up to me expecting nothing but a good time," he replies. "Because I have no problem giving them one as long as they know it's just once and it's just for fun."

I swallow but my mouth is dry. "You must have had a girlfriend at some point."

He shakes his head. "Nope. Never."

"Never?" I repeat in disbelief. "Not even before hockey? Like when you were in high school or something?"

His expression grows dark before he bows his head. "Not a lot of girls want to date a homeless guy. Although there was one girl who used to sneak me into her basement and let me sleep there if I fooled around with her. She wouldn't admit we were messing around in school because she was embarrassed, but I guess she was as close as I got to a girlfriend because it was a regular thing for a while."

My heart aches for him, but I try not to let him see it. I know he might construe it as pity and I don't want to upset him. "Can we talk about that? Your childhood?"

"I don't like to."

"I know. I don't like to either." That makes him look up and meet my eye again.

"Len mentioned she thought I would understand you better than that asshole you were dating," he tells me and I bite back a smile.

"You might," I admit and pull my knees up, wrapping my arms around them. "And there's no need for name calling."

He balks at that. "I heard him at the fund-raiser talking

about you like you were his property or his project. He's an asshole. You might have a lot in common with him like the way you grew up or the schools you went to, but he is nothing like you and you deserve more than him."

Those butterflies are taking flight again. "I don't have that much in common with him, actually. I mean I know it looks that way, but his idea of struggle is having to wait so long for a cab that he contemplates taking the subway, which he never has by the way."

Alex laughs at that and gives me a sheepish smirk. "I hate to say it, but that's what I thought of you too."

"And you're wrong, but I see why you made that assumption. My parents are rich and my dad's family has been wealthy for generations too," I explain and hug my knees tightly to my chest. "But technically I'm a Bennett by name, not by blood. My mom hates when I point that out because she says I'm her daughter because her heart chose me not her DNA. But what I'm trying to say is I was adopted."

"Is it a secret?"

I shake my head. "No. But like I said my mom doesn't like to make the distinction. Probably because of the way I was adopted."

"How were you adopted?"

"Nope. Your turn," I counter and give him a small smile. "How were you able to play hockey if you lived on the street? You said yourself it's not a cheap sport."

I figure that's an easy first question—not too invasive and shouldn't upset him too much, I hope. He runs both his hands through his hair, leaving it mussed up in a deliciously sexy way that I purposefully try to ignore so I don't get distracted, and then he leans back on the sofa, his back against the other arm so we're facing each other. "I grew up in Quebec and like the rest of Canada, maybe even more so, they take hockey very seriously. They offer a lot of free programs and equipment when you're really young. When I was nine I ended up in a group home for troubled boys and they put us in one of the free programs hoping it would help curb our aggression. I was addicted the minute I stepped onto the ice. A coach saw potential in me, and he made sure I had the necessary equipment. The next coach did the same thing and then passed my name on to a Juniors coach and they helped me to keep playing."

"And you ended up getting drafted?"

He smiles at me. It's boyish and sincere. "Oh, if only it was that simple. I entered the draft but wasn't selected. I barely finished high school so playing in college wasn't an option so I sweet talked an assistant coach on the Quebec Royales into letting me attend their development camp for undrafted players. I worked my ass off like my life depended on it because it honestly did and they signed me."

"That's an amazing story." I'm in awe. "You need to tell the kids about that. It shows that you can accomplish everything you want to, despite a rocky start."

His expression dims again. "Like I said, I don't talk about it. My teammates don't even know about my childhood."

I drop my knees and lean forward. His right knee is bent, lying up across the couch cushion and so I extend my own legs so my foot brushes his knee. He looks down at it, reaches out and lays a hand over my ankle. One of his fingers brushes against the small patch of bare skin between my sock and my leggings and it sends a gratifying shiver up my body. "Don't be ashamed. You should be proud. You've overcome so much."

He won't look at me. His eyes focused on his hand and my leg. "I'm not ashamed. I just don't like talking about it. I've overcome my past, like you said, so why would I want to re-live it by talking about it?"

"But you relive it anyway, don't you?" I can't help but ask and he stops moving his thumb softly across my ankle. "The way you react to small spaces has to do with your childhood doesn't it?"

He pulls his hand back and leans away from me. I want to kick myself. I feel like I've gone way too far and he might leave but he does something else, just as bad. He puts on one of his cocky, flirty grins, which I now know for sure are an act. He's hiding himself from me again. "Take off your shrink hat. We're two friends talking, remember? I'm not your patient."

"I'm a psychologist, not a psychiatrist," I clarify and smile. "And I think we're kind of past the friends stage, aren't we?"

As soon as the words leave my mouth I realize how wrong I am. The smile on his face disappears and the storm always swirling behind his eyes turns into a category five. I pull my leg back instinctively, but he reaches out and stops me. His hand wraps around my ankle and he grabs my other one too and he yanks me closer. Now I'm almost sitting in his lap. Letting go of my left ankle he cradles my head and leans in. The kiss is long and hard, his lips rough and his tongue forceful as it dominates mine. I feel that crazy, inexplicable instantaneous fire again and find myself crawling into his lap as his hand delves deeper into my hair. I wrap my arms around his neck pulling myself closer to him. His hands side down my back and cup my ass, pushing me higher, off his thighs and onto his lap, and I feel him rub, rock hard, against my center.

Against every animal instinct I have, which seem to be my only instincts right now, I break the kiss and struggle to find my sanity. "We shouldn't do this without finishing our conversation."

His eyes remain closed and he sighs softly. "I know. But I had to kiss you again and I know when we finish this conversation, you won't want to let me do that again."

The butterflies that have been fluttering inside of me suddenly turn to stone and drop like a cold mass of dread into the pit of my stomach. I move off him and back to the other side of the couch. He runs two hands through his hair again this time pausing to pull on it gently out of frustration. "I'd be lying if I said I didn't like you," he says but somehow looks stricken, like the admission is horrifying or painful or something. "And I mean, obviously I'm attracted to you."

His eyes drop down to the bulge in the front of his jeans and mine can't seem to help but follow. Yeah, he's definitely hard. It makes me flush but his next words are like being doused in cold water. "But I can't be anything but your friend."

"Why not?" It's a simple, honest, yet painfully needy question. And I can't help but ask it.

"Because I'm different," he replies gruffly and stands up creating an even bigger void between us, which I hate. "I don't just mean because you grew up differently than me. I guess that's the root of it, because it made me who I am, but it's not that I think we can't make something work because you grew up with everything and I grew up with nothing. It's not that. It's just I can't be someone's boyfriend. I'm not capable of that."

My mouth falls open and I find my heart wanting to scream the words "I don't care" but the fact is, I do care. My heart wants him—as is, with all the broken pieces, and even if some pieces are missing. But my brain knows who I am and what I need from a relationship and it's more than just sex. "I can't be someone's bed buddy. I'm not capable of that."

His face falls, like he was hoping beyond hope for another response. "I know. So I kissed you because it's going to be the last time. Because we want different things."

I'm not buying it. I stand up too and cross my arms. "You want to be single forever?"

He shrugs.

I glare. "That's not an answer, Alexandre." I say his name with a rolling French R and it gets under his skin, I can see it.

He shoves his hands in his pockets defiantly. "I'd rather be single than be rejected because I can't be what someone needs."

"How do you know what I need?" I ask. "I'll be honest, I don't even think I know what I need. I just know that everyone who seemed right so far, didn't feel right. And this thing with you is different...and overwhelming and confusing and even a little terrifying. But that feels right."

He wants to consider the possibility that I'm right but he doesn't. Instead he steps over to the window and glances out at the street below, face set in the mask of cocky smile again. "You're beautiful and sexy and we could have a lot of fun together. But that's all it would be. I'd love to have fun with you. Friends with benefits is my thing. It's my only thing. I'm trying to be a good guy here and be honest up front. I've never lied to a girl about it before and I certainly don't want to lie to you. I do think you're special, Brie, but I can't be your boyfriend."

"I guess we've found something you're more afraid of than closets." It's mean and I instantly hate myself for it. I should know better. His claustrophobia is real and I just shamed him for it. I step closer. "Alex, I'm sorry."

"Don't be," he replies in a hard clipped tone but he still sports that stupid, easy smile. "I should get going."

I follow him as he makes his way to the front hall and slips on his shoes. I'm still feeling like a massive pile of shit for what I said. I lean on the archway that separates the living room and hall. "Alex. I'm just...disappointed. And confused. I don't get it. I just don't."

He's not about to try and explain it to me again. He gives me an authentic smile instead of one of his fake ones. "I hope we can be friends. I still want to volunteer and hang out with Mac too and I hope that means I can see you and maybe hang out together."

"Is that going to be easy for you?" I have to ask because I know the answer for me. It's not going to be easy. I like him.

I want him. Pretending those feelings don't exist is going to suck beyond words.

He's already opening the front door but he pauses and looks over his shoulder to meet my eye. "No. It's going to be hard as hell. But that's the story of my life."

He walks out without another word.

Chapter 16

Brie

I feel like I shouldn't even be going. I haven't heard from Alex—not a word—since we ended whatever it was we were trying to start. He's purposely showed up at Daphne's when he knows I'm not there. Not just last Saturday but again on Wednesday when I was at court with Laura and Mackenzie, which he knew because I texted him to tell him she had another hearing. He responded with nothing but a "Thanks" and a crossed-fingers emoji. When he texted me hours later to see how it went and I told him, he responded with a smiley face and a thumbs-up. I forced myself not to respond with the middle finger emoji. I hate that he's just walked away from me. And I hate that not wanting him to walk away makes me feel like a lovelorn fool.

Still, when Rose Caplan and her sisters sent me an Evite to his housewarming I accepted. I would have invited Len for moral support, but she offered to stay at my place and unofficially babysit Mac, who pitched a fit when I used the actual term "babysit."

Yeah, she's almost fifteen but I still feel like someone should be with her. She thinks it's because I don't trust her. I do, but I'm new to this guardian thing and I'm terrified something will happen if she's alone at night, like a murderer will try and break in or the gas will leak and explode or something. What if she goes to sleep before I get back and gets woken up by a sound and thinks someone is trying to break in and terrifies herself? I did that the first night my parents left me alone to go out to dinner when I was thirteen. They came home and I was hiding behind the couch, holding a croquet mallet and sobbing. I don't want Mac to have to freak out like that. Is this the level of worry my parents went through when I was a kid? God bless them.

Anyway, I really should have lied and said I was busy, but Rose mentioned that her sisters were really hoping to talk to me more about Daphne's House and there was no way I was going to miss the opportunity to get any kind of help for the place. If they were interested in donating or volunteering it would be stupid to miss out on that because of a guy.

I turn onto his street in Tribeca and start looking for his address. It's a loft building. There are many in this area and none of them is cheap. I'm not shocked he wanted a loft, with his aversion to small spaces. I'm greeted by a smiling doorman and tell him I'm here to see Alex Larue. He grins. "The housewarming. Head right up."

Everything about the building is big and airy from the lobby to the hallways and I see, as he opens the door, his loft. He gives me a tight smile and motions for me to enter.

Everyone is already there and the people I've previously met call out greetings. I wave and smile and walk slowly into the expansive, sparsely decorated space. He's got twelve-foot ceilings and enormous windows on two sides. His bedroom is a large nook. You can see a track where there used to be sliding doors but he's removed them. The bed is positioned to face out into the living room, toward the giant windows, none of which have curtains. I'm sure someone tonight will make a joke that he's an exhibitionist, if they haven't already. I'm also sure he's used to it. I have a feeling he's never lived in a space with many walls or curtains.

"Thanks for coming," Alex says but his tone is gruff and cool.

"Yeah, you sound super excited to see me," I scoff back and move quickly toward the kitchen to Rose and her sisters. Their greeting is much warmer and much more believable. Each of them hugs me and thank me for coming.

"Please excuse your host," Callie adds with a smirk. "The guy who will talk to anyone in a skirt is suddenly as perky as Oscar the Grouch."

Alex rolls his eyes and walks over into the living room area where a bunch of guys are drinking beers and talking. I recognize Devin, Jordan and Luc, but there are other guys here too who, judging by their hulking sizes and in some cases scars and bruises, are also Barons players.

I spend the first forty minutes at the party talking to Rose, Callie and Jessie. They're genuinely interested in the charity and they tell me tales from their own childhood. There's no love lost for their grandmother and they don't hide it, but Callie tries to find a bright spot. "In the end, Lilly did us a solid when she kicked the bucket because that's the only reason we went back to our hometown. If we hadn't, Jordan wouldn't have found Jessie again and I might not have found Devin, and Rosie would still be wishing she could make Luc notice her."

Rose gives Callie a shove. It's light but it makes her clutch her stomach and turn green. I worry she's about to puke, but she seems to gain control of the situation. Jessie narrows her green eyes suspiciously. "You've had the flu for a while now."

"Uh-huh." Callie grabs the glass in front of her that is filled with what looks like sparkling water.

Rose watches both her sisters carefully for a second and then the oven bings behind us and she jumps off her bar stool. The delicious smell of caramelized onion and melted cheese fills the air as she opens the oven door. Except Callie turns green again and jumps off her own stool. "I'm going to go ask Devin something."

She's darting across the living room before either of her sisters look up. Jessie looks suspicious again. She grabs her glass, which also appears to be filled with water, and follows her sister. I watch Rose take a tray of bite-sized appetizers out of the oven. She looks around for her sisters. "This is Callie's favorite. Goat cheese and caramelized onion in puff pastry. Where did she go?"

I point to the living room. Rose's dark eyes dart from Callie to Jessie. "And why is Jessie wearing a baggy sweatshirt to a party? Sure, she's glamming it up with a scarf but I didn't even know she owned a sweatshirt."

I smile and Rose starts to smile too. "Oh my God...I think they're both..."

"Pregnant?" I conclude for her and she immediately starts to tear up.

"Oh my God, you think so too? Oh my God!" I step closer to her and put a hand on her shoulder to calm her down.

"It's just a guess. Don't freak out until you know," I advise her cautiously but I have a feeling nothing about these girls is cautious.

Rose walks around the island, puts her hands on her hips, one of which is still covered in an oven mitt and asks in a loud voice that seems very un-Rose-like, "Are you two pregnant?"

The room is suddenly and completely silent. Jessie and Callie both look up at their sister. And then turn to each other. I feel like I'm watching a reality show on TV, but judging by the way these girls act no one is surprised by this and honestly, their honesty and bluntness are refreshing.

"You girls are horrible liars and ridiculously bad at keeping secrets so I'm going to tell the truth for you," Alex says firmly.

"Alex..." Jordan and Devin both say in a warning tone and then they're looking at each other, baffled.

"They're both pregnant," Alex announces firmly.

Rose starts screaming. Callie and Jessie start screaming and pointing at each other. Alex walks over to watch the show next to me. He leans down and with a half smirk on his lips whispers, "And not by me. I thought I should make that clear since people think I like to mess around with my friends' girlfriends and wives."

I roll my eyes.

Two hours later, everything is back to normal. The night turned out to be really fun. Everyone I met was great. Most of the guests have left and Callie has offered to teach the kids the tips and tricks she learned when she started cooking for her sisters as a kid, and Jessie has offered to give a talk on what her childhood was like. And all three of them have offered donations.

Now the only people left are Jessie and Jordan, me and Alex. Jordan helps me pick up empty glasses and carry them to the kitchen area while Alex loads his dishwasher.

"So where'd you get the name for the place?" Jordan asks casually. "Who is Daphne?"

"She was my birth mother," I tell him and Alex stops loading the dishwasher. "She died when I was almost two."

I can feel Alex's eyes on me, but I don't look over. Jordan looks the way people always look when I tell them—stunned and sad. "I'm so sorry."

"Thank you," I smile softly and out of the corner of my eye I see Jessie yawn where she's stretched out on the couch. "I think you need to get her home. Congratulations, by the way."

Jordan looks back at Jessie and his face softens into pure love. It's the kind of look you see in movies or read about in romance books and dream someone will give you one day. It's nice to know it actually exists.

"Thanks. I'm thrilled," Jordan replies. "And I think having Callie going through it too will be great for Jessie. And hysterical for me. So there's that."

He chuckles and walks over to the couch. "Let's go home, babe."

Jessie stands up and smiles at me. "It was great seeing you again, Brie. And I can't wait to come by Daphne's."

I give them a little wave as they head for the door and glance around for my purse so I can get the hell out of here too. Being alone with Alex doesn't seem like the best idea, even though he did seem to relax as the night went on.

I see my purse hanging on the back of one of the chairs by the island so I walk over and grab it. Before I can tell him I'm leaving he curses in French. "How do you work this thing?"

He doesn't know how to work the dishwasher? I walk over and watch him stare helplessly at the inside as he holds a small detergent pod in his big hand. "Where the hell does this thing go?"

"You've never used your dishwasher?" I ask.

"I've always had one but never used it. I usually eat out, and I hand wash the one or two plates I use." He looks up at me with helpless, almost puppy dog, eyes.

"*Mon Dieu.*" I say with a smile and my use of French makes him smile too. I walk over and take the pod from him. I pop it into the little holder on the inside of the door and close it then punch the appropriate buttons on the front. It makes a soft gushing sound as it begins its cycle.

"*Merci,*" he replies softly.

"Anything else you need help with?" I ask and I can't help but flash him a cheeky smile. "Like how to use a washing machine or set your alarm clock?"

"You're hilarious," he snarks back. "Making fun of a man in need."

I roll my eyes. "You're a big boy, you can handle it."

He's standing so close I can smell the woodsy scent that engulfed me seconds before he kissed me the other night. My skin starts to tingle. I try to take a deep breath, but it's hard suddenly. He's smiling but it's dark, in the most delicious way. "You have a nice place."

"Thanks."

"Very open."

"Yeah. I like open spaces," he says. "You know why."

I adjust my purse on my shoulder and suddenly remember. "I brought you a housewarming gift."

"What?" He looks startled and not in a good way. He takes a step back and blinks. "I told the girls to make sure no one brought gifts."

"I know. I wasn't going to, but there's this little store near the courthouse." I feel suddenly stupid again. Why does he always make me feel like this? "I bought it on a whim. It cost nothing and if you really don't want it, I'll keep it for myself."

I pull out the bag and shove it into his chest. He doesn't take it so I just hold it there. My knuckles are between the gift and his chest and it's like pressing them into a rock. He's pure, solid muscle. I think of how he looked in that tight shirt after the game and I flush. "Just take it. It's not a big deal."

He makes a noise almost like a groan and finally takes the bag. It's a simple paper bag. The gift is unwrapped inside because I wasn't lying when I said it really wasn't a big deal. He looks inside. The scowl on his face softens and softens until it's nothing but amazement. He pulls out the tiny metal, handmade fleur-de-lis with little LED lights hammered into it.

"It's not a nightlight, but it's not like a real light. It's kind of useless really but it's a fleur-de-lis," I explain even though it's obvious. "and I rarely see those around New York and it reminded me of you. If you don't want it, I'll keep it."

"I'm keeping it," he replies quickly and turns it over and pushes the little switch on the back. The tiny lights come on. "It's perfect. I use ambient light all the time. I don't sleep in the dark."

He points and I follow his hand and notice a tiny light in a socket in the corner of the living room. I force my face to remain neutral but holy shit, is this big, hulking, man afraid of the dark? Once again he's making my heart ache. He turns it over and stares at the lights twinkling off the metal.

"People don't buy me things," he mumbles softly.

I look around at the sparsely furnished apartment. There's a sectional, an ottoman, but no chairs, bookcases or pictures. The nook for his bedroom only contains one three-drawer dresser. His bedside lamp is on the floor beside the bed because it doesn't have night tables. "You don't seem to like things."

He shrugs and those deep blue eyes find mine. "I don't have a lot of things from my past worth holding on to."

Oh this man...I reach up and gently cup the side of his face. He reaches up and grasps my hand and I think he's going to pull it away but he doesn't. He holds it to his face and pushes into it. He's like a puppy looking for love and I want desperately to give it to him. But he won't let me. "And you seem to want to throw away things now that are worth holding on to."

I force myself to step back and start walking toward the front door because if I don't leave now I'll let things happen that are going to mean more to me than they should. Than he wants them to. But he speaks and his words stop me in my tracks.

"I don't know how to be a boyfriend, Brie." The look of pure confusion on his face would be comical if we were still talking about dishwashers. But we're talking about feelings here. "The only thing I've ever committed to was hockey and even it tried to reject me. Hell, in a way every time I get traded I feel like it still is. But it's a thing, not a person, and I can force hockey to stay in my life simply by working harder and finding my niche. Right now I'm a third line center. Then I'll be a fourth line. Then I'll find a coaching job somewhere. Hockey is staying in my life whether it likes it or not. It doesn't have a choice, but you do."

I start to walk back into the kitchen as he turns away from me to look out the window. "People who have had the choice to keep me in their lives never have."

Thank God he's turned away because I actually press my palm to my heart at that statement to keep it from cracking. Holy shit. I have no idea how anyone would walk away from him—the man and his big, broken heart—because what I want to do is run to him. "Give me that choice and I'll change that track record."

He grunts at that and turns back to face me. His smile is weary, his eyes filled with disbelief. "You're this amazing, stubborn, gorgeous woman who wants more than the one thing I know I can give. And as much as I suddenly, for the first time in my life, want to try and give more, I'm also so fucking clueless as to how."

I walk right up to him so we're toe to toe. "You want to know how? You just do it. You let me in. You take the chance, like you do every time you step onto the ice. You don't know if you'll win or lose, but you play the game anyway and you take the shots on net even if you don't know if you're going to score. So tell me you want this. Take the shot."

He nuzzles my hand and but then turns his face and kisses my palm. When he turns back to me he looks so serious it's startling. "I want this."

I feel my smile from my toes to the roots of my hair. "Game on?"

He smiles back, raw but darkly playful. "Game on."

I step into him and up onto my toes and then I use my hand to guide his face down to mine. When our lips connect again it's as perfect and sensuous as it was last time. Except this time, he has no hesitation. He quickly takes control and uses his lips to open my mouth and slip his tongue inside.

He holds my head, hands tangling in my hair and pushes me until I'm pressed against the island. All I feel is his hard, warm body pressed into me, the urgent push of his tongue against mine and the gentle but forceful tug of his hands in my hair.

But I also feel the hesitation start to seep back in. His tongue pulls away, his lips start to leave mine and his fingers start to slip out of my hair. I circle his neck with my arms and hold him in place. "Don't you dare fucking stop."

"I'm not just going to kiss you."

"Good."

The next several minutes we're like horny teenagers in a dark corner of the prom—making out, groping, grinding. He grabs my hips and lifts me like I'm made of paper, dropping my ass on his island. He pushes my knees apart as his perfect and skilled mouth finds its way to my neck. Holy shit, the roughness of his stubble and the softness of his mouth together, at once, are sending direct pulses of pleasure to my clit.

I tip my head to give him better access. My God, I had no idea someone's lips on my neck could feel like this. I feel his teeth gently tug my earlobe. I reach for the bottom of his shirt and start undoing the buttons as fast as my fingers can. I'm quaking with anticipation. I want to feel his skin against mine. With every button I undo, I pause and touch the skin exposed. His stomach is warm and hard and my fingertips graze over his treasure trail. It makes him suck harder on the skin just above my collarbone, which then makes me arch my back.

He moves his hands around my lower back and under the hem of my sweater. I feel his palms splay out across my back, warm and strong. He yanks me closer, to the edge of the counter and I panic he might be pulling me off the counter and to my feet—and be ending this. So I wrap my legs around his waist, keeping both of us in place. I manage to get the last button on his shirt undone and slip my hands inside it, wrapping them around his back

We're hugging now—tightly—and it feels overwhelmingly right. I'm flooded with warm contentment, security and affection. But also lust. The feel of his skin, pressed against me, even through my sweater is intoxicating. I need more of it. I pull away only enough to be able to take off my sweater. I drop it to the floor next to the island and cup the back of his head and claim his mouth again.

His hands slide down my back, stopping to unhook my bra, and then continue lower to cup the top of my ass and hold me on the edge of the counter. His hips shift forward, pressing into me, and I can feel he's thick and long and so incredibly hard. "You want me."

I didn't mean to say it and I definitely didn't want it to sound so damn surprised. He pulls back and covers the side of my jaw with his palm and says in more of a growl than a whisper, "I want you."

"I want you too." I move my shoulder, my bra straps slipping down my arms. His gaze slips with them, from my face down to my bare breasts. The weight of his stare makes my skin prickle and my nipples raise. He cups them, running his thumbs over them before he kisses and sucks each. My hands curl in his hair and my head falls back.

He's worshipping me, there's no other word for it, and I get why this man has women swooning. He is pure desire, lust and sex. Everything he does makes me feel sensual and sexy and fills me with hunger.

I slip my hands over his shoulders, pushing his shirt off him and onto the floor. He lifts his face from my breasts and covers my mouth with his. His hands move to grab my ass and, because my legs are still hooked behind his back, he easily lifts me off the counter and starts walking us back to his bed. I wrap my arms tightly around his neck so our torsos are pressed into each other and I can feel all his delicious skin. I can't get enough contact. I want to touch him every second, everywhere. So I tell him.

"I want to touch you too," he confesses. "Everywhere."

The idea of him everywhere...oh God. I swear I'm on the edge of an orgasm just thinking about it. As soon as we enter the bedroom nook, he reaches out with one hand, still holding me up with the other, and hits a panel on the wall. All the lights in the apartment turn off but his night-lights kick in. Between those and the lights twinkling in from the cityscape beyond the curtain less windows it's still easy to see everything. I'm grateful because I don't want to miss anything.

He climbs onto his bed and lays me down in the middle of it. He slowly, forcefully grinds his cock between my legs as he comes down on top of me. It's powerful and instinctive. I have never felt so visceral about a sexual connection before. I've had good sex, loving sex, hot sex, but this... this is a whole new level.

He's kissing his way down my body and by the time he reaches my belly button, his fingers have managed to do undo my jeans and are pulling them down—along with my underwear.

His mouth follows his hands, nipping my hip, kissing the inside of my thigh, the side of my knee. He tugs everything fully off, removes my socks and drops them at the foot of the bed. And then, kneeling between my ankles, he starts to undo his own jeans. He's not wearing underwear and his cock is on full display before his pants make it halfway down his thighs. It's long and thick, and suddenly all his swagger is justified. The man is well endowed, to say the least. He stands up at the foot of the bed to kick off his jeans and his left hand wraps around his cock. I'm sure his eyes are roaming my naked body but I don't look up to find out. I'm glued to the way he grips himself, slowly stroking, almost absently.

Before he realizes what I'm doing—hell, before I fully comprehend what I'm doing—I'm on my knees in front of him, my hand curled around his and my lips at the tip of his cock. I lick away the droplet of desire there, then slide down his length. I feel his whole body tighten instantly and his legs quake.

"Brie...baby."

I slip my mouth back and forth a few times, swirling my tongue around him as I go, but that's all I get—a few quick moments—and then he's stepping away from me.

"Was it not...?"

"It was too good," he tells me. "I won't let this end before it begins, *ma belle*. I can't."

He turns away from me, toward the dresser and that's when I see the tattoo for the first time. It starts at the base of his spine and climbs all the way up stopping just below his neck. A tree. It's got gnarled roots, curled, crooked branches and it's barren—leafless—except for the very tip of the top branch on the left, just over his shoulder blade. There's one, small leaf dangling off the end of the branch.

It's beautiful, in its design and detail but it's also sad. Haunted. He turns from the dresser leaving the drawer open and holds up the condom, tearing it with his teeth as he walks toward me. And then we're kneeling, inches from each other, face-to-face on the bed. As he slips his hands between us, he leans forward and kisses me. It's hard and yet needy. He must have the condom on because now his one hand is on my hip and his other is between my legs. A finger slides slowly across my opening.

"So warm and soft," he whispers against my lips. He pushes two fingers inside me curling them toward himself and I instantly gasp. "You're going to feel incredible."

"You already do," I pant as he pulls his fingers out a little and pushes back in curling them again at the right moment, the right way, so I see stars.

"Lay back," he demands pushing into me so gravity helps me obey his command. I'm flat on my back now and he's still kneeling between my legs, his fingers still working magic. When he pulls them out I whimper. I watch wide eyed as he brings his fingers to his mouth and tastes me. He closes his eyes and makes a sound of pure satisfaction that sends heat crawling up my face. No man has done that with me before and it's so fucking erotic it makes me hotter.

He lies on top of me, one hand beside my head the other somewhere lower. Then I feel him slipping over my opening. I open my legs farther and reach up and grip his shoulders.

He's inside me in one long slow push. I feel deliciously full, like every nerve ending is suddenly short-circuiting. I twist my hips and arch my back, my hands stretching out above me. He drops his full weight onto me and immediately begins moving his hips. His pace is unexpected—slow, rough and deep. He grabs one of my legs under the knee and pulls it up, twisting his hips a different way and that spot he was hitting with his fingers he's now hitting with his cock, and I moan out his name.

He likes that and lets out a growl before he bites my shoulder. Every thrust his cock is creating shoots stars of heat through my entire body and then finally, I'm falling too, just like a star, cascading into orgasmic oblivion. I am not a loud partner. I've honestly never let out more than a coo. But tonight—here with this man—I am moaning and panting and begging him for more even though I can no longer feel my body.

He pulls himself up on his knees, yanking my ass into his lap and holding me still by my hips as he pushes harder, faster, deeper and then a groan rumbles out of him as he comes. His fingers grip my hips so tight I'll probably have marks, and I like that idea. That his fingers will leave their imprint on my body the way his soul seems to be leaving an imprint on my heart.

Chapter 17

Alex

What the fuck just happened? My head is spinning like I just got off a Tilt-A-Whirl. Is this real life? I'm in a relationship. Me. Someone wants me and I want her and this is happening. My heartbeat hammers and my limbs tingle from my orgasm. Brie looks euphoric and beautiful. I feel like I'm dreaming because this can't be real.

This wasn't my storyline. I'm the guest star in life, not the romantic lead. I've never had sex with someone like her—someone who doesn't put on a show. There were no fake noises or overblown words of encouragement. More than that, I've never had sex with someone who knows me like she does. I've told her things I've told no one. I was real. The sex was real. And it was amazing.

I reach over and brush back a lock of her long, silky hair. "That was incredible," she says softly.

"You're amazing," I reply. She gives me the warmest, sweetest smile. I lean over and kiss her, long and deep. And then I sit up, swing my legs over the side of the bed and pull off the condom. As I tie it and lean forward to toss in the wastebasket, I feel her fingertips on my back. She's tracing the lines of my tattoo and I try not to tense. I hate when people touch it.

"There're bumps..."

That's why I tense. I hate talking about it. So I never do. I lie. I am dreading lying to her so I don't answer. I just close my eyes and enjoy the feel of her fingers fluttering over my back. I feel her thumb glide over another scar.

The bed dips behind me and I know she's moving closer to examine it. I force myself not to sigh. God, I hate this. "Are they scars?"

"Uh-huh," I grunt more than speak. "Hockey scars."

I lie to her like I lie to everyone. But this time it bothers me. Still I'm overwhelmed with everything that's already happened tonight. I can't add this truth to the pile I've already unloaded. Even if she thinks she can handle it, I know I can't.

"Really?"

I turn and lie down beside her again. Closing my eyes, I take her hand and run her fingers along my cheek by my eye, where I have an actual hockey scar and down to my chin where I have another one. "I'm full of scars."

"Scars are badges of honor," she says softly. I've let go of her hand, her fingertips still drift over my scars, and it's soothing. "It's proof something or someone tried to break you and failed."

My eyes flutter open and find hers. She's looking at me with compassion and something else. Something I'm not ready to see. Like I said, I've faced too many truths tonight as it is. So I give her one of my best snarky smiles. "Where did you hear that? Fortune cookie or yoga class?"

She blinks and for second I think she might be offended, but then she grins. "Pinterest."

I laugh. She laughs with me, dropping her head onto my chest. This is good—being here with her. It feels right in ways I can't remember ever feeling with a woman before. But I still can't let her spend the night. I still don't want to risk subjecting her to what could happen if I have another nightmare. As our laughter dies, I start to worry about how I can get her to leave without offending her. I really don't want her to be upset. I don't want her to think I'm treating her like a booty call because we've already promised each other it isn't.

Luckily after a few minutes of me running my hands through her long, soft hair and her drawing circles on my chest she lifts her head and looks at the clock beside my bed and her face clouds over a little. "I should get home."

"Okay," I say quietly, trying not to sound relieved.

Our eyes meet and she looks curious. "You're used to women running out after you give them incredible orgasms?"

I grin at the word incredible. "I usually have such a busy schedule that I don't tend to have sleepovers."

"That's a polite way of saying you kick them to the curb."

"You're not any woman. You're my girlfriend. I am not going to kick you to the curb." *But please leave because I'm not ready to tell you about the nightmares.*

She smiles so beautifully it makes it hard to breathe. And then she kisses me, making breathing impossible. "I'm your girlfriend," she repeats and then her expression sobers. "And I have to leave because Len is at my place with Mac, and I promised I wouldn't be late."

"Is it still going well?" I ask.

"It is except she hates school and she skipped yesterday. She says she started to feel sick on her way there, so she came home. But she didn't tell me and when the school called, I freaked out thinking she'd run away." Her brows pinch and she frowns at the memory. "I rushed home and found her eating a bag of chips and channel surfing and we had a huge fight. She hates school and says she has no friends and she's too far behind and wants to drop out."

"She's too young to drop out," I state the obvious. "And the judge isn't going to let her live at Daphne's if she's not in school."

"I told her all that, so she agreed to a tutor," Brie confirms as she gets out of bed and starts to get dressed. I have an overwhelming urge to stop her and pull her back into bed and have sex with her again, but I know I can't. "A bunch of teachers come to Daphne's twice a week to do group tutoring sessions. Rose is actually joining this week and so Mackenzie will go to that. Even though she's already complaining about it."

I groan. "She's her own worst enemy."

"We all were at her age. She's just being a kid." Brie pulls on the last of her clothing, then smooths her hair.

"You're going above and beyond for her."

"She's special to someone who is special to me."

Her words make me feel warm and my chest feel tight—in a good way. It's the most surreal feeling ever.

"And honestly, she's a special kid. I really like her. She reminds me of me when I was her age. There are rough edges, sure, but there's a diamond in there waiting to shine."

I want to laugh at that. "Pinterest again?"

She grins. "Motivational poster at my dentist's office."

I get out of bed and follow her into the main living area. She's walking a little in front of me, so I put my hands on her waist and nuzzle the side of her neck.

"I'm sorry I acted like you were a one-percent, puddle-deep rich girl," I whisper against her skin. "You're clearly more than that."

"I'm a hell of a lot more than that," she replies. She grabs her purse off the floor where she dropped it and her coat off the back of one of the bar stools and walks slowly to the door. I follow beside her and she glances down. "You know you're still buck naked in a Manhattan apartment with no curtains. And you're half hard."

"I've got nothing to hide," I say with a shrug and glance down. "And that's not half. It'd be bigger if it was half. You should know that now."

I grab her hand and spin her around right next to the door, pressing her against the wall I kiss her again. I can't get enough of her, the softness of her lips, the warmth of her mouth, the eagerness of her tongue. It's more intoxicating than alcohol.

But she breaks the kiss before it can develop into anything more. I know it's for the best but I still frown and try to pull her mouth back to mine. She laughs softly and slips away, grabbing the door handle, ready to make her escape.

She pauses and looks up at me. "I'm sorry I acted like you

were a cocky playboy, incapable of serious feelings," she tells me quietly with the hint of a smile. As the knob turns in her hand, she adds, "Because you're more than that, and you might not truly believe that yet, but I do."

With one more soft, quick kiss, she's gone.

Chapter 18

Brie

Four days later I wake up and the first thing I do is check my phone. Alex is on a road trip playing Vegas and Seattle so I knew I'd be asleep by the time he got back to the hotel and we wouldn't be able to talk like we did the last two nights. But there's no text. No missed call. No email.

I have to put aside my disappointment and pull on my big-girl pants here. I know this. He's not ignoring me. He's not used to being in a relationship and I'm not used to being in one that's long distance every few days. Maybe I'm expecting too much. He's home today and I'll get to see him again and that's what counts.

I sigh and get out of bed, wandering into the kitchen to make myself a cup of coffee and some toast before work. Mac grumbles something and sits down beside me with a bowl of Cheerios and begins to cut a banana into it. Her eyes seem barely open, but she doesn't sever a finger and manages to pour the milk in the bowl anyway.

I keep quiet and stalk Alex on Instagram. He's posted two photos since he's been on his road trip and neither are the usual hotel bathroom towel selfie. The last time he posted a selfie with a hot girl hanging off him was before he moved to Brooklyn, before I met him. His two shots from this trip are caption-less artsy photos he's taken. One, a cityscape shot of Seattle at night and the other a black-and-white of a cactus in Vegas. The comments under them are mostly complaints he isn't posting half-naked selfies anymore, and proclamations of love and offers for a good time. He never responds. This morning there's a new post. It's in black-and-white and it's of the light I gave him. There's a caption: *My new favorite thing.*

I smile so big my face hurts and Mac gives me a weird look, like she thinks I'm insane, but I ignore her as my worries disappear and my heart catapults itself back into my chest.

Four hours later I'm sitting behind my desk going through paperwork and still feeling awesome when there's a knock on my door. I wasn't expecting him to come straight here from the airport, so seeing Alex standing there in a suit and tailored wool coat is pretty overwhelmingly awesome. The grin on my face must make me look insane it's so big, but I can't contain it. A slow smile starts to spread across his face until it's almost as big as mine, and as he walks into the room, he pulls the door closed behind him.

I stand up and walk around my desk.

"Hey," he says simply, his French accent thicker than normal.

We're standing so close I have to tilt my head back to look at his face. "Hey."

"I have a work thing I have to go do, but I wanted to swing by and see how Mac's doing," he says.

Oh.

"She's at school. She skipped again yesterday, so I grounded her," I explain and take a step back. "She was pissed but didn't run away. At least not yet..."

"I think her birthday is coming up," he says, shoving his hands into the pockets of his jacket. I take another step back. "She mentioned something about it being this month when I met her."

"Yeah. It's Sunday," I reply. "I asked her if she wanted a party and she said no, but that it would be cool if you and maybe Len came over. Are you in?"

"Of course," he says. "Great. I'll get her something too."

"Is there something else?"

Please let there be something else.

He clears his throat. "I missed you. Like crazy."

"I missed you too." I bite my bottom lip, feeling light and coy and kind of giddy.

He reaches up and gently holds my chin using his thumb to pull my lip from my mouth. "Do you want me to talk to Mac? Like back you up or something?"

"Right now all I want is for you to kiss me." My voice is barely a whisper because he's dipping his head and our lips are closer and closer, and then he kisses me. It's as passionate and carnal as I remember.

There's a knock at the door and we leap apart. I run my fingers gently over my lips and call out. "Come in!"

Rose Caplan opens the door and steps inside. She smiling warmly but does a stutter step when she sees Alex on the other side of the room, rubbing the back of his neck and staring at his feet. I can feel the heat in my own cheeks so I know they're pink...maybe even red. We not only look guilty, there's an air of guilt in the room.

"Hi. Sorry," she says awkwardly. "I didn't know you were busy. I just wanted to say hey. I'm here for the tutoring session with the kids. I'm early but I thought maybe you'd want to grab a coffee."

"Yeah. Sure," I reply casually, like I didn't just have my tongue in her friend's mouth.

Alex strides to the door, freezes, and comes back to me, cupping my face and kissing me hard on the mouth. "Bye. I'll call you later."

He walks back to my office door, right by Rose, who is grinning like a love-drunk fool. "Bye, Rose," he mutters, not making eye contact.

"Toodles!" Rose sings.

As soon as he's out the door, I reach for my purse. When I turn around, Rose is still standing there grinning at me. I blush. Again. She laughs and hooks her arm through mine as we start down the hall. "I'm going to buy you coffee and you're going to pretend it's truth serum and tell me *everything*."

"There's not much to tell." I shrug and try not to grin. "My boyfriend just stopped by to say hi."

She rolls her big brown eyes. "Honey, don't even try to downplay this. I want all the details and I'm going to squee like a total fangirl."

"Wow," I huff and I can't help but smile in awe. "You're intense, Cupid."

She pats my arm as we step out into the chilly fall afternoon. "I know they're the picture of wedded bliss now, but both Jessie and Callie were their own worst enemy when it came to true love. So yeah, when love happens easily, I'm going to bask in it like a warm summer day."

I find that hard to believe. Both her sisters are madly in love—and are loved madly—it's obvious. But Rose isn't a liar, so there must be one hell of a past I'm unaware of. We reach the corner and wait for the light so we can cross to the Dunkin' Donuts across the street. "I don't know Alex really well, but I know him well enough to know he likes to pretend he's undatable. Obviously you busted through that bullshit."

"I think he still believes that, but he's willing to try with me anyway."

She waves her free hand in the air, waving away my concern. "Pish. Nobody is undatable. Love is something every person on this planet wants...whether they know it or not."

"You are quite the lover of love," I remark.

"Yup!" she says with a shameless grin. "So details please! When did it start?"

I laugh. "I guess technically the night of the housewarming."

"I knew it! I thought I saw you guys checking each other out."

We order our coffees, and as we wait for our orders she leans close to me and asks, "So how'd you handle your first road trip as a girlfriend?"

"I missed him."

"Not going to lie, it can get hard. Especially on the long

ones or when they're in playoffs," Rose confesses and sighs before leaning closer again and flashing me a devilish grin. "Skype sex helps."

I laugh. "I'll keep that in mind."

They call our orders and we grab them from the counter.

"Does Luc get banged up a lot?" I can't help but ask as we make our way out of the coffee shop. "Alex seems to have a lot of scars."

Rose's smile slips a little. "Yeah, the injuries can be brutal, and Luc isn't exactly a passive player. He likes to get into it. He kind of has to because he's a defenseman. He's had pucks to the face, fists to the face, a stick to the face. Luckily nothing has left too big a mark."

"What would cause scars on the back? A skate or something?" I didn't mean to say it aloud. I just couldn't help it. Rose looks at me, puzzled. "Alex has little scars on his back. He's covered them with a tattoo but you can feel them."

Rose's grin is back and she wiggles her dark eyebrows almost frantically. "You've felt his back? Shirtless back?"

I know I have to be the shade of a fire engine right now. Ugh. I cover my face with my hands. Rose takes pity on me and hugs me quickly as the light changes and we start to cross the street. "Okay, okay, I won't press for details...right now. But I don't know anything in hockey that would give him a bunch of scars on his back. They wear pads and jerseys and maybe once, if he was really unlucky a skate might pierce all that but I doubt that would happen more than once. How many does he have?"

"Umm...like seven or eight." I feel kind of guilty bringing this up with her because I doubt Alex wants me to talk about him, or this, with anyone. Especially if he lied to me about the origin of the scars, which it's definitely beginning to seem like he did. "Forget I said anything. It's not my place to talk about this, you know."

Rose nods and brushes back her long black hair as the cold wind whips it across her face. "Jordan played on the same team as Alex for years and didn't know his background. He knew his family never came to games, but Alex never told anyone why. He recently opened up a bit to Callie and admitted his parents have died."

"I know." I sip my coffee and leave it at that.

"Jordan was shocked Alex never told him, but I think Alex picked Callie because she was the most like him before she finally admitted she loved Devin. Dear God, that girl tried so hard to keep herself from happiness it was maddening."

She proceeds to tell me a brief summary of Callie and Devin. It's a wild, heartbreaking tale. Callie, I can tell even from the brief time I've been around her, has a giant heart and is fiercely in love with her family and Devin. Her face lit up like a Christmas tree when she told me about her stepson at Alex's party. It's almost impossible to imagine she'd have tried to walk away from that.

"Callie was hell-bent on spending her life alone," Rose says as we cross the street and head back toward Daphne's House. "Look at her now. She's happier than she ever thought possible."

"I don't know them well, but it seems impossible that Callie or Jessie would ever have been like that," I confess as we reach Daphne's House and start up the steps. "It gives me hope that if they can end up in love and happy then maybe Alex can too."

"Good. It should," Rose says as I unlock and open the front door. "Happy with you."

That additional statement makes my heart skip. Rose freezes and her face lights up like she just remembered something. "I think this means you'll be coming to my wedding!"

"What?"

She's absolutely glowing. "He's invited, obviously, and you can be his plus one now! I was going to invite you anyway, but thanks to Cupid I won't need to. I love love!"

Selena walks into the hall from the classroom. She claps her hands excitedly. "Kids are all set to go, and the other teachers are here if you're ready."

"Yeah. Of course!" Rose says excitedly and hugs me before disappearing into the classroom. I peek in and am pleased to see five kids there, including Mackenzie. She glances up at me and gives me a hard smirk as if to say *Happy now?* because I'm making her attend. I smile back at her because yes, I'm happy now. In more ways than one.

Later that night, as I watch Mackenzie's favorite show, *Riverdale*, with her, my text message alert goes off.

> Rose: Hey. Know you said to forget it but mentioned the scars to Luc.
> He said Alex got them when he was a kid. Fell on glass or something.

I read the text over and over. I can't pull my eyes away. All the words circle around in my head, swirling and banging together. He fell on glass. When he was a kid. The story isn't complete by any means, but there's enough of it for me to make the connection to my own life. And the similarity has me dazed.

"It can't be . . ."

"Who cares? It's Archie. I only watch this for Jughead," Mackenzie replies, her eyes still glued to the television. She thinks I'm talking about the show. My phone buzzes again with another text.

Rose: Anyway, I won't bring it up again. I promise.
Unless you change your mind and want me to.
See you Thursday!

I text her back with a simple "okay" and then stand. Mackenzie looks up. "I need to grab something of mine from the closet in your room. Okay?"

"It's your room, your house. You don't have to ask me," she replies quietly. "Do you want me to pause the show?"

"No. Keep watching." I start toward the hall but stop. "And it's your room. Okay?"

She nods cautiously like she doesn't believe me, but I know that will only change with time, not with words, so I leave her to her show and head up to her room. It's a bit of a disaster with her clothes in random piles and the bed unmade, but I don't care. It's actually nice to have her here. Her mess is somehow comforting. I didn't have a messy room as a kid because we had a maid that came three times a week. I always wanted a messy one though. It seemed like a "normal kid" thing to have and I was always struggling to feel normal. I head to the closet and the small filing cabinet I wedged in the back corner when I moved in. I pull open the top drawer and it only takes me a minute to find the file.

My parents gave it to me when I really started hounding them with questions when I was fourteen. I always knew I was adopted and what had happened to my birth mom, but eventually I started to ask a lot of questions about the time between my birth family and my adoptive parents so they gave me my file from the social worker.

I move Mackenzie's backpack off the corner of her bed and sit down with the folder in my lap. I haven't opened this in years. I don't like revisiting it; besides, once I read it at fourteen the information was seared into my brain. I flip it open and scan to the section that Rose's texts made me think of.

I read the words over and over and over. *Removed from home when it became apparent that children were being physically abused. A child found locked in a closet in the basement. Another child had been pushed through a window.*

I must've been staring at it for a long time because Mackenzie appears in the doorway. "You okay?"

I blink and nod. "Yeah. I just...Something made me think of my childhood and I wanted to look something up."

That couldn't be vaguer if I tried but she doesn't question me. Her pale eyes fall to the folder and she narrows her eyes on it. "Gabrielle Laflamme. Is that you?"

I nod. "It was before I was adopted. When I was in foster care like you."

"How did you end up there?" she asks, leaning against the

door frame. "Was your mom a selfish crack head like mine?"

I try not to frown. There is work to be done on her outlook on her mom, who died of an overdose two years ago, but now is not the time. I shake my head. "My mother was a single mom, like yours, but mine was older. She was forty-one when she had me, by herself. No husband."

"On purpose?"

I smile at that. "Yes. On purpose. She wanted a family so she had me on her own. But then she got cancer and died before I turned two."

"Holy shit," she gasps. I glare at her and she covers her mouth but argues. "Come on. If ever there was a legitimate holy shit moment, it's now."

"No swearing," I reply sternly.

She walks into the room and plops down next to me, her eyes back on the file. I slide it over so she can see it. "She was an only child. Her mom had already passed away and the only family left to take care of me was my grandfather. He took me in until he had a stroke and had to go into a home. So that's when I ended up in the system."

"When were you adopted?"

"At four," I reply and smile. "Well, at four I was placed with my parents, but the official adoption happened when I was almost seven."

"You're so lucky," Mackenzie comments. "People like the little ones. They have a better chance because they're usually less fu—messed up."

I smile because I appreciate her stopping herself from swearing there.

"I wasn't exactly unscathed." I sigh and look down at the

file. "This file says some pretty bad things happened, but I just don't really remember."

She glances down again and begins to read the file. I let her, watching her eyes flare. "Some kid went through a window?"

I nod. "It was on the news. I guess the place they put me after taking me from my grandpa was a really bad home. The other kids there were being abused. I was only there for less than a week before the kid went through the window and they figured out what was going on."

"It's screwed up, but it doesn't surprise me," Mackenzie replies. "That kid going through the window was probably the best thing that could have happened to you because you got out of the house quickly."

I nod and close the file. "I think you're right."

God, how absolutely crazy would it be if Alex was that same kid? It can't be... the chances are one in a million.

"Too bad my mom didn't drop dead when I was little, so I would have had a chance at being adopted," Mackenzie blurts out in a hard, pained tone. Before I can react, she's up and walking out the door calling over her shoulder. "I'm going to take a shower and go to bed. Night!"

Oh God, that poor girl. She's right, though. Her chances of being adopted aren't as good. Of course the fact that she ran away from two foster homes and skipped school a lot has already labeled her with a behavioral problem, even though she's been great with me.

I look back down at the file in my lap and reach for my cell phone. My dad answers on the second ring and I'm grateful it's him and not Mom. He has an easier time talking about this stuff than she does. She still gets upset thinking about my early years.

"Hey, princess!" I know it's silly that he calls me princess at twenty-six but I love it. "What's up?"

"I have a weird question that you probably can't answer, but I have to ask," I say quietly.

"Okay... that sounds ominous. Talk to me, Goose."

I smile again at his *Top Gun* reference. He's obsessed with Tom Cruise movies, which is pretty ridiculous for a refined, retired CEO of a Fortune 500 company, and it's one of the things I love most about him. "I was wondering if you guys knew the names of the other kids that were in that foster home I was in."

"The one with the abusive assholes?"

"Yes."

"No, princess, that level of information on the other kids would have been private," he says, explaining what I already know. "We were only given access to your file."

"I was just wondering if the social worker mentioned it or it slipped out or something," I say as I stand up and put the file back in the closet, knowing Mackenzie will be out of the shower soon and will need her privacy. "I thought maybe you could casually bring it up with Mom. She remembers every detail of all that stuff. Maybe she'll remember a name."

"I can try, but you know how worked up those memories get her," he cautions. "If she gets all moody, I'm making you come over for dinner so she remembers how perfect you turned out."

I laugh. "Okay, deal. And Mackenzie too."

"How's that going by the way?" he asks, his tone growing somber again.

"Good," I reply as I leave her room and walk down the hall to my own. "We've got little bumps but no major ones. Not yet."

"And how long is she staying?"

"Haven't decided," I explain. "It's up to the judge. I'm holding the spot in Daphne's for her as soon as they say she can live there."

"Hmm..." my dad says and it sounds like he's got an opinion he doesn't want to share.

"What?" I say as I gently close my door and drop down on my own bed.

"Nothing," he says, even though I know it's something. "Anyway let me poke your mom's memory and get back to you Sunday at Mac's little shindig. Why don't you send Mac on by for dinner tomorrow night. We only got to meet her briefly last week and we'd like to get to know her better."

"You've got a deal, but I'm warning you, she has trouble getting a handle on her potty mouth," I smile. "Night, Dad."

"Night, princess."

I dream that night of things that haven't haunted my brain in decades. A cold hand around my arm. A deep, cooing yet menacing voice. Sickly sweet breath. A child screaming and the sound of cracking glass.

Chapter 19

Brie

Almost twenty-four hours later I'm staring at Alex and it's impossible not to laugh. He looks so damn confused and out of place and maybe even truly terrified that I am completely and profoundly amused. With each store we go into, his anxiety and confusion seems to deepen. I thought it was bad in Sephora, but now that we're in Forever 21 he's basically apoplectic. I really shouldn't laugh, but as he picks up an off-the-shoulder shirt that clearly wouldn't reach the belly button of anyone over the age of five, his eyes bug out of his head and his brow furrows and his nose crinkles. I can't help it. I burst out laughing.

He turns to me, butt hurt. "I'm glad you find my confusion and fear so delightful."

I cover my mouth with my hands hoping to keep the giggles from escaping. "I'm sorry. I am. It's just you look so damn cute."

He startles at that. "I do?"

"Like a puppy seeing his reflection in a mirror for the first time," I reply and he frowns. "Eager and confused and scared all at once."

He puts the shirt back on the rack and turns to me, his face serious. "No man wants to be compared to a puppy. 'Cute' is not a compliment."

"I wasn't trying to compliment you," I reply softly as he takes a step toward me. I love that he asked me to help him find a birthday gift for Mackenzie. Still for the first hour we've been shopping he's been a little distant. I'm hoping joking with him will loosen him up.

"I was just stating facts," I continue. "And you know what? It's kind of nice to see you vulnerable. You're always so cocky with the right comebacks, or pickup lines, for everything."

He smiles so deep it makes a dimple appear on his cheek that I'd never noticed before. It's tiny, just below the scar on his cheek, but it's damn sexy. He reaches out and takes my hand in his. It's a subtle thing, his fingertips just lightly clinging to mine, but it changes the energy between us— makes it electric. "I'm not good at being vulnerable. I don't like it. Cocky is better. It's easy. It gets me what I want."

"And what is it you want?" I ask, my voice taut with need. His smile deepens and darkens in the same instant.

"Other than to find a gift Mac won't laugh at?" he says with a chuckle and steps closer again so now we're standing almost on top of each other in between racks of discount clothes. "I want to take you home and do exactly what we did the other night, only better."

I smile. "Better? I don't know how you improve on perfection."

He grins again and his hand leaved mine and circles my waist pulling me to him. Our bodies connect and he feels warm and hard—especially the part pushing into my hip. Honest to God, my knees get weak. His hand slides to my ass as his head dips to my ear. "So stop poking fun at me and help me find the perfect gift, so I can get you home and give you the perfect orgasm."

"She likes music," I sputter suddenly. Apparently the promise of the perfect orgasm has given me inspiration. "She sings a lot and she mentioned she used to want to learn an instrument. She didn't say which one."

He grazes his lips across my cheek, like a kiss but with much more friction thanks to his perfectly unshaven face. I feel that friction through my entire body. His hand on my ass squeezes and then it's gone and he's grabbing my hand again. "*Viens*. We need to find a music store."

Alex buys her a guitar at a store near my place and a lesson package too.

"Mackenzie's at my parents' place for dinner, so she won't see us with it and we can hide it under my bed," I explain.

"So we'll be alone, in your place, in close proximity to your bed," he says and winks at me. "I love it when a plan comes together."

As we exit the store, his phone starts ringing. He glances at the screen and scowls before hitting the ignore button.

"Everything okay?"

"Yeah," he mutters. "I'm just going to be a healthy scratch again."

"What does that mean?" All I can think about is the scars on his back as soon as he says "scratch."

He adjusts the guitar case in his hand and we continue down the street. The store is only a short walk from my place, but it's blustery out so it won't be a leisurely stroll. "It's what you call it when the coach doesn't let a guy play even though he's not injured."

"Why would he do that to you?"

We turn the corner onto my street. "Because he's trying to make me do this fucking TV thing and I keep blowing off the producers when they call. I don't want to do it."

"Can't you just tell him that?" I ask. "Instead of wasting everyone's time."

"I tried, but he's insisting. I thought if I blew off the producers long enough they'd give up and go for someone else, but instead they complained to management," he explains. "Coach said I either give them the segment or I can kiss my ice time good-bye, which makes him an asshole because I've been playing really well lately."

"Why don't you want to do it?"

"The same reason I wouldn't let you put my name on your auction flyer," he replies and shifts the guitar case to his other hand, then takes mine with his free one. "I don't want to have my personal crap out there. This show profiled Devin a couple of years ago when he was married to his first wife. They filmed his house, his kid, his wife cooking dinner. They asked him like a thousand questions about growing up and his family and even interviewed his parents for the segment."

Oh. I get it now. I hold his hand a little tighter. "Is there any way you can set the rules? Like tell them it has to be about the present and not the past? Or that you only want to focus on hockey and not your family?"

"I doubt it, which is why I'm just avoiding the calls and am about to end up in the press box." Another scowl darkens his face but he fights it this time and tries to smile at me. "Tell me something good from your day to get my mind off this."

The memories of my day come filtering back and I frown. "My day was beyond shitty. There was a leak in one of the bathrooms upstairs at Daphne's House and it turns out we have a burst pipe in the ceiling and the plumber swears we need to replace everything. Before it really starts to freeze outside or will have pipes bursting every five seconds."

"That sounds expensive."

"He quoted me eight grand." I get the heavy leaden feeling in my belly like I did when the plumber first told me. "I'm getting a second opinion tomorrow, but if it's true and I have to replumb the place I'm in serious financial trouble. I have to raise our profile and get in some more donations as fast as I can."

The setting sun softens his face, but the worry painted across is still visible. "I can make a donation."

"You already do. Your time," I remind him firmly as we start to climb the stairs to my place. "And I know you made a hefty donation at the fund-raiser."

I slip my key into the lock and open the door. "You mean the Barons tickets and the false promise of sex to the winner?"

I turn and look up at him, giving him a hard glare and he bats his eyelashes at me innocently and tries to pretend that wasn't a comment meant to tease the hell out of me. He lives off his sex appeal. I bet he's gotten out of more traffic tickets with just a wink and a smile. "I mean the check you wrote. Len showed it to me. It was more than generous and I can't ask you for more."

"You aren't asking. I'm offering," he replies as we step into the hallway and I close the door.

"I appreciate it and I may have to take you up on it, but what I really need is media coverage," I explain. "I did get an email from *The Times* asking me a few more questions about a press release I sent a while ago, so fingers crossed they write a story."

We kick off our shoes and coats and head straight for the bedroom. I help him tuck the guitar case under the bed making sure the big bow they put on it doesn't get squashed. As soon as I stand back up, his lips are on mine.

I still want to ask him about his foster home and maybe share my suspicions. But after the day we both had and how good this kiss feels, I decide to wait. Mac will be back sooner rather than later and I want some adult time with him before then. So when he deepens the kiss and starts to undress me, I not only let him but I return the favor.

This time the first orgasm he gives me is with his perfect mouth. Without even letting me lie down, he kneels before me, tugging my pants down my legs along with my underwear and he starts kissing me. First my thighs, then my clit and then I feel his tongue and I shudder and sigh at the incredible sensations. My hands curl into his thick, soft hair and he murmurs something I don't catch, but I don't care. I'm too consumed by the way his mouth is moving over me. His hands slip around my thighs and he grabs my ass tight.

I'm still standing, but I can't feel my legs. My whole body is quaking and my neck snaps back and stars shoot across my closed eyes as I come harder than I've ever come before. My knees are suddenly made of Jell-O and I start to drop vaguely hoping I land on the bed, but I'm too spent to care either way. He's on his feet, his arm around my lower back, holding me up as he buries his face in my neck and lowers me onto the bed. "You're going to wreck me," he whispers into the crook of my neck. "And I'm going to let you."

My eyes flutter open and our eyes connect, and I'm breathless at the pain in his face. Oh my God, what the hell happened to him. I slide my hand down his cheek. "Alex . . ."

He silences me with a kiss. His lips never leave mine long enough for me to speak—to tell him I would never hurt him—and I think that's intentional on his part. The sex is incredible. He's this mix of rough and gentle, fast and slow and he knows exactly how to hit a G-spot. He gently sucks on my neck and tells me confidently, "I'm going to make you come again now," and then moves his hips a different way and it's like he tapping a button and my whole body detonates. I fight off the wave of oblivion long enough to clench down on his dick and he swears in French and the vein in his neck throbs and he comes with me.

He gets up to remove the condom and then lies back down next to me, pulling me into his chest. We don't bother with blankets because we're both still sweaty and panting. I listen to the thump of his heartbeat against my cheek as he runs his fingertips up and down my back. "This is nice," I confess softly.

"Mmm..." he responds, his voice heavy and deep.

I blink, take a breath and tell him what he wouldn't let me tell him earlier. "I'm not going to wreck you."

He doesn't say anything for so long that I worry he didn't hear my words. But I can't bring myself to look up at him. I don't want to see his face because I'm worried he'll look pained again or worse, angry. "I've had my share of empty promises in my life and I don't want to add you to that pile. So just don't make any promises okay?"

It's not okay. And I want to promise—to come out and declare—the exact opposite. That I won't wreck him. That I'll do everything I can to make sure no one wrecks him ever again, but I bite back the words because he won't believe them anyway. So I'll just have to show him. So for now I change the subject. "Are we going to tell Mackenzie about this?"

"Us?" he asks and I nod against his chest. "Yeah, I guess we have to because I intend to be around a lot and I'm pretty sure it'll start to get obvious."

"Should I just tell her, or do you want to? Or should we do it together like we're starring in some awkward sit-com?" I joke, and I feel his body shake with a laugh. "No matter how we do it, I don't think she'll care. She likes having you around."

"And by the time we start to turn into a bickering old couple, she'll be living at Daphne's on her own anyway," he replies and I feel a tiny little void start to open up in my heart at the thought of her moving out, which jars me a little bit. "Man I wish they had a place like Daphne's when I was a kid. Would have made life so much easier."

"You never told me how you ended up in a group home for troubled boys," I say and reposition myself so my hands are laced on his chest and my chin is resting on top of them. "Why did they move you there from foster care?"

His face doesn't flicker or twitch. No frown or scowl takes over. He remains passive but his eyes change. The color seems to darken and the softness is gone, the glassy postorgasmic quality hardens. "It's a long story."

"We've probably got an hour before Mac comes home."

"I'd really rather not get into it tonight." His tone is stern and foreboding like he's warning me to stop. Change the subject. Let it go.

"You don't know how I learned French, do you?"

He looks down at me finally, instead of up at the ceiling. "I assume it was a summer in Paris or a winter in the Alps or however it is that princesses get their linguistic skills." He winks as he teases me.

I lift one of my hands and flip him the bird. He laughs. "*C'est pas jolie, ca.*"

I ignore his comment and tell him my mom was French Canadian.

"Quebec?" he asks, his accent in full force and it's hot as hell.

"*Oui.*" I take in the happy surprise on his handsome face. "That's where my parents—the Bennetts—adopted me from."

I wait for him to let that information sink in. He rolls me over so he's on top and kisses me slowly. When he pulls back he's all mischief again. "Finally something about Quebec that I like."

I smile at that and fight the urge to close my eyes and moan as he starts kissing his way down my neck. I can feel his cock coming to life against my thigh and as much as I would love a round two, I want to talk more. "I was in one foster home before they adopted me. How many were you in before the group home?"

"Fuck," he says lowly and starts to untangle himself from me and stand up. I get to my knees as he swings his legs over the side of my bed, and I drop a hand on his shoulder to stop him, just above the branch of his tattoo with the single leaf. He shrugs it off though and stands up anyway. He paces for a second, running his hand through his hair, his eyes on the fluffy fake fur rug by the side of my bed. "I told you, I didn't want to get into it."

"I'm sorry, Alex. I didn't mean to push. I just—"

He swears again and reaches for his jeans. "You just felt like hearing a sob story? That's what you like after some hot sex? To make me feel weak and vulnerable. Is this what people do in a relationship? Should I make you talk about how your mom died and why you don't have a dad?"

He's being mean and hard, and I'm suddenly feeling like an idiot sitting here naked so I get up and grab my robe as he yanks on his jeans and reaches for his shirt.

"Ovarian cancer. That's how she died. And I don't have a dad because he was a sperm donor. From a clinic, not like a one-night-stand kind of sperm donor," I explain sharply. "I'm not trying to make you feel weak or hurt you, Alex. And I wouldn't bring up all this shit except that I think that we've lived through the same shit."

"Why? Because we're both from Quebec? Big deal. I'm sure there's a bunch of orphans in Quebec," he mutters, twisting his shirt in his hands. "I can name four that I lived with. Jayla, Andre, Kenny. Of course they're all dead now. Jayla ran away because the foster monster was touching her, became a prostitute and was killed by her pimp. Kenny overdosed, and Andre was killed after he joined a gang."

"Jesus Christ," I whisper in horror at the pure tragedy.

"Exactly. That's why I hate talking about it. I truly fucking hate it. So can you please just stop."

He grabs me roughly by the waist and pulls me into him, dipping his head to bury it in my shoulder. I wrap my arms around his neck and press my mouth against his neck softly. His pulse beats rapidly under my lips. "You can talk about your past. Tell me whatever you need to or want to and I will listen but please, don't try to dig up mine."

I hear a noise downstairs. A rattle, a click, a thump. It's the front door. Shit! Mackenzie is home. We both stare at each other in fear. He's barely dressed. I'm not dressed at all. Oh crap! I put my hands on his chest and push him back into the corner of the room behind the door. "Stay here until I can distract her and then sneak out. I don't want her to find out like this."

He nods. I rush to my bedroom door and scurry down the hall, reaching the stairs just as she's shrugging out of her coat and toeing off her boots. I hate that ratty coat of hers and I keep telling her I want to buy her a new one, but she doesn't want me to. She says I've done enough. It's still got the rip in it from when she hurt herself. I smile trying to look casual. "Did you have a good time with my parents?"

She nods. "They're cool people. And your mom makes great food. She gave me cupcakes to bring home."

She pulls a Tupperware container out of her backpack. She looks at me again, her eyes sweeping up and down, taking in my outfit. I play with the tie on my robe and lie. "I was going to take a shower."

"Oh. Okay." She walks past me, toward the kitchen. "I'm gonna eat another cupcake and watch TV."

"Sure." I should ask her if her homework is done and make her do it before TV and sugar, but right now I need her tucked away at the back of the house so Alex can leave.

She pauses and looks at me again. I feel like she wants to say something, but she doesn't. She heads into the kitchen. As soon as she's out of view I rush back to my room and swing open the door. I motion for Alex to come and he does. He's got his boots on now and his jacket in his hand. His shirt is on inside out and backward. We both tiptoe down the stairs and into the front hall. I watch him reach for the front door, opening it but pausing to look back at me. That pained, suffering look is on his face again—the one that makes me believe he tortures himself with his own thoughts.

"I'm sorry," he whispers.

"So am I," I reply because there's so much more I want to say but it's not the time now. Maybe it never will be.

He bends down and kisses me quickly then disappears out the door, leaving nothing but cold night air in his wake.

I sigh, lock the door and turn around to find Mackenzie standing at the end of the hall holding a half-eaten cupcake and a glass of milk, staring at me with a knowing look in her eyes.

"Called it!" she announces and then disappears into the living room.

Chapter 20

Brie

My front door opens and I glance over to see Len walk in, her arms loaded with grocery bags. There's a bunch of balloons tied to her wrist too. She went overboard, clearly, and that's why I love her. I smile. "You're too much."

She grins. "She's probably never had balloons. Every kid should have balloons at least once in her life."

"True."

"I'm the coolest aunt in the world," Len proclaims. "It's a role I've always wanted to play and now that I have my chance I'm not giving it up."

I watch her as she walks toward me and into the kitchen, the balloons banging against the chandelier in the hall and the opening to the kitchen. She drops the grocery bags on my tiny kitchen table. "Premade party platters and almost every chip flavor in the store. Oh and guac. Every party is better with guac."

"Ain't that the truth." I start to unpack the groceries as

she begins to untie the balloons from her wrist. "So I got her a fifty-dollar gift card to Sephora because what teenage girl—or hell grown woman for that matter—doesn't love that place? And also the cutest loungewear I've ever seen. Oh and a poster of a Banksy piece because she said loved his work. You better let her hang it on her bedroom wall. With thumbtacks. Don't be like my mom and insist on the gummy glue stuff that always falls off. Let the kid be a kid and put holes in your walls."

"She can use tacks, I promise. And that's a very generous gift," I can't help but mention.

"I told you I'm going for the best aunt in the universe. Also the craziest and the funnest," Len explains. "And yes I know 'funnest' isn't a word."

I smile. Len suddenly stops and lets the balloons rise to the ceiling. She looks me dead in the eye and I freeze with a tub of guacamole in my hand. "You're keeping her, right?"

"I don't know," is my answer because I don't. Having Mackenzie here has been a lot of work in some ways and no work at all in others. And I like her. A lot. I kind of adore her actually.

"You've always said you wanted to foster," Len reminds me. "She's a good kid. Her rough edges are totally buffable. She likes you. You're financially and emotionally stable. You should keep her."

"'Buffable'?" I have to chuckle at her choice of word. "I'm definitely considering asking her if she wants to stay. But it's up to her. The judge may let her move into Daphne's House and what independent kid is going to pick living with a boring spinster over getting their freedom?"

"You're not a spinster! You're dating a hot, rich professional athlete," Len exclaims dramatically. "She'll say yes because the two of you are the foster parent jackpot and Mac's not stupid. She knows it."

"She doesn't get both of us. Legally, she just gets me. And I think she likes him more," I kid, but it's kind of true. I don't blame her. Alex saved her.

"Well, he'll be around if she sticks with you," Len says. "And she gets me. And Helena and Baxter, who are the coolest foster grandparents a kid could ask for. They make up for any lameness she might think you have."

I full on burst out laughing at her now. "Thanks for that."

"What are best friends for?" she coos back. "Now can we get back to your sexy boyfriend? How are things going?"

"Good." It's only been a couple of days since Mac caught us, but he's hung out here with us both nights. Even though she knows and doesn't seem bothered, I suggested he still not spend the night yet and he agreed. I haven't brought up anything about our childhood, but I've wanted to. "We're still in the getting-to-know-you phase, I guess. And it could take a while because Alex is kind of private."

"Yeah well I'm betting you're not exactly an open book." Len jumps for the dangling balloon strings to pull them down from the ceiling. "Have you told him about your past?"

"I've told him most of it, yeah." I go back to unpacking the groceries.

"Did you tell him your stance on kids? You know, the biological kind?"

I shake my head. "It hasn't come up. We've only been together for like a millisecond."

Len jumps again, grabbing the last balloon string and then pushes her hair out of her face. She walks over to the dining table and starts tying them to a chair. "I'm thinking you should tell this one sooner rather than later. He's a pro-athlete. Don't those guys always want to spread their seed and create mini-mes to carry on their athletic dynasty?"

I make a face at her choice of expression. "They're not cavemen, Len."

She shrugs. "Maybe not but still, I would lay that out. Don't get me wrong, I understand your logic and I agree with it. But if you want him to be an open book, you should be too."

I just nod and turn around to find my chip bowl. Leave it to Len to make perfect sense. He said I could talk about my past so I will. I'll tell him that there's a hereditary component to ovarian cancer and that's why I won't have my own kids. I can only hope he'll take me seriously, unlike Victor.

"He's still coming this afternoon, right?" Len asks.

I nod and pour one of the bags of chips she bought into the bowl. "He's with her now. She's in his running group and they'll come back here together."

The doorbell rings. It's got to be my parents because those are the only other people invited. Len rushes to the front door to let them in. They greet Len the way they always do—with giant hugs, like she's their second daughter. And they greet me with the same affection. I don't know what happened in that foster home when I was four, but I'm glad it did, because if it hadn't, these two wouldn't be my parents.

We spend the next half hour setting up and putting out

the food and then, just as I'm paying the pizza delivery guy, Alex appears on the front steps. I look behind him for Mackenzie, but I don't see her. He smiles at me. "Hey! Am I late?"

He bends down to kiss me but I don't let his lips touch mine. "Where is she?"

He blinks. "What?"

I step onto the stoop and glance down the street. "Is she still at Daphne's?"

"What? No." He's as confused as I am. "She didn't come to running group. Was she supposed to?"

"Oh fuck." I turn and leave him on the stoop as I run back into the house and straight for her room. It's clean. Her bed is made, the clothes I've bought her are folded on the bed, her school books are stacked neatly on the desk, but her knapsack is gone and so is her coat. There's a piece of paper torn from a notebook in the center of her desk. I walk over and read the note.

Thank you for everything. I mean it.

"Alex, she's gone."

I don't let myself cry until three in the morning as Len and I walk down what feels like the millionth alley. My feet and back ache, but not nearly as deeply as my chest does. And as reality settles in, the ache grows deeper. "I'm going to have to call the cops in the morning and report her. And Laurie will have to tell the judge. Even if they find her, she won't be allowed back with me."

"Can't you wait to tell them?" Len asks, and when I shake my head the first tear tumbles.

"I can't. I have to follow the rules. I don't want to lose my ability to foster," I explain, although I'd rather throw my heart into a food processor than even think about doing this again. It would be less painful. I wipe at the tears and Len walks over and hugs me, smashing my face into the puffy down of her black ski jacket and she rubs my back with her mitten-covered hand.

"You should go home," I tell her. "You can look in the morning."

My parents stayed at my place in case Mac comes back. Len insisted on coming with me and now she's refusing to go. "I am not leaving you out here alone. As long as you're out here, I'm out here."

"Thank you." I sniff and wipe at more tears. "We're stupid to think we'll find her in this city."

Len shakes her head and readjusts her wool cap. "We have to try,"

My phone rings. I have the volume set on high to ensure I don't miss it since it's tucked into the pocket of my wool coat. It echoes off the concrete walls. I rush to pull off my wool gloves so I can answer it and drop one on the litter-strewn ground but I don't care. It's Alex.

"I've got her."

My whole body floods with relief and my eyes blur with tears. "Thank God. Is she okay? Where are you?"

Len starts to jump up and down in excitement. "She's being an asshole, but she's fine. We're heading back to your place."

"We're on our way." I hang up and grab Len's arm. "He's bringing her home."

I burst through my front door ten minutes later and march through the townhouse and find them in the kitchen. She's at the table, a plate of snacks from her now defunct party on a plate in front of her. She looks up at me, her expression cold. But her eyes are bloodshot and puffy, and her nose is red. I notice a wad of used tissue on the table beside her plate. She's been crying.

"Your parents went home but said to call them if you need them," Alex says. I nod, my eyes still glued to Mackenzie.

"Are you okay?" I ask. It's the first question my parents always asked me in a crisis or drama and this feels like both.

"Yeah."

"I'm going to head home," Len announces from behind me and I feel her give my shoulders a squeeze. "Happy birthday."

Mackenzie looks up at Len and her eyes start to water and she looks away. A minute later I hear the front door close. I lean against the archway, suddenly exhausted. "Why would you do this?"

Alex stands up and reaches for me as he glances over at Mac, who is staring at the floor. "Tell her what you told me," he demands before pulling me off the wall and giving me a strong, warm hug and kissing the top of my head as he gently pushes me down into the chair he vacated across from Mackenzie.

"Mac," Alex says her name sharply. "Tell her what you told me."

"I couldn't do this fucking birthday thing," she says in a choked voice. "You made a fucking cake and you were all going to get me presents and there's no point. I don't know what's going to happen down the road, but chances are at some point I won't have a house and I'll probably end up pawning whatever nice shit you give me because I'm not going to get into Daphne's House. Not anytime soon and you've got him now, and you'll want to get your life back and be a normal couple. You're too young to have a kid like me. You were just doing him a favor probably because you liked him. And now you're, like, together which is great because you're both awesome, but I'm a third wheel and the stupid asshole judge won't let you put me in Daphne's House and I don't have anywhere to go. I stayed up all night worrying and then I realized I needed to just go. I shouldn't hang around because it was just going to make it worse. So I left . . ."

"You created a whole shitload of drama in that head of yours, Mac," Alex says.

"I told you, it's not drama. It's fucking fact."

"Language!" I bark and she looks stunned by that, like the rules suddenly don't apply. I reach across the table and grab her hand. "Are you happy here?"

"What?"

"With me. In this house. Are you happy?"

Her tiny shoulders lift toward her ears and then drop. "I hate school, but I always hate school wherever I go and I'm too young to drop out yet, so it is what it is. But I finally like coming home from school. I mean . . . you aren't mean or high and the rules aren't stupid."

"Because I love having you here and I want you to stay." I squeeze her hand under mine. "If you're okay with it, I think we should decide to forget talking to the judge about

Daphne's until next year, when you're sixteen. He's more likely to let you live there then anyway. And so let's both agree to keep this arrangement and we can discuss it again next year. Discuss. Together. Do not assume you know what I'm thinking and make a decision on your own, okay?"

She nods, but she looks skeptical. The scar weaving its way through the caramel skin of her forearm catches my eye. I lean farther forward and lay my hand over it. "Here's a little secret I haven't told you. The only kids I ever intend to have are foster kids. Now granted, I didn't expect to have one so soon, but I adore you, Mac. I'm happy with this. With you."

She tears up again but quickly brushes them away with the back of her hand.

"I told you, you big dummy," Alex says to her, trying to be lighthearted but his voice is thick.

Mac gets up and leans into me, hugging me tightly. Every single fiber of my being warms like it's in the hot summer sun. "Go to bed."

"I'm sorry," she whispers before she pulls away.

"Get some sleep because we have a birthday do-over in the morning," I say and watch her disappear from the room. Then I cover my face with my hands and exhale a shuddering breath. I feel Alex's hands under my elbows and he pulls me to my feet and into his arms.

"I didn't know you don't want to have biological kids," he murmurs against the top of my head. I try not to bristle because I can't decipher his tone and that makes me nervous.

I look up at him. "Ovarian cancer and breast cancer can be caused by a gene mutation that can be passed on to children.

Even though my grandmother died of ovarian cancer and had the mutation, my mom didn't get tested."

"And she had it."

"She did and she died."

He studies my face and I can see the color drain from his. "And you have it?"

"I was tested." I pause and feel that familiar sense of frustration. "And then I decided I didn't want the results yet, so I never picked them up from my doctor's office. I'm a coward like my mom. I want to live in oblivion. But I'm smarter about it because I'm not going to orphan any kids if I do have it and get sick." He looks at me with a strange expression I can't read, and I'm too exhausted to try. "I need sleep."

"Me too. I have to meet with those stupid producers tomorrow," he tells me and keeps his arm wrapped around me so I'm snugly tucked under his shoulder as we walk downstairs to the front door.

I hesitate as we reach the front hall. "You can stay. It's got to happen eventually so why not tonight?"

He shakes his head. "No, baby, not tonight."

I feel a wave of disappointment, but I'm too tired to convince him with words so I just tilt my head up and kiss him. I think I meant for it to be a gentle, quick gesture but as soon as my lips press to his, he takes control and his intentions aren't subtle. His tongue finds mine and with that one hand wrapped around my waist, he lifts me off the ground and walks us back toward my bedroom, his mouth never leaving mine.

Chapter 21

Alex

Tonight was everything I swore I could never handle. I got too close to a street kid and she almost ripped my heart out. And worse than the worry and the pain I was in thinking about Mac being on the street again was the worry and pain I saw in Brie's face. I realized as I walked the streets looking for Mac, that if Brie's heart was broken over this, it was my fault. I brought Mac into her life.

I couldn't stand the thought that I'd caused Brie pain...because I was falling in love with her. Another thing that I swore I would never do because I wouldn't be any good at it. But Brie, right now, as the emotional dust of this day settles around us, is looking at me with tenderness and relief, like having me here is making her life better and not worse. She needs me and I am not failing her, not because I learned how to be a boyfriend but because I somehow just instinctually know how to be what she needs. It feels natural and right.

And as soon as our lips connect my whole body relaxes.

Muscles I didn't even know I had start loosen. I hold her hips and pull her closer but when our lips touch, I let her control the kiss. She starts slow, easy, gentle and then her tongue finds mine and she teases, touching and retreating and then touching again. For the first time in my life I understand all those lyrics from love songs, the ones about falling in love and the ones about getting your heart broken. Because this woman . . . she is the only person that's ever made me feel this good, which I know means she can make me feel worse than I've ever felt too. I push that fact away as she walks back toward her bedroom, still holding on to me, her lips still on mine. She lets go and quietly closes the door, leaning against it as she looks up at me. "We have to be quiet."

I smile. "I know. But I don't intend to make that easy for you."

She grins. "Do your best." And pulls her shirt over her head.

I reach behind my back and pull my shirt over my head too. Her hands are on me before it even hits the floor, sliding up my abdomen leaving a trail of gooseflesh in their wake. I take her head in my hands and kiss her—hard and deep.

The sex is different and not just because it's slow and gentle. It's different for me because I'm letting myself feel more than just her body. Not that her body isn't enough. She's wet and warm and tight in all the right places and it would be great sex no matter what. But for the first time I'm feeling more than just the physical act. I'm feeling the unspoken words in our kisses and the promises in our touch. I have no idea how to make love to someone but I hope she knows that's what I'm trying to do.

When I come, I bury my face against her neck to muffle the groan I can't contain and to hide the look on my face because I know it's pure need. I've never needed anyone, my whole life, and now I need her.

I clean up, throwing the condom in her trash and lie back down in bed beside her. I pull her into my chest and she rests her head on my chest. "You think she heard us?"

"No," she whispers back. "She's got to be passed out cold with exhaustion. I know I'm about to."

She tilts her head so she's looking up at me, but her eyelids are heavy and start to flutter closed immediately. Watching her makes me realize how tried I am. I look around the room. It's got a decent-sized window, but heavy curtains that are drawn shut. And Brie has a canopy bed frame with gauzy, sheer white curtains. They're drawn back in each corner right now but the idea of sleeping here still makes me feel a little claustrophobic, which means I'll most likely have nightmares. Between that and the fact that I've come to realize they're triggered by change or uncertainty—like getting traded or moving or other big life events—I'm almost guaranteed to have one tonight.

"I won't be here in the morning," I tell her. "I can't spend the night here."

"Oh." She looks confused and even a little hurt. Fuck. I'm already ruining things.

I run a hand over the back of her head, my fingers slipping through her hair. "I'm a restless sleeper on a good night. And my claustrophobia issues, which you've witnessed, sometimes kick in when I try to sleep in small rooms."

I watch her big brown eyes dart around the room. "This is

a decent-sized room for New York," she defends, but the hurt is gone from her gaze. "I mean it's not a twelve-hundred-foot loft but it's decent."

I smile. "Even that loft feels claustrophobic sometimes."

She places a palm on my chest just over my heart and rests her chin on top of it as she looks at me and softly asks, "What happened to you to make you claustrophobic?"

I shrug. She's not buying it and I didn't expect she would but it's instinct to deny, evade, lie. But she's not going to let it go. "Alex, I won't judge you."

"You should," I reply and kiss her forehead before gently nudging her off me and standing up. She reaches out for my hand, stopping me. I look down at her, all messy sex hair and swollen lips and flushed cheeks. She's stunning.

"I think you might have PTSD," she says quietly.

"What?"

"I don't know for sure, but that's what it seems like, Alex."

I frown and shake my head. "Soldiers get that."

"Lots of people get that," she counters calmly. "Especially children who have been through a traumatic event. Did someone hurt you when you were a kid?"

I hesitate, then nod. "And I'm not ready to talk to you about it." I walk over and cup her face in my hands. "I want this, but I have to...you have to give me time. I don't talk about this—ever with anyone."

"What about seeing a therapist?" she asks. "A clinical psychologist could help you."

"Like you?" I feel instantly uneasy. She can't be my shrink.

"No. I can't. I'm not practicing and if I was, I'm not supposed to get orgasms from people I treat," she says, smiling softly. "But I can recommend someone."

I take a deep breath. "I'll think about it." She nods and I bend down and kiss her softly on that pretty mouth of hers. I glance at the clock behind her on the night table. "I should go."

She nods again. I finish getting dressed and she follows me out to the front door.

"Would you like to go on a date?" I ask her before I open her front door. "A real date, just the two of us. Like a couple."

She looks shocked but happy. "Yes. When?"

"I have a game tomorrow night so how about the night after?"

"I'd love to." She rocks up on her tiptoes to kiss me good night.

I head out into the New York streets filled with emotions I'd never thought I'd feel—happiness and hope.

Chapter 22

Brie

I kiss him, but he doesn't really kiss me back. It's adorable. I look over my shoulder to ensure we're alone and then I give him a playful smile. "My dad doesn't own a shotgun. And even if he did, you've been a delight tonight. He's not going to shoot you."

Alex smiles at that. "I did good, eh?"

I grin and cup his cheek. *"Très bien. Ils t'aiment."*

They do love him. And I loved watching them love him. He was so adorable helping my mom with the dishes and trying so hard to be polite and complimentary to my dad. Mackenzie loved having him here too. I think it made her less uncomfortable. She told me she never did Thanksgiving with her mother. Her mother didn't do any holidays so she wasn't sure what to expect. Having Alex here, who also clearly isn't one to celebrate holidays, gave her an ally. They both did great and I think they enjoyed themselves.

"Are you sure you don't want me to wait and walk you two home?" Alex asks.

"Mac and I are going to spend the night here," I explain. "But I'll see you tomorrow?"

He nods. "I'll pick you up at noon. The flight is at two."

I nod and try not to look as excited as I am. Not just because it's Rose and Luc's wedding, which I'm sure will be lovely, but because Alex and I are going to have a sleepover. A bona fide, full-fledged, out-of-town sleepover.

It's been two weeks since Mac ran away and everything has been amazing, with her and with Alex and me . Three one-on-one dates as well as two outings with Mackenzie for ice cream one day and to see a movie the other. And he dropped by after his last home game for a what was supposed to be a beer and some conversation but what turned into quickie and then he left.

I'm not complaining about the quickie. I had watched the game on TV and the camera loved to focus on him—on the ice and the bench. He was getting lippy with the other team and it was fucking hot to watch him fearlessly taunting the other team, getting under their skin. I never thought I liked the troublemaker bad boy, but damn, it made me wet. So the quickie was as much my doing as his, but then he left.

He still hasn't spent the night, and as much as I wish it didn't bug me, it does. I've tried to talk to him about it a little more—his past, why he won't stay over—but he just says he's not ready. I want to ask him about his foster homes, about those scars on his back and if he got them falling through a window. If one of the other kids in the home was a tiny, scared four-year-old with big brown eyes named Gabrielle. But any time I try to bring it up he gets upset. So I've just been trying to enjoy him—us—and be patient.

He kisses me again, this time less PG and with a little tongue. "*Á demain, ma belle.*"

"Yes, see you tomorrow."

He heads out into the stormy night, and I watch him go until he's disappeared from sight. I close the door and walk back through the large Upper East Side penthouse I grew up in to the kitchen. Mackenzie is helping my mom load dishes into the dishwasher while my dad puts the extra food into Tupperware. My dad smiles at me as I stretch out on the bench seat in the little eating nook. "I like him. He's much more interesting than Victor ever was."

I laugh. "You used to say Victor was a nice boy."

"He was. You know what else is nice?" my dad counters with a wink. "Vanilla ice cream. White toast. Plain milk. This guy has character and personality. Like sourdough toast or a milkshake or chocolate ice cream."

"More like Rocky Road," I murmur but no one catches it.

"I think it's so magical that you found a boy with French roots just like you," my mom interjects. "Are his parents still in Quebec?"

"Alex doesn't have parents," Mackenzie replies before I can explain. "He grew up in foster care, like me. And he ran away like me. Only he didn't have someone to take him in. But he has hockey, so there's that."

Now both my mom and dad have stopped their tasks and are staring at me. I glance over at Mackenzie. "Why don't you go pick out a movie for us to watch? It's family tradition we watch a Tom Cruise movie after dinner every Thanksgiving. You'll find a pile of them on Blu-Ray in the cabinet under the TV."

"Tom Cruise?" Mackenzie repeats and the look on her face says she's completely baffled. "We're not Scientologists, are we?"

My heart swells at her use of the word "we." She feels like she's one of us now.

"No. It's strictly a respect for his work," my dad tells her. She still doesn't get it—judging by the way her eyebrows and nose are all scrunched up and her head is tilted—but she shrugs and walks out of the room. My dad turns his attention back to me. "Is Alex the reason you were asking me about your case files a couple weeks ago?"

I nod and sit up, worried about the pain that's creasing my mother's porcelain skin. It's like talking about what I went through physically hurts her. "Did you know him back them, Gabrielle?"

"I don't know. I was so little, but...I think I might have."

My mother seems to grow even paler, and she closes the dishwasher and walks over to me. I move over so she can sit beside me. "There were four other kids, three boys and a girl, in that first, horrible place you were in and then, the place they moved you before we took you had one other child, a girl."

"Do you remember their names?" I ask.

She shakes her head. "No, but I know they were all older than you. The first place had an eight-year-old, two ten-year-olds and a twelve-year-old. The second place had a fourteen-year-old."

"Alex is four years older than me, so he would have been

eight when I was in the first home," I tell them quietly and gently lay my hand over my mom's, which are curled together on top of the table. "And he has scars on his back that he doesn't tell the truth about. He says they're from hockey, but they can't be."

My dad frowns. "You think he's the child who went through the window?"

I look up at him. "I don't know. Maybe."

"Oh my God, Brie, honey, the odds of that are virtually impossible..." My mom's voice trails off and she swallows as her eyes grow misty.

"I know, but...what if?"

She lets out a shuddering sigh and leans in to hug me. "Well if it's true then I'm just happy he seems to be doing well now. And he's managed to keep his heart open."

Has he? As I hug her back my dad leans over us and ruffles our hair. "Come on. It's movie time," Dad says. "'My name is Joel Goodson. I deal in human fulfillment. I grossed over eight thousand dollars in one night. Time of your life, huh, kid?'"

I groan. "We are not watching *Risky Business* with Mackenzie, Dad. I'd rather watch *Top Gun* for the billionth time."

He chuckles as he leads the way into the living room.

Later that night, I'm lying in my childhood bed in the middle of sending Len a text when my phone rings and it's her. I pick it up smiling. "Hey are your ears burning? I was just texting you."

"Nope. And if you're texting me that means you're not in postcoital cuddle sesh, which means Alex didn't spend the night," Len replies. "Brie, this is weird."

"Mackenzie and I stayed at my parents' tonight," I reply. "Our first sleepover is not going to be in my parents' house. And I told you, he's got claustrophobia issues."

"Can't he take a Xanax or something?" Len asks and I can't help but laugh because she seems to be more frustrated by this than I am. "I'm living vicariously through you, remember. I can't find my own happy ending so I'm stalking yours. And happy endings include sleepovers and cuddle sessions, Brie."

"Well thanks to my parents watching Mackenzie for the rest of the weekend and Rose and Luc's wedding in Maine I'll be able to get in the first sleepover," I remind her. "Although I don't know how much sleeping will happen."

She laughs. "Even an athlete built for sex needs a catnap."

"Probably," I reply, although with Alex, I'm not convinced. "I'm glad Rose invited you too."

"So am I," Len tells me. "I love her. She's fantastic and a weekend away at a wedding full of hockey-playing guests, maybe I'll find my own Alex, minus the claustrophobia issues."

"It's really not that big a deal," I tell her even though I know it will be if we don't get through it.

"See you tomorrow at the airport," Len replies. "My first private plane experience. So exciting!"

I say good night and then put my phone down, turn off the light and snuggle deeper under the covers. I'm excited about tomorrow too.

I don't sleep very well for some reason—it's either nerves or excitement. In the morning I have breakfast with my family, leaving Mackenzie there, and then head back to my place to get ready. Alex shows up an hour early and I'm in a towel, fresh out of the shower. When I swing open the front door I can see his eyes darken with lust. Twenty minutes later the towel is on the floor in the front hall, his pants are at his ankles and I'm bent over the couch falling into a blissful orgasm.

He keeps trying to fool around as I pack and get ready, even after the mind-blowing living room sex, so we end up getting to the airport with barely any time to spare. I've never been wanted the way Alex wants me. It's so visceral, like he's just instinctually attracted to me. It's not a choice, it's a requirement, like air and water and food. I feel the same way about him, which is why it's so scary. I don't have control over it.

Len and everyone else taking the private plane to Maine are already there. They all greet us with warm smiles. Jessie is looking pregnant now, with a little yet distinct bump. I hug her and tell her she looks fantastic. "We had to alter the bridesmaid dress last second. I just picked it up at the tailor on our way here and haven't even had a chance to try it on. I hope it fits. I feel like this kid is growing by a foot every day."

"Meanwhile over here I just look like I ate too many burritos," Callie says and pulls her shirt tight against her own stomach. She's right. She kind of just looks bloated.

Devin walks over and pats her belly while giving her a kiss on the cheek. "Don't worry baby, you'll be so big you can't see your feet soon enough."

She punches him on the arm and he winces but laughs. I catch Alex watching everything from the back of the plane where he's sipping a bottle of water. I can't help but think he does that a lot, watches his teammates interact with their loved ones, like it's a movie he wants to see but can't be a part of. I get that. I was there too.

I walk over to him and rock up on my toes to give him a quick kiss. "You okay?"

He nods and sips his water again. He smiles at me, but it's forced. "Let's grab some seats."

The plane is small but comfortable. I sit in one of the oversized leather seats and Alex sits next to me. Len sits across from me. The flight isn't long but because I didn't sleep well I doze off. When I start to wake up again, Alex is still talking with Jordan. Jordan's words quickly pull me out of my sleepy state, but I don't open my eyes or move my head off Alex's shoulder where it must have dropped when I nodded off.

"So no one is coming? Not even Brie and Mac? You haven't brought anyone to family day, like, ever have you?"

"I have you guys and your crazy families to amuse me," Alex jokes back, but I can feel the tension in his body.

Jordan laughs. "Yeah, we do tend to be entertaining."

"Nothing is going to be more entertaining than watching you try to be a dad," Alex laughs. "This kid is in for a hell of a ride. Hopefully I'm on this team long enough to see it myself or else I'll have to have Jessie send me videos of all your epic diaper-change and burping fails. Have you bought the kid a helmet and protective suit yet? You know you're going to drop it at least once."

"Fuck you, buddy," Jordan jokes. "You can bust my balls all you want, but I think you're not so different from me anymore. So remember, payback is going to be a bitch."

"I am not the family-man type," Alex says.

Jordan makes a noise in the back of his throat. "Yeah, well you're fooling everyone right now. Even yourself."

I know he's referring to me and I can feel their eyes on me. I know a flush is imminent so I stir, moving my body Alex and tilting my head toward the window so they don't see my face. I still pretend I'm asleep though, because I need time to absorb what I just heard.

"I know you always said you break headboards not hearts," Jordan whispers but I hear it loud and clear. "But this thing with..." He doesn't say my name but I'm betting he's gesturing to me. "Feels like more than a broken headboard and I have to say, it suits you."

"It is." His answer is terse. "Now shut up."

"You're a headcase you know that, Rue," Jordan says with a slight chuckle. "You're lucky chicks think you're cute."

"They think you're cute," he retorts back. "They think I'm a god."

"Ha!" Jordan balks at that and I shift again, this time opening my eyes and praying I look groggy and like I just came out of a coma.

"Hey. Have a good nap?" Alex asks and kisses my cheek. I nod and plaster a fake smile on my face and glance across from us at Len who is still sound asleep. I'm guessing she's not faking it by the snoring. I lean forward and give her a gentle shake.

"We're landing soon," I tell her and she nods, rubs the sleep from her eyes and mumbles something about freshening up and heads to the bathroom.

Alex reaches over and takes my hand in his. His eyes cloud over. "Are you okay?"

I nod. "Sure. Have you been to Maine before?"

He nods. "Yeah for Jordan's wedding. And a couple times before that during the summers to visit him. I spend most of the off-season bumming around visiting teammates."

"So most players go back to their hometowns when they aren't playing?" I question.

"Yeah."

"When was the last time you went back to Quebec?"

He looks startled by that question but he answers it. "I haven't been back since I was started playing professionally. No point."

"What's the family thing Jordan was mentioning?" I ask bluntly. Now his startled face morphs into a guilty one because he knows I heard his conversation.

"It's nothing."

Okay then. I lean forward and turn to look at Jessie across the aisle. "Jessie, what's family day?"

"With the Barons?" she questions and I nod. "It's a day near Christmas where the families come to the arena and skate on the ice. We bring toy donations for charity and there's food and Santa usually makes an appearance for the kids."

"It's a way for hockey players' extended families to get to know each other," Callie adds as she shifts in her seat across from Jessie. "Devin's parents always come down, and Luc's mom showed up last year."

"With her new boyfriend. Who is now her old boyfriend," Luc adds with a roll of his eyes. "She's actually flying solo to the wedding thankfully."

"Maybe she'll pick up a player," Callie replies and Luc groans. "Come on, maybe something younger will do her some good."

"Stop talking now before I barf," Luc warns, and I laugh at the look of horror on his face. But Callie started something that no one but Luc wants to let go of.

"Chooch is single," Alex tells everyone. "He's coming, right?"

"Stop," Luc warns.

"Right! Chooch could use the gentle touch of an older woman after that viper of an ex-girlfriend," Jordan announces and Luc looks like he might be physically ill.

"No seriously, stop," Luc begs and covers his hears with his hands.

"What's a Chooch?" Len asks as she sit back down.

Rose's eyes light up and I swear I can see hearts floating in them. "Actually, you know what? You're going to find out what a Chooch is. I'm going to sit Mike at your table!"

"You're in trouble now," Callie tells Len. "My little sister is the matchmaker from hell."

"Truth," Jessie adds with a grin.

"I was going to focus on Alex here, but seems like that work is done so you're my next victim!" Rose looks absolutely gleeful.

I don't know whether to be concerned for Len or excited. She looks like she's not sure what to feel either. I look over at Alex who is chuckling at the whole thing, but when our eyes meet he seems a little guarded. I wish he had invited Mac and me to this family day thing. The fact that he didn't makes me worry that I'm moving faster than he is and it's the worst feeling ever.

The plane lands and there are two SUV cabs waiting to take us to Silver Bay. All the guests are staying in the same lakefront inn so we all get dropped off first and then the locals get taken to their homes. We agree to meet up later tonight, after their rehearsal dinner.

Len checks in and tells me to text her once I get settled because she wants to go for a walk around town and explore. I agree and watch her trot off to the elevator as Alex talks to the front-desk clerk.

"You'll be in room 304," he tells Alex and slides the key card across the polished wood countertop. "And Miss Bennett is in room 303, just across the hall."

He slides a second key card across the countertop and my heart hits the floor so hard I'm surprised it doesn't crack the tile.

Chapter 23

Alex

She hasn't said a word since we checked in. I've been talking. She's been nodding as I babble on about this little town, but I know she's pissed. I should have said something before we got here, but what the fuck could I have said? "Hey honey, I got you your own room because I don't want you to have a black eye at the wedding."

Jesus, she's going to run so fast in the other direction. We get to the third floor and she walks to her door. Without looking back at me she says, "I'm going to unpack and then head out with Len to explore the town."

"Oh. Okay." I should say more here. Stop her? Beg her to not be mad at me? Have sex with her? I don't know but something. This feels wrong. But I don't do anything more than watch her disappear inside her room.

I head into mine, drop my overnight bag on the bed, hang my suit in the closet and text Avery to see if he got here yet. He texted back that he and Stephanie are having a late lunch down in the tiny restaurant attached to the inn. Five minutes later I'm standing next to their table. Avery looks confused by my appearance. Steph can see the tension radiating off me and pulls out the extra chair at their table. "Sit."

I do what she asks and she smiles gently. "What happened?"

"Nothing yet, but I'd bet money I'm about to get dumped," I admit and drop my elbows on the table and my head in my hands.

"Wait. What?" Avery asks. "From the Barons?"

"No. A girl."

"You're dating a girl?" Avery croaks out his tone drowning in wonder. "Like exclusively? You have a girlfriend? A real one, not one you blow up?"

I lift my head long enough to glare at him. He laughs a little and tries to cover it with his hand. "Sorry, but come on. It's like unheard of that you're exclusive with someone. It's against your personal brand or religion or whatever."

"You of all people should know things change," I retort.

"Yeah, but I smartened up. I didn't think you were capable of that," he quips and I glare at him again. "Sorry. But seriously, you were single by choice. I was single because I had to be. So this is a shock."

"Well she's going to dump me anyway," I tell them. "Because I have no idea how to do this and I fucked up."

"How?" Steph pats my hand and pours a glass of water for me from the pitcher. "You can tell us. I won't judge and if he gets snarky again I'll kick him. I promise."

Avery rolls his eyes but says. "I promise to quit with the jokes."

"Tell us about this mystery girl," Stephanie commands. "And why you think you blew it."

I give them a quick rundown of how we met, how amazing she turned out to be and then tell them about the current situation.

"I booked us separate hotel rooms," I admit. "Because of the nightmare situation."

Avery and Steph are the only two people who know about my nightmares and I didn't tell them by choice. I had a bad one this summer when I was visiting them. Avery burst into my room and tried to wake me, but I was thrashing so hard I clocked him in the head and gave him a black eye.

"So you've been dating her for a couple weeks and you've never…" Avery's eyebrows lift as his sentence trails off suggestively.

"Are you stupid? Of course we have. A lot," I clarify. "I just haven't slept over afterward. You saw what can happen."

"You're still having nightmares?" Avery asks. "I thought that was a random thing."

"I've been having them on and off my whole life. Anyway, I can't do that to her. I would never forgive myself. And I can't explain that to her because…she'll think I'm crazy."

Stephanie gives me a little shrug. "I'm betting she's pretty fabulous if you're dating her. You don't date just anyone. So why not give her the benefit of the doubt?"

"Yeah, I mean if she's crazy enough to give you any kind of shot in the first place, she can probably handle it," Avery adds and bursts into a giant grin when I glare at him again. I feel the table shake and his face contort. "Ouch!"

Steph kicked him. Good.

"Oh come on, Steph!" Avery gives his girlfriend a pleading look. "He's made it his mission to take the piss out of us when we're in relationships. Now it's my turn!"

"Avery, my love, can you run off and see if Seb and Shayne are ready to head into town? Since I have some experience with hiding stuff I shouldn't from boyfriends, I'm going to keep talking to our clueless friend here."

Avery pushes back from the table and stands up, leaning across it to kiss the top of Steph's head. "Meet you in the lobby when you're done," he tells her and then reaches over and squeezes my shoulder. "Good luck, buddy. I know you need it."

"I want to tell you to fuck off, but I do need it," I mutter back and he walks off.

Stephanie watches him go and then turns to me with a clear, calm expression. "'It's not ruined. Avery knows you're right for him. The kid isn't as stupid as he looks. It'll be fine, Steph.'"

"What?"

"Your words to me when Avery found out about my past," she says. "You said it better than I ever could."

"Yeah, but I knew Avery well. You've never even met Brie," I remind her.

She shrugs. "Yeah, but I know you. And this girl has to be special if she's got you feeling something."

I smile sheepishly. "We have similar pasts. She just had better luck."

"Your luck will only change if you let it, Alex," she says. "Let her in. If you think you're going to lose her either way, then what difference does it make? Give it your all."

"I'll take your advice," I tell her and let out a long, slow breath.

"Good. Now go find her and fix this," she says shooing me from the table as she stands up. I stand too and she wraps her arm around my shoulder reaching up to kiss my cheek. "And remember, no matter what, you've got us."

I leave her in the lobby but not before saying hi to Sebastian and Shayne, who are also there now with Avery. They invite me to join them, but I decline and head upstairs, knocking on Brie's door. She doesn't answer so I text her but she doesn't answer that either so I call her. It goes to voicemail.

Fuck.

My chest tightens and I start to feel cold—on the inside. I don't know how else to explain this sensation I used to get as a kid every time I felt rejected, by a classmate or another foster kid or when the social worker explained to me that my family couldn't...wouldn't take me. It's this feeling of frost growing in my veins and I hate it. I've had little flickers of it resurface when I get traded from a team, but although one team is rejecting me another team wants me. But now the feeling is back with a vengeance. This is exactly fucking why I never wanted to be involved with someone. Because they'd reject me. Everyone always rejects me if I give them enough time to do it.

Fuck this.

I grab my phone and my wallet and storm out the door.

Six hours later I'm on the back end of buzzed, sliding face-first into full-on drunk. And it cannot come fast enough. I

walked around town for about an hour aimlessly. I was hoping
to find Brie but eventually I ran into Seb, Shayne, Steph and
Avery, who were on their way to dinner. I joined them, refusing to talk about Brie when Steph tried to ask me the million
questions she had about why I wasn't with her right now. I
barely touched my food while downing three scotches. Then
the guys went to the local bar owned by Jordan and Devin's
younger brother Cole, to meet Luc, Jordan and Devin and the
girls broke off and went to another to meet Rose. It was their
version of a bachelor and bachelorette.

I didn't try to text her or call Brie again. With every drink
my resolve grew. She was cutting ties—just like I knew she
would, just like everyone does—so I was going to let her. I
would help her. Fuck this. The night though, was annoyingly
low key. The guys just wanted to sit around Cole's bar and
play pool and shoot the shit. And by ten o'clock there were
mutterings they were about to call it a night.

"Are you serious?" I asked. "It's your last night as a free
man and you're turning in before midnight? Barely drunk?
Luc, you're doing this wrong."

"I'm doing it very, very right my friend," Luc replies and
sips his beer, which I swear he's been nursing for like an hour.
I bet it's even one of those ridiculous nonalcoholic ones. "Besides, I haven't been a free man in years and I'm happy about
it. This is just a piece of paper to make it legal to other
people."

"What about you two?" I ask turning to Jordan and
Devin. "Let's have some fun before you're both on diaper
duty."

Jordan shakes his head. Devin grins. "Dude, Callie is in

the horny stage of pregnancy. I'm not giving up any extra time at home right now, especially because my parents have Conner for the night."

"Don't you want to get back to the hotel to see Brie?" Sebastian asks me. "This is your first weekend away together as a couple isn't it?"

"I need a fresh drink," I announce and down the rest of my scotch. I start to stand to head to the bar, but Cole interrupts me.

"The waitress is on her way over," he says and he turns to look at Luc with a devious grin. The next thing I know the future Mrs. Richard is strutting our way holding a tray in a short, even by my standards, jean skirt, a tight little tank top and cowboy boots.

I try not to let my jaw drop to the floor, because it's inappropriate, but then I notice that every man in the place had their mouth hanging open. Still I snap mine shut and look at Luc who I think might try to hump her right here on the table judging by the look on his face. Behind Rose I see Callie, Jessie, the blonde Cole is married to, Len and Brie. Our eyes connect but she looks away.

"What can I get you boys?" Rose asks.

"Is this a role-playing wedding or something?" I whisper to Jordan who laughs.

"Rose used to work here," he explains. "And dressed like that to get tips. And to drive Luc crazy."

He grabs her by the waist and pulls him to her. "I need to take you home before someone else in this bar tries to."

"I just have to finish my shift," she jokes, and the next thing I know he's picked her up, over his shoulder and is carrying her out of the bar.

"Wait! You can only keep her until midnight!" Callie is calling as she chases after them. "She's sleeping at Jessie's tonight or else it's bad luck!"

Devin stands up. "I'm going to go get my superstitious wife and head home. Night guys."

Jordan stands next and I almost tackle him to stop him as he reaches for Jessie. And then it happens, the way it always does, one by one my friends couple up and leave. Now it's just Brie and Len standing awkwardly in front of the table where Chooch and I have been abandoned. Brie looks at me again. I stare back, trying to look like I'm not a giant mess inside. But I must be failing because Chooch, my only single ally left, stands up. He smiles at Len in his totally uncool, awkward way and clears his throat. "I know we've never met, but they seem to have some stuff to work out. Can I buy you a drink?"

"Sure." Len smiles back at him all bright and bubbly like she always is.

"Rose is right," I mutter more to myself than Brie, but she hears me.

"About what?"

"Well, a lot of things." I stare at my empty scotch glass for a moment before looking up at Len and Chooch by the bar. "But today she's right about that. Len is exactly the kind of woman Chooch needs."

Brie looks over at them for a moment, her long hair falling over her shoulder and shielding her expression from me. "That's Chooch, huh? He seems nice. Len needs nice."

"He's one of the best," I say. "Almost too nice. He gets taken advantage of a lot."

"Len too," Brie replies and then turns back to me. I had all these ideas of pushing her away, playing it cool, being aloof. But now that she's in front of me, looking beautiful but guarded and maybe a little weary, I just want to fix this. "I'm sorry. I should have told you I booked us separate rooms."

"Or you shouldn't have booked us separate rooms," she counters.

"I had to." The tension and that cold prickle start to develop again, despite the scotch in my system.

"If you think that's what you have to do, then I have to do this," she retorts and starts for the door.

I watch her walk all the way across the crowded bar. I watch her swing the front door open. I watch her step over the threshold and I watch the door start to swing closed behind her.

I should move. I want to move.

I can't move.

Chapter 24

Brie

The wedding is truly beautiful and one of the most emotional ones I've ever been to. Rose was walked down the aisle by Jordan and Devin's dad. Her sisters and Cole's wife were her bridesmaids just as Cole, Jordan and Devin were the groomsmen. From the second I entered the church with Len until now at the reception, there is so much love in the room it's palpable. As I eat my piece of delicious strawberry wedding cake with buttercream frosting I can't help but look at Alex. He was assigned to my table, obviously, since Rose and Luc thought we were coming together, but Len quickly moved the name cards when we got here so she was sitting next to me and bumping Alex to the other side of Chooch.

He's been silent all day, barely speaking a word to anyone and as I look at him now, I can't figure out if he's feeling the vibe of this wedding as much as I am—as everyone else is. I've spent all day feeling like I'm treading water with bricks tied to my ankles. I think we just broke up. I mean, it hurts like we did. And more than the pain I feel a whole lot of frustration and anger about what could have been.

Len did a good job of distracting me for most of the day before the late-afternoon ceremony. We went to brunch and got mani-pedis and did some shopping. This little town is cute. I imagine that growing up here without your parents was a little easier than growing up on the streets of Montreal alone, like Alex did. I have to keep reminding myself of that because otherwise I think about how even Callie, who everyone will quickly tell you was a card-carrying commitment-phobe, was able to let Devin in.

Len leans closer. "Do you want me to kick him out? The meal's over. They're going to start the dancing soon. I could tell him to go take his brooding ass to another table."

I shake my head. "No. It's fine."

It isn't, but I want Len to just go back to enjoying Chooch's company because I haven't seen her smile so bright in a long time and definitely never over a man. The music gets louder and Rose and Luc step onto the dance floor and begin to dance to "All of Me" by John Legend. Len sighs and puts a hand to her chest. "I know. It's perfect," I smile.

I feel his eyes on me so I look up. Alex doesn't speak or move, just stares at me with those lost, stormy blue eyes. So I stare back, taking in every scar, every feature because after tonight I probably won't see him again. I have to make a point of not seeing him again because it'll be too hard if this really is the end. I finally pull my gaze from him and whisper, "God, how the hell does he not see we have something special and I'm worth letting in?"

"I have no idea," Len whispers back. "But he's going to regret it."

Halfway through the dance, Cole, who is the MC, tells everyone to join in. Luc swings Rose and then lets her go. He walks over to his mom and brings her onto the dance floor and Rose starts dancing with Mr. Garrison. Chooch is looking hopefully at Len so I nudge her. She laughs. "Would you like to dance?"

He basically jumps out of his seat instead of saying yes, and I grin at them as they make their way onto the dance floor. Alex is looking at me again, I can feel it, but this time I refuse to look back. I have to move on. I have to . . .

Then suddenly there's a hand, palm up, in front of me. I look up. "Please," he begs.

I shouldn't. But I do.

It feels good, dancing with him, being touched by him. I wish it didn't. He pulls me closer, so that our bodies are grazing and his cheek is brushing against mine.

"I was born in Montreal. My parents were young and happy. We lived in a very small apartment on Saint Denis Street." His voice is low and clear, but thick with emotion. "They both worked two jobs because it was the only way they could afford the place. I went to a daycare across town. I liked it there. The lady who ran it was nice. The other kids were fun. My parents only had one car, so they used to drive together to and from their jobs. They died in a car accident on their way to pick me up at daycare when I was five. I remember waiting and waiting and being upset that I was the only kid left. I remember the lady was annoyed until the police car showed up. I remember the officers took her into the kitchen and told me to stay in the play room. I heard her start to cry anyway, but I didn't know why. And then they told me they were taking me for a ride and I was excited because they were going to let me go in the police car."

I try to pull back a little so I can look at his face, but his arm around my waist gets tighter, holding me in place. He doesn't want me to look at him. I give his shoulder a little squeeze to let him know it's okay.

He takes a deep breath that I can feel quake through him, but he continues. "I don't know where my father's family was or if he had any. I don't ever remember meeting them. We did the occasional Thanksgiving with my mom's parents and her siblings. They lived somewhere up north. I remember it was always colder there and it took almost a day to get there. Anyway they came down and stayed at our house until the day after the funeral and then they left. But first they introduced me to a lady they said would take me to my new home. It was a social worker."

I bite my lip to keep from gasping or swearing. What fucking monsters do not take in a little boy they're related to? Oh my God. I close my eyes. The music has changed. Now an upbeat tune by Katy Perry is playing. We're still standing on the edge of the dance floor, motionless now, like a statue of a couple mid-waltz. "Anyway I ended up in a few different foster homes, but none of them kept me. No one wanted to keep me."

I feel hot tears prick at the corners of my eyes, but I refuse to cry. He doesn't want my tears. So I take a deep cleansing breath, and when I'm sure I'm in control and my voice will be steady I say, "Will you come with me? Right now?"

He lets me pull back so I can see him nod. Without another word I take his hand in mine and lead him out of the inn's restaurant and back to my room. We take the stairs because I don't want to wait for the elevator, which isn't in the lobby when we walk toward it.

But when we get up there I realize I left my purse with my key card in it on the table. Shit. He must realize that because without a word he walks over to his own door, pulls out his key card and opens his door. He holds it open for me to enter. I turn to him as soon as we're inside.

"You think I'll leave you, like everyone else has," I state. "That's why you're holding back."

"It's more than that." He runs his hands through his hair.

"So tell me more," I beg and blink because the room is getting blurry. "Like how you really got those scars on your back."

He shakes his head no, and I move to the bed and sit down on the corner of it. "After my grandfather had a stroke, they put me in foster care."

"In Montreal?" I nod and he swallows hard, his Adam's apple bobbing.

"I was in a home for a week. It was bad. I don't know exactly what happened. I can't remember. But I know that police came and took everyone away." I swallow before I continue. "I also remember a boy fell through a glass window."

The only thing I hear is the thumping of my heart, and maybe even his, and then he says in a low, firm voice, "No."

"What?"

"You don't remember that. Someone told you," he argues,

his voice taut with fear and anger as he rises off the bed. "You read my file."

I shake my head, my heart pounding harder. "I read *my* file."

His eyes get dark. He shakes his head again. I stand up. "Brie is short for Gabrielle. My birth name was Gabrielle Laflamme."

"Oh God." Suddenly looks at me like I'm someone else. Because now I am. I'm a four-year-old girl he knew for a week in a nightmare he lived. "It was you?"

"It was you," I reply. "You're the boy who fell through the window."

"I did. On purpose," he tells me, still looking at me like I'm a ghost. "They were abusing all of us, locking us in a closet in the basement and then after a few years when Jayla, the girl in the home, got older the man would go up into her room when his wife wasn't home and lock the door. We could hear her crying and she told us he was touching her and making her do things. No one would tell anyone because they were scared, and when I tried the social worker told me I was a liar."

He pauses and lifts a hand to run through his hair. He's shaking, but I don't dare try to touch him because I don't think it would help. "I was going to run away, like Andre did, but then they dumped you there."

He cocks his head to the side and blinks. "You were scared and quiet, but you didn't cry and you seemed so . . . normal. I wasn't going to leave you there to get fucked up like the rest of us. I didn't want you to experience that cement room in the basement and I knew eventually he would do things to you like he did to Jayla. I knew it."

I shudder violently at the thought.

"I was too young to handle this, you know? Only eight. And no one would listen to me. So I had to do something they couldn't ignore," he says, walking over to the bed. He sits on the edge and runs his hands through his hair before resting his elbows on his knees and hanging his head. "One night they'd already locked Kenny in the basement for something stupid like not eating all his dinner and Jayla was in her room, and the guy said I needed to go in the closet too so he could spend some time with you and Jayla. You were sitting on the floor just staring at us, and I was standing by the coffee table refusing to go into the basement. I felt so sick and panicked. He reached for me and I jumped up on the couch and I screamed as loud as I could. I just wanted someone to hear me and see what was going on. The couch was in front of the bay window and it was dusk and there were people outside, walking their dogs and I thought, *Fall through the window and tell everyone he did it.*"

"Alex, oh God." I can't imagine the desperation that would lead a child to do that.

"So when he tried to grab for me, I did," he says quietly. "I was young and stupid and didn't understand I could have died. I got up on the couch and just hurled myself backwards through the window. I got hurt worse than I thought. And they labeled me a problem child, but...it worked."

He lets me pull him to his feet. I wrap my arms around him and he collapses into my embrace and I start to cry. I think he might be crying too. "My parents were living in Quebec for my dad's job. They were having trouble conceiving and had been trying for years. They'd already agreed to look into adoption and fostering when my mom saw the story about the home on the news and there was a clip of me crying, being taken away by the police. That's how they found me. Because of you."

He pulls away and turns toward the window. He reaches up and wipes at his eyes and takes a shuddering breath. "Good. Then it was worth it."

"Alex, I'm falling in love with you," I confess and it's terrifying. "I know you're not ready for that. I'm sorry."

He finally turns and looks at me.

"I know there are a million things I can say to you, as a trained psychologist, to try and console you or change your thought patterns," I tell him quietly as I cross the distance between us. "I can point out to you how loved you are by your friends. The people downstairs would never hurt you. And I can remind you that Mackenzie, in all her lippy teenage cynicism, idolizes you. For a girl who hates the world, that speaks to how lovable you are."

I reach up and lay my palms on either side of his face. He closes his eyes at my touch, the hard lines on his face relaxing a little. "But I'm not your shrink. I'm just this girl who sees you as this amazing human being and who is tripping all over herself to make you see it too so you'll let me love you."

He opens his eyes. "I get nightmares."

His words swirl around my brain as I struggle to focus again after the kiss. Nightmares? I blink. "Is that why you won't sleep with me?"

He nods. "They can be violent. I thought I had them under control, like if I drank enough or was tired enough, they wouldn't happen. But then I had one this past summer at

Avery and Steph's place, despite being tired and drunk, and he tried to wake me up and I accidentally hit him."

"You're scared you'll hit me." Realization dawns on me.

"I don't want to lose you," he whispers, closing his eyes and resting his forehead against mine. "But I need to get my head on straight. I'm going to fuck this up again if I don't. I want to see that shrink you mentioned."

"I'm going to give you the time you need, the space you need," I tell him, even though it hurts so much I can barely breathe.

But I'll do anything for him, even if it means letting him go.

Chapter 25

Alex

I smile up at them as the final buzzer sounds. Not only did we win the last game before the Christmas break, but I scored and Brie and Mac were here to see it. Life is good. I hurry through the shower and rush to get dressed. Devin watches me, perplexed.

"Why is your ass on fire?"

"I'm meeting Mac and Brie for dinner," I explain. "They're waiting."

"Really?" Devin looks intrigued and a little amused. "You dating again? Or is it still? I don't know what the hell is going on."

"It's complicated," I reply and grab my coat.

I've been in therapy for a few weeks. Brie and I never said we were breaking up, but we've definitely put the brakes on our relationship. I've been seeing a therapist twice a week and I've made some progress, but I have a long way to go. But it's amazing how the mental exercises and meditation the therapist has given me are working.

"Later, guys!" I call before anyone can make any more comments or ask any questions.

In the hallway the coach barks my name. I turn and see he's almost smiling. "Great game," he says gruffly. "I'm liking you're play lately."

I want to pump my fist and scream *Fuck yeah!* but I just nod. "Thanks, Coach."

I'm grinning as I leave the building. Brie and Mac are waiting across the street as planned. I burst into a grin at the sight of them. Mac runs to me jumping up and down. "You scored! How cool is that?"

"Pretty cool," I laugh. Brie walks over and gives me a kiss on the cheek. "It was a goal, not an assist. It deserves more than a kiss on the cheek."

Brie grins and rocks up and kisses me gently on the lips.

"Gross," Mac announces, but she laughs.

We go to an Italian place and share an extra-large pizza and then, despite being full, Mac asks for a double order of chocolate cake and three forks. By the time we get to Brie's house she's told us all about her school day, asked a thousand questions about hockey and listed all the songs she can now play on the guitar. She's a turning into a normal teenager. It's fucking fantastic.

She plays us one of the songs, then heads to bed. "I'm going to sleep with my headphones in tonight. Just so you know. And we have enough cereal for three bowls in the morning."

"Oh my God," Brie groans. Mac waves good-bye and disappears down the hall. I hear her bedroom door close and I laugh.

"What kind of cereal?' I ask and slide across the couch so I'm right next to Brie. "Anything good like Cocoa Puffs or Sugar Smacks?"

"I am not sending that child to school full of sugar," Brie tells me. "We have Chex or Cheerios."

"Honey Nut?" I ask and raise an eyebrow. She laughs and I kiss her.

The sex with her is amazing the way it always is. God, I can't believe this woman puts up with me. That hits me at least once a day. She's sticking around, she's loving me even when I don't know why she is. She's lying beside me breathing hard with pink cheeks, and I feel like my heart has suddenly grown so big it's going to crack my ribs. I reach over and brush a lock of her hair off her forehead. "I love you."

She stops breathing. Her brown eyes find mine. "I love you too."

"I know." I swallow and fight the flutter of fear that has started in my gut. "That's why I wanted to ask you if you and Mac would come to the Barons family skate Saturday. As my guests."

"Really?"

I nod. "I know we're like taking it slow, but that stupid TV crew is finally doing their piece on me and they're filming me at the skate. They want to see me being myself and I'm myself when I'm with you."

She lifts herself up on her elbow, eyes still glued to mine. A smile starts to bloom on her lips. "I would love to."

"They also insist on a segment away from the rink," I explain and grit my teeth.

She reaches up and palms my jaw softly. "Don't grind

your teeth, they're under enough stress with all the sticks and pucks they have to avoid."

I smile at her snarky comment and force my jaw to relax. "I really fucking hate sticking my life out there, but I thought if I had to do it I might as well bring them to one of my volunteer shifts at Daphne's. I can turn the exposure I hate into exposure you need and make it bearable."

"Are you serious?" she asks, excitement filling her voice. "That's national exposure."

"I know. So that's a yes?"

"That is a yes!" She kisses me and then drops down onto my chest.

"Are you going to tell them why you volunteer here?" she asks quietly a moment later.

"Maybe. I don't know," I confess. "I'll see if it feels right at the time."

She snuggles closer and I start to trail my fingers up and down her back. This is our thing. We lie like this after sex for an hour, sometimes more, and then eventually I go home. I haven't had a nightmare in a while—almost two weeks— but I still worry. I run my fingers through her long, silky hair, playing with the ends before dropping them and sliding through it again. My body is particularly wrecked after the game and the sex. I yawn. I need to head home soon, but she's just so warm and soft and there's something soothing about running my fingers through her hair . . . the last thing I remember is blinking.

"Babe?" Her voice is raspy and filled with sleep. "Alex?"

I must be dreaming. I feel her hand on my shoulder. She

squeezes it softly. "Alex, I have to get up and make sure Mac gets off to school."

My eyes flutter open. "What?"

Morning light floods through the windows. I sit up quickly, startled. She looks worried. "I slept over?"

"You slept over," she confirms. "I didn't even realize it. I fell asleep and when I woke up, you were still here."

I glance at the small digital clock on her nightstand. It's ten to seven. Holy shit. She slips out of bed and grabs her robe off the back of the door. "Are you okay?"

"Yeah." I nod and blink. I can't believe it. I'm flooded with relief and happiness.

She walks over and runs a hand through my bed-head and smiles. "Just so you know, even if you have a nightmare, it'll be okay."

"I'm beginning to think you're right," I reply.

She leans down and kisses me quickly. I cup the back of her head so she can't pull away and I kiss her again and then I tell her something that's been on my mind for a while now. "And just so you know, whether you carry that gene or not, it'll be okay too."

I drop my hand and she stands up her beautiful face swirling with ugly emotions—fear, shock, maybe even a little anger. I stand up and reach for her hand. "It'll be okay because I'm not having kids so I won't leave them alone."

"Sweetheart you have a kid," I remind her softly. "You're the closest thing to a good mother Mac will probably ever know, so you bet when you go, no matter how or when, she'll mourn you the same as any biological kid now."

She looks so pained, but I know this is a conversation we

have to have. "Are you saying this because you want kids or something?"

"I just want you to know I've been reading up on this. Even if you have the gene, it doesn't mean you're going to get sick and people get cancer without the gene too." I pull her into my arms and press my lips to her head for a moment before speaking again. At first the idea that she might be taken from me sent a cold flash of fear right through me. But I realized that it was a risk I had to take. I wasn't going to walk away from the only woman I've ever loved—who has ever loved me—because of a what if. Any time with her was better than no time with her. "I'm saying this because I want you, kids or no kids, and whether you get the test results or you don't, I'm always going to be here for you. You're stuck with me."

There's a thump down the hall and then Mac's voice bellows through the apartment. "Brie! Have you seen my backpack?"

Brie steps out of my arms and gives me a shaky smile. "Are you okay?"

She nods. "I am. I promise."

She slips out of the bedroom, closing the door behind her. I lie back and stare at her ceiling. I feel this overwhelming sense of peace, which is crazy because when I look at my life now, it's like I'm a different person. I don't even recognize myself anymore . . . but it's no longer terrifying. It's incredible.

Chapter 26

Alex

Are there always so many fucking people involved in this type of thing?" I growl as Luc and I watch ten people zip around the sidewalk carrying camera equipment.

"You act like you've never been on camera before." Luc grabs my shoulder and gives it a squeeze. He saw how stressed out I was at the Barons family skate with the camera crew and producer following me around. I think he felt bad for me so he stopped by to see how I was doing while we film the final segment here at Daphne's House. "You've done probably about four hundred postgame interviews in the locker room. Remember that."

I shrug and run a hand through my hair, which makes the hair lady frown. I give her a quick apologetic smile. "In the locker room I'm in my element. I'm comfortable."

"Why because you're half naked and panting?" Luc quips.

"Maybe you should do the interview shirtless like you do after games," Brie suggests. She's standing beside Luc looking at something on her phone but clearly listening to our conversation. Some things never change. "I can get you hot and sweaty too if that helps."

I smile down at her and wish I could kiss her right now but we have to keep this professional. "I am definitely taking a rain check on that."

She smiles and quickly lets our hands tangle, giving mine a squeeze that is way more comforting than the squeeze I got from Luc. *Mon Dieu,* I love her so damn much. "I'm going to go check on the kids."

She gives me one more supportive smile and then walks over to where the kids are clustered together on the sidewalk a few feet away. Luc watches her go and then looks at me with an awed grin. "I can't believe that Starbucks encounter turned into this."

"Neither can I." I smile at the memory.

He claps my shoulder again. "I'm going to head out unless you want me to stay."

"Nah. It's good. I've got more than enough eyeballs staring at me while I do this. Thanks though for swinging by." I'm grateful for his friendship. It's funny how life can change in just a few short months.

"You've got this, man. Just be yourself." Luc gives me a smartass grin and glances at Brie again. "Somehow that seems to work."

"Please know I am mentally flipping you the bird right now."

He chuckles and waves before turning around and heading down the street.

"Alex," the producer says and marches over. "We're good

to go. Sit there, in the middle on the top step okay?"

I go to sit down. The stylist charges over and starts to fix my hair.

"Now just do your thing and pretend we're not even here," the producer says with a smile and I try not to roll my eyes. This whole day is contrived and set up just for them. They followed me for part of my run with the kids earlier and now they want some of them to stay and ask questions and chat with me on the front stoop, something that we'd never do normally. If they have questions, they ask me on the run or later in the house. She turns and starts to point at them, one by one, and tells them where to sit. She tells Mac to sit on the bottom step, the farthest away from me, but Mac ignores the request and sits to my left on the step beneath me. The producer starts to open her mouth, but the look on my face stops her.

"Okay . . . start rolling!"

Oh God, someone shoot me now. Reg starts it off as he looks up at me and asks me a question about whether I run because it's part of my hockey training or because I like it. I tell him it's the latter and how I used to run a lot as a teen because it got me out of the house. I tell them that I mostly did it in the summer when there was no ice hockey, since I couldn't afford to pay for time in indoor rinks.

The questions keep coming, ranging from running techniques to hockey questions to general health stuff. I have no idea how any of this will be interesting to hockey fans who watch this show but hey, they're the experts. After ten minutes the producer says it's done and everyone gets up to leave, but Reg has more question. "You said you couldn't afford indoor hockey in the summer, so like were your parents poor?"

My heart beats faster at the mention of my parents.

"I got into hockey when I was nine, which is considered late for most. I was playing on the free rec leagues until a coach saw my potential and got me on a team where the fees were waived and equipment was supplied."

I feel a weird lump forming in the pit of my stomach. It's guilt. I feel bad I'm giving him kind of a half-truth or half an answer. My eyes catch Mac's. She doesn't look disappointed by my answer, but I realize I am. I don't want her to think that she has anything to be embarrassed about just because she's not growing up the way people think you're supposed to.

I look back at Reg. "And no, my parents weren't poor. They passed away when I was little. I was in foster care and didn't have the best luck there, so I left and ended up kind of homeless for a few years because there was no Daphne's House for me. But I had hockey, thanks to some great coaches who helped me stay in the game."

I glance up and realize the camera guy is still filming. The rest of the crew is staring with most of their mouths hanging open. The producer is furtively leafing through her notes, probably wondering where the fuck that detail was in her research on me and how she missed it.

"Have you talked about this before?" the producer asks, finally giving up on her notes and staring at me in stunned confusion.

I glance at the camera. Still fucking rolling. Okay well...I guess I'm doing this. And honestly, it doesn't feel wrong, even if it is fucking uncomfortable and terrifying. I shake my head. "Never. I had misplaced shame. I think all kids in this situation do, even if they didn't suffer the abuse in the system I did. So when I finally got that first NHL contract, I decided to be the person I always wanted to be—the fun, easygoing guy living his dream without a care in the world. The player who hurls as many jokes as pucks." I smile, just like the Alex they know would. "I didn't want to be that guy with the tragic past. The sob story turned success story. I just wanted to be normal."

"You did a good job," the producer replies. "So why talk now?"

"Two reasons. Because I realize normal is a myth." I pause and let my eyes find Brie. She's standing off to the side, a proud smile on her face and her beautiful brown eyes swimming in tears. "Even the person who looks successful and privileged and 'normal' has fought a battle that's left them with scars, be it mental, physical or both. And I want people to know that. I also want people to know that giving to places like Daphne's House, whether it's time or money, actually makes a difference. I didn't have a place like this, but if I had my life would have been easier. These kids—whether they are homeless or in foster care or here at Daphne's—these kids can become something amazing. I'm living proof. But people can't know that unless I tell them so I'm telling them. If it means more people will help kids in the situation I was in, then it's worth talking about it."

The entire crew starts clapping except the hair lady, who's dabbing her eyes with a tissue instead. I have never been so uncomfortable in my life. Mac launches herself off the step she's sitting on and wraps her arms around my neck in a hug so tight she's kind of strangling me. And yet it feels fucking fantastic.

"Okay. Well, honestly, Alex I think we got more than we came for. We're gonna wrap this." The producer steps forward. I shake her hand keeping the other one around Mac, who's still hugging me.

Mac finally lets go and her face is all pinched like she's fighting her emotions. "You're a badass," she announces, standing up. I stand up too and watch with relief as the camera crew starts toward their big white van parked down the street.

"Language," Brie warns her as she walks up. "But yeah, he kind of totally is."

Mac rolls her eyes at the language police and heads inside. "You two look like you're going to kiss so I'm outta here."

The door closes behind her and Brie climbs the steps to join me on the stoop. She stands right in front of me. "Was that honestly okay? Did I sound like a fool?"

"You sounded like a goddamn hero." She reaches up and wraps her arms around my neck. "And you are."

She kisses me and once again my self-doubt and anxiety starts to melt away. Yeah, it was worth it. Everything that I've gone through. Everything that got me here, to this place with her, was worth it.

Epilogue

Alex

18 months later

I watch Mackenzie as she sits in a chair next to Brie at the edge of the surf. Brie is telling her something, but I can't hear what. Mac is listening and smiling with an occasional nod. I wonder if Brie is asking her? If she is, I'm too late. Fuck, I need to grow some balls already and just do it.

"Hey, burger boy," Jordan yells as he walks across the patio toward me. "I don't like mine charred."

I look down at the patties on the grill and start to flip them with the spatula I forgot I was holding. I look back up and smile at Tate, the little boy strapped to his chest. His big green eyes are barely visible under heavy lids. I coo at him and he gives me a sleepy smile. "You are so lucky this kid looks like Jessie. He's got a shot in life now."

Jordan flips me the bird above his son's head. "I'm just happy he's a boy. Devin is going to have his hands full with a daughter from the Caplan gene pool."

I glance past Jordan to where Callie is sitting under an umbrella trying to keep a sun hat on her daughter's head, while Olivia—who everyone calls Liv—repeatedly removes it and Devin splashes in the water with Conner. "Yeah, I don't envy him either but it's going to be a riot to watch."

Jordan laughs. I flip the burgers on the grill again and glance back to the beach. Mackenzie has gotten up and is walking into the ocean where Jessie, Rose and Luc are already swimming. "I have to say," Jordan says. "I didn't expect to ever be having a family-friendly preplayoffs barbeque with you at your long-term girlfriend's Hampton summer home."

I grin. "It's an unexpected plot twist for sure."

"Things are still good with Brie obviously," Jordan remarks and I nod.

I nod. "They're fantastic."

We sold her grandmother's place four months ago and bought a place together. It's not as open as my loft but it's a big, spacious brownstone that Mac loves because she's got her own floor since her room is by itself in the attic. I've only had one nightmare since we moved in. And last month Brie decided to face her own nightmare and had herself tested again and I went with her for the results. When we found out she doesn't carry the gene her mom did. The doctor asked her if that meant she would try for children and Brie simply said. "I already have a daughter."

And it was that night she told me she was going to ask Mac if she wanted to be adopted.

I turn away from the burgers and watch Brie stand up and join everyone in the water. "I was planning on asking Brie to marry me tonight, actually, after all you goofballs leave."

"Get the fuck out!" Jordan says, his eyes bulging out of his goofy head and his mouth hanging open. He glances down at the fuzzy blond head. "You didn't hear that, Tater."

"He's asleep," I assure him. "And I'm not kidding. I have been trying to work up the courage to do it for a couple of months. I want it to be memorable and all that crap you know. But she told me last night she's going to ask Mackenzie if she wants to be adopted today. And so I kind of want to do it now, so I can adopt her too."

"Holy shit..." he says, which is kind of the reaction I expected but then he starts laughing. Loudly. So loud that it wakes Tate and he starts to cry. "Sorry. I just...you're the guy who used to brag about leading the league in sleepovers and you acted like love was a terminal disease you were afraid to catch."

"Yeah. I was an idiot," I retort and smirk. "Keep rubbing it in, arsehole, and I'll bring up your past. At least I did the player thing well, you were a train wreck."

"True that." He puts down his beer next to the grill and lifts a still crying Tate out of his carrier. "Come on, son. Let's hug it out."

He cradles his tiny human to his chest. Watching this kind of thing—family, a clear sign of love—used to feel so foreign to me. Now I'm no longer just a visitor in other people's families; I've got one of my own. I just have to make it official.

I hand the spatula to Jordan. "Man the grill. I'm going to go ask Brie to marry me."

"What? Now? But...what? For real?"

I walk across the patio and hurry down the stairs to the beach below. It's low tide so I have a lot of beach to cross, but my confidence grows with every step. Mackenzie is waist deep, jumping waves with Rose. Brie is only knee deep, watching them. I walk right up to her and circle her waist from behind. She tilts her head and smiles up at me.

"Have you asked her yet?"

"No. I almost did..." Brie explains. "I'm nervous. I can't figure out the perfect way to bring it up."

"I have the same problem," I confess and she gives me a quizzical smile.

"With what?"

I don't answer her. Instead I call Mackenzie. She turns and looks at me and I wave her over. Brie stiffens in my arms. "What are you doing?"

"Relax," I reply and kiss her cheek softly. "Sometimes you have just take a chance."

Mac jumps to a stop in front of us but not before splashing us playfully. "What's up?"

"So Brie has been wanting to ask you something important," I start and Brie whispers my name under her breath followed by an "oh God." She tries to step out of my embrace, but I hold her to my chest. "She's too nervous to ask you, so I figure I'll ask for you, Brie."

"I'm confused," Mackenzie says, her brow furrowing.

"Mac, Brie would like to know if you'd like her to adopt you, because she would really love to adopt you," I tell Mac and her face instantly looks stunned.

"Oh my God..." Mac whispers her hand covering her mouth as she gasps. My eyes fall quickly to the scar on her forearm and I think God, that was a lifetime ago. "Really? Are you shitting me?"

"No. Not shitting you," Brie manages to squeak out. "But don't worry if you don't want to it's okay. I get it. You can still stay with me until you're ready to apply for emanci—"

Mac starts to cry. "No. I want to be adopted. By you. I do."

Mac throws herself on Brie and the hug would knock them both over if I wasn't there for support. They're both crying now and I have a lump in my throat the size of a damn baseball. I try to clear it out. "I love you, Brie."

"I love you too."

I turn to Mac. "I love you like a daughter, even with your attitude and potty mouth."

She smiles. "Then you should get in on this and marry her so I can be adopted by both of you."

"Mac!" Brie gasps and starts to blush.

I laugh and splash Mac. "Way to steal my thunder, kid!"

"What?" Brie looks at me with complete confusion.

"I have a ring upstairs in my bag. I have been carrying it around for two months trying to find the right time to ask you to marry me and if I can adopt this goofball with you and maybe even a couple more one day," I tell her. "So Gabrielle Bennett, what do you say? Want a husband to go with your kid?"

"As long as it's you, yes," she says and launches herself at me. I catch her in a hug. "One hundred percent yes."

Mackenzie squeals like only a teenage girl can and jumps on both of us causing me to lose my balance and we tip backward into the water, one big happy family.

My family.

Keep reading for a preview of

SLAMMED

A San Francisco Thunder hockey novel

Available December 2017

Prologue

DIXIE

*C*ome on...where is the damn elevator?

I glance at my phone to check the time and then shove it into my blazer pocket. Tonight is not going as planned. I was almost late getting to the arena because of an accident on the freeway, and as soon as I arrived I realized I forgot my employee pass. So I had to skip the PR briefing and run to security to get a temporary pass. I managed to print out the press list, but now I'm late for a meeting with the owner of the team, Ryanne Bateman. She's the reason I wanted to work for the San Francisco Thunder hockey franchise to begin with, and I'm about to mess up my first impression. The thought has me so panicked my skin is itching.

I jam my thumb into the elevator button again. And again.

"Punching it repeatedly doesn't make it come any quicker, you know." The voice rumbles through me like an earth-quake. My first thought as soon as my eyes land on him is

Ooh...he's pretty. If a scientist mixed the DNA of a Disney prince and an action hero, this guy would be the result. Tall, dark, rugged, muscled and exuding calm confidence. Who the hell is he?

I glance at his chest, which is expansive, to say the least, looking for the pass that should be around his neck if he's a guest or staff, but there's nothing there. My eyes move up from his chest to his face, and on the way they land on a scar. It's hard to miss because it's pink and puffy and takes up a lot of real estate on his strong neck, moving from below his ear to an inch or two from his Adam's apple. There's only one person with a scar like that who would be in this arena.

"You're Levi's brother," I announce, like he doesn't know his older brother is captain of the Thunder.

"Just Eli is fine," he corrects and his voice is even deeper than before, which is both unbelievable and unbelievably attractive.

He's in a suit that fits him like a glove, and the charcoal gray color compliments his shock of thick, dark hair. His eyes are...green? I'd have to step closer to find out, and I almost do but catch myself. Then he smiles, something that his constantly brooding brother rarely does, and it's sexy as all hell.

"Are you lost? Are you looking for the friends and family lounge or something?" I ask and glance at the elevator, which still isn't here. "I'm heading down that way. You can come with me."

Eli's sexy smile grows bigger. "There's nothing I'd rather do."

He winks at me. Wow. Talk about cheesy. So why am I smiling? I bite the inside of my cheek to stop it from spreading as he takes a step closer so he's standing right beside me now. He's looking down at me with those definitely green, like dewy moss or freshly cut grass, eyes. Wow. He's hot. Am I breathing? I don't think I'm breathing. I take a deep, deliberate breath. "You're going to need to get a pass from security." I hold up mine as an example. "All non-players walking around the VIP areas need a pass on game days."

"I don't need a pass," he replies casually and then dips his head a little to read the name on my pass. "Dixie Wynn, PR intern."

I glance down. "Crap. They printed my old title. I'm PR staff now. Since June," I mutter, annoyed. "Also, I know you're the captain's brother, but you still need a pass."

He smirks at that. "I don't."

Wow. He's entitled. I decide not to argue with him. He'll find out quick enough when the security guard at the players level won't let him off the elevator.

The elevator dings and the doors open. No one is there. That's weird. Why was it taking so long if no one was in it? I step inside and he follows, once again standing right next to me even though we have the whole elevator to ourselves. It's disconcerting and yet somehow flattering at the same time. I keep my eyes focused on the elevator panel after I punch the bottom floor.

"There might be something wrong with my eyes," he murmurs and his rough, deep voice seems to reverberate off the walls of the elevator. I look up at him and he smiles. "Because I can't seem to take them off of you."

Oh God. Is he serious? Who uses lines like that? Our eyes

meet and he grins, and it makes me grin. Damn it. I'm enabling him.

"That was cheese-tastic. You need to work on your pickup lines," I say. "On someone else."

He chuckles lightly. This guy must think because he's the captain's brother he can do whatever he wants.

"You clearly don't know why I'm here, so how did you know who I was?" Eli asks, and it makes me look up at him again.

"You're here to visit Levi, obviously, and I recognized you because..." My eyes linger on the scar instead of his face, and when I do make eye contact I can see a scowl cross his face, but he quickly smiles.

He raises his hand to his neck. "I got it saving orphans from a knife fight."

I bite back a laugh. "Do you actually tell women that?"

He nods. "Sometimes. Other times I say I was saving puppies from a hostage situation. Women love heroes, Miss Wynn."

"Are you for real?" I ask, and I can no longer hold back my laugh. "Do cheesy pick-up lines and ridiculous lies honestly work for you?"

He laughs too. "Yeah. Because it gets women to laugh and it starts a conversation. And it takes the stick out of even the tightest little asses, like yours."

"You really can't talk to me like that!" I warn him, but I can't sell it because I'm not all that angry—just mostly stunned. "Are you sure you share DNA with Levi? He's way more...refined than you."

He chuffs at that. "Refined? You mean boring."

Before I can answer there's a noise—a horrendous grinding sound that makes the hair on the back of my neck rise—and then the elevator shimmies and stops abruptly. I reach out and grab for the small railing along the walls, and he reaches out and grabs me. His hand around my waist is tight and firm and it causes a tingle that has nothing to do with the fear from the faulty elevator. I can't remember the last time I was this close to a guy this hot, which seems pathetic, but I've been busy with work, and since I found out about my dad being sick, I haven't exactly been in the mood to go out and meet people.

When I'm convinced it's not going to move again I step forward, out of his protective embrace, and look up at the lights telling us what floor we're on. No floor is lit up. I punch the bottom-floor button again. Nothing happens.

"No," I say out loud. "Just no."

Eli steps forward. I can feel his whole body like a warm, muscled wall behind me. "It's stuck."

"No."

"Yes."

"Fucking hell. Fuck my life!" I blurt out and instantly hate myself for it. I couldn't be more unprofessional right now. Embarrassed by my outburst, I step away from him, closer to the panel of buttons, and hit the one marked Call. A ringing sound fills the elevator.

"It's okay. We'll get out of here," he says in a soothing tone. "It's not going to turn into a survival movie where one of us has to eat the other. Although I'm open to that..."

I snap my head up to stare at him. He's grinning again. Jesus, does this guy take anything seriously? Why is everything sexual? And why is it suddenly warm in here?

Before I can chastise him the ringing stops and a voice comes out of the little speaker above the floor numbers. "Security."

"Hey! We're trapped in an elevator!" I blurt out, panicked.

"Okay ma'am..." the security guard says. I bristle at that term and see Eli chuckle. "We have fourteen elevators in the building, so can you read me the number at the top of the panel? It's engraved in the metal. That will tell me which one you're in. I don't see an alert on our system."

Oh fuck. That can't be good. "S4," I say.

"Okay..." His pause fills me with dread. "We'll figure this out. I will send someone over there to see if they can manually reset it and call the elevator company immediately. It will take a little bit of time though, so hold tight."

"How long?" I ask and the anguish in my voice is more than a little apparent. It's so strong Eli drops a hand on my shoulder and squeezes. "I have somewhere to be."

"We'll work as fast as we can, ma'am."

"We'll be fine. Thank you," Eli says. "We'll buzz you again if we need an ETA."

He hits the button again and the little light that was lit up fades. I look up at Eli. "What did you do?"

"Ended the call so he can get to work getting us out of here," Eli explains casually. I want to argue with him, but I don't know why. He didn't do anything wrong. I'm just raging inside that yet another thing today has totally backfired and I want someone to blame. Being late makes me crazy. I'm always early to everything—meetings, parties, doctor's appointments, funerals.

I pull out my phone and pull up my boss's number. I text Mr. Carling that I'm running behind. I'm about to make a bad first impression on a woman I've studied and admired since college.

"Who are you texting? Your boyfriend?"

I roll my eyes. "My boss. He was going to introduce me to the team owner, but now I've screwed that up."

"It's not your fault the elevator crapped out," he reminds me.

"Yeah, she's not going to care. She's just going to see me as a screw-up," I tell him, my voice filled with disappointment. "In her memoir Ryanne says all mistakes must be owned, and nothing is out of your control. If something goes wrong, there's a reason, a choice you made, that should have been different. Like I could have taken the stairs."

"Wow, you've read her memoir?" he says, his green eyes wide.

I nod. "She made her first million by twenty-eight. She's a marketing genius and the only woman to own a professional hockey team. And the Thunder are the most popular California hockey team in the league, thanks to her marketing savvy."

Eli's expression seems to cloud a little, dimming the flirtatious twinkle in his eyes. "I'm sure she has flaws. Maybe even a dark side."

I roll my eyes. "Yeah, men often say that about successful women."

He chuckles. "I'm just saying. We all have a little fault in our stars."

I glance at my phone screen to see that Mr. Carling replied.

> She's done meeting staff, gone to meet with the team. Maybe I can introduce you after the game. Hope you get unstuck soon.

I slump against the wall and cover my face with my hands for a moment, fighting to rein in all these hideous emotions. "Dixie? Tell me what I can do to help."

He's suddenly serious and it radiates through his tone. It's low and rough and I *feel* it inside me like the bass in a song coming out of kick-ass sound system. I drop my hands and look up into his eyes. "Your voice is so deep it's kind of insane. It sounds like sandpaper but feels like velvet."

He stares at me. His expression intense, but his face passive and calm in an unnerving way. "You *feel* my voice?"

Somehow he said that with even more sandpaper and velvet. I feel it *everywhere*. I try to swallow and nod my response. The elevator suddenly feels claustrophobic and hot. I move away from the wall, and him, and shrug out of my blazer. The air swirls around my bare arms, and I pinch the front of my sleeveless silk shirt and move it, creating a breeze.

"If it makes you feel any better I have somewhere important to be too," Eli tells me quietly, still serious. "And I could use a little luck right now too."

I have no idea what he's talking about and I open my mouth to ask at the very moment the elevator lurches up but stops just as abruptly as it did before. It makes me squeak in shock at the sudden movement and stumble, but he grabs me again, this time with both hands on my waist, and I face-plant into his chest. It's rock-hard and warm, and he smells unbelievable. I look up at him. "I guess we both need something good to happen."

"So let's make something good happen." Before I realize what he's doing he's got his hands against my cheeks and he's tipping my head back.

His mouth hovering so close to mine as he tilts his head slowly. His lips part just a little bit, as his mouth gets even closer. I feel like the whole world has stopped just like this elevator. We're frozen in this almost kiss. And then his lips are against mine. It isn't sudden. It isn't rushed. I'm not taken by surprise. I knew exactly what he was going to do and I let him do it. Still somehow I'm surprised. My pulse races and my breath catches, but I kiss him back. With everything in me, I kiss him back.

It's long, it's deep and hot and perfect, and I find myself suddenly begging the universe to leave us here in this elevator forever. But the universe isn't taking my calls right now, obviously, because the elevator shudders and starts moving down. This time it doesn't stop.

He steps away from me abruptly and my hand flies up to cover my mouth. He just stares at me, a victorious smile on his lips. "That was something good," he says in that deep velvety voice.

Oh my God. Suddenly he's way more than just a pretty face. And just like that I am totally, fully and completely crushing on Elijah Casco.

The elevator stops, smoothly this time, and the doors slide open. I rush out. He follows. We're on the player level, my original destination. I turn to him and I start to open my mouth because I need to say something—but what? Do I ask for his phone number? Do I ask him out for drinks? Do I act like that kiss just didn't curl my toes and set my insides on fire?

"Dixie!" Mr. Carling's voice shatters the euphoric post-kiss haze that had engulfed me. "You're out!"

I spin to face him as he approaches. "Hi Mr. Carling. Yes. We're out."

He glances past me at Eli and his entire face lights up. "Elijah! You were trapped in the elevator too? We've been looking for you everywhere! The rest of the team is already dressing, and Ryanne wanted to meet you before the game."

Rest of the . . . *what?* I blink. My eyes fly up to Eli. He's giving Mr. Carling an easy smile. "Sorry. I would have called but my phone is in the locker room."

"You still play?" I blurt out, stunned and horrified. Eli's nods. His back is to Mr. Carling because he's about to walk away, so Mr. Carling doesn't see the smug smirk and the wink. That's just for my viewing pleasure.

Mr. Carling looks at me with confusion and a little judgment, which makes me feel like I just let him down somehow. "You didn't know?"

"I mean, I knew he played in college . . . " I mumble like an idiot. "I saw the news reports on the accident a couple years ago, but I assumed he quit hockey after that."

Eli frowns, hard, but I ignore him and concentrate on Mr. Carling, who's still looking at me like I've just failed some test. "He's been with our farm team for almost a year now. We called him up for the game tonight. I guess you haven't see the team roster yet."

"No. Sorry," I mumble, stunned and confused. It's like the world just stopped and started spinning in the wrong direction.

"I figured you wouldn't even need the roster since Levi is best friends with your brother. I'm surprised Jude didn't ever mention Eli was playing in the organization," Mr. Carling glances past us, down the hall, and smiles. "Oh! There's Ryanne. Let me go get her."

He starts to march down the long, curved corridor. I try not to fall headfirst into a panic attack because holy shit, the hottest kiss of my life just turned into a giant mistake. There's a strict policy against fraternization between employees and players, and I'm fairly certain having Eli's tongue in my mouth in the service elevator counts as fraternization. I don't break rules. Ever. Especially ones that can cost me my fledgling career.

"Why didn't you tell me you're a Thunder player?" I whisper harshly when Mr. Carling is out of earshot.

"Why didn't you tell me you were Jude Braddock's sister?" he counters, looking just as stunned as I feel.

"Because I don't tell anyone. That's why I use my middle name as a last name," I reply sternly. "I don't want the team to think he got me the job, so you can't tell anyone. Just like you can't tell anyone about that kiss. *Please.* Because this is the only good thing I have in my life, and I'm not losing it over a kiss."

"For the record, I didn't tell you I play for the Thunder because I don't. I play for the Storm," he tells me calmly. "And

I won't tell anyone your real last name, but who cares who knows about the kiss?"

"I care! They have a strict policy about that stuff here," I explain. My eyes keep darting down the hall. Mr. Carling is coming our way now with Ryanne. "That kiss could cost me my job."

"Okay. Okay. If you want me to pretend that incredible kiss didn't happen, then I will. But I don't think either of us will forget it," he manages to whisper before Mr. Carling and Ryanne are standing in front of us. She looks equal parts power and beauty in a pair of tailored black pants, with her long dark hair pulled back in a low ponytail that looks as silky as her red blouse. I open my mouth to introduce myself, but her eyes are on Eli, not me. She extends her hand to him. "Mr. Casco. I'm looking forward to seeing what you can do out there tonight."

He shakes her hand and flashes a confident grin. "I'm looking forward to impressing you."

Ryanne glances at Mr. Carling. "This one is much bolder than his brother. Let's hope he can back it up."

"I should get into my gear," Eli says and then puts a hand on my back which makes me bristle. "I'll leave you to talk to your best and brightest communications team addition. Nice meeting you."

Eli walks away and I'm left frazzled again, but I try not to show it as I look up at Ryanne and give her what I hope is a poised smile. "Dixie Wynn. I'm very happy to meet you, Ms. Bateman. You're the reason I wanted to work here."

She smiles and shakes my hand. "I'm flattered. Your whole

department—hell, the whole organization—has nothing but positive remarks about you."

I smile brighter, my nerves starting to dissapate. She leans in and winks at me. "And I admire the fact that you haven't told them who you are. You earned your fantastic reputation on your own."

She stands straighter and turns to Mr. Carling again. "I'm heading to my box. Looking forward to seeing you all at the party later tonight."

And just like that she's off down the hall, her four-inch heels clicking loudly against the concrete floor. That went way better than I thought it would after all the drama leading up to it. I turn to Mr. Carling. "I'm going to go brief the team on the media info for after the game."

His phone buzzes and as his eyes slide to the screen, I leave him to head into the locker room. I march right in, even though some of the guys are in various states of undress. I learned early on that being timid or shy with these boys caused them to give me more grief than if I just walked in on them when they're half naked.

"Boys! Listen up!" I bellow and ninety percent of the heads in the room snap to attention. Only one of them is glaring at me in horror—my brother, Jude Braddock.

"Hey, Ms. Wynn," he says, accentuating the Wynn part. "Maybe knock before entering or something."

I give him a quick *I don't give a fuck* smirk. He knows the look well, and I know it annoys the hell out of him, which is why I do it. The only thing I love more than Jude is irking the hell out of Jude.

"I'm not the Virgin Mary, Braddock." I let my eyes sweep

the room, but they somehow get stuck on Eli. His jacket and shirt are gone. His chest is wide and smooth and his abs are hard and rippled . . . I blink and wrench my eyes away. "Nothing I haven't seen before."

I shoot out my directions about press after the game like a drill sergeant, explaining it's a light schedule tonight because the media only want to talk to the Casco brothers after the game. The irony is I was holding this list the entire time. If I'd just read it in the elevator I would have known Eli was playing for us. I leave, forcing myself not to look back at Eli even though every fiber of my being wants to. I have to let it go—forget the kiss and how attractive I find his bold, goofy personality.

Fifteen minutes later the players are filtering out to take the ice. Eli is the last one out of the locker room and as his eyes connect with mine, he grins and gives me a wink. Everyone continues down the hall chattering away, excited for the game. Eli pauses for just a second right in front of me and in a rough whisper says, "Admit it. That was one hell of a kiss."

"Go!" I command sharply and he struts off down the tunnel with the rest of the team.

Alone in the hall, my fingertips brush my lips absently, my breath hitches. He's not here to see my response, but I can't help nodding my head in agreement.

About the Author

Victoria Denault loves long walks on the beach, cinnamon dolce lattes and writing angst-filled romance. She lives in LA but grew up in Montreal, which is why she is fluent in English, French and hockey.

Learn more at:

VictoriaDenault.com

Facebook.com/AuthorVictoriaDenault

Twitter: @BooksbyVictoria

CPSIA information can be obtained
at www.ICGtesting.com
Printed in the USA
FFOW03n1156260817
39256FF